COMMANDER-1

A DELACORTE PRESS BOOK

New York

COMMANDER-

BY PETER GEORGE

Whoso diggeth a pit shall fall therein: and he that rolleth a stone, it will return upon him.

Proverbs 26;27

. . . . but war is the most natural, the most everyday matter . . . War is life.

A. Hitler
(To Rauschning, 1933)

I wonder if we could contrive some magnificent myth that would in itself carry conviction to our whole community.

Plato's *Republic*

FOR STANLEY KUBRICK

COMMANDER-1

PEACE: DECEMBER 24/25, 1965

War was no longer possible, everyone agreed.

The President agreed, the Premier agreed, everyone felt the same way. War would be profitless, pointless, futile. What use was war when you—anyone—couldn't win it? A test-ban treaty had been signed, and a hot line was in operation between the President and the Premier. So war was impossible, and peace was here. It was the eve of Christmas, and there was goodwill to all men in all people.

In a suburb of Johannesburg a Negro ran through the streets. He ran with desperation but without strength, because he was hungry. Three days ago he had eaten, and then only a half-loaf of bread. He had never been educated, so he did not speak English or Afrikaans. He had no permit to work, no permit to be in this area, because he did not understand these things. For three days he had wandered the streets, sleeping at night in the darkness of alleys. Instinct warned him to keep clear of the police. But hunger finally drove him to snatch a purse. The woman screamed. Men rushed to join the chase. He turned into a blind street, and as he tried to climb the wall at the end of it they dragged him down. Two police-men, fifty yards away, saw them catch him. They began to walk, at a dignified, leisurely pace, toward the mêlée. In the few seconds before he died under the clubbing fists, the swinging boots, he saw their one face, the single face of mob hatred. The face was white.

The thousand eyes of Rockefeller Center beamed down on the skaters gaily circling the outdoor rink. David's gloved hand pressed tightly in his mother's as he watched with delight the gyrations of the skaters, felt the excitement of happy, laughing people who pressed past them, and absorbed with the clean wonderment of young eyes the newness and joy of it all. Bernard saw David and Myra from the other side of the rink. He stopped for a moment to watch them, feeling as always a slow gathering of excitement because of their nearness, a sense almost of disbelief that he should be so lucky. That the serene, lovely girl, the merry, volatile little boy, should be his! For this, it was worth the long hours at the agency, the grinding work at home. They were his, and he was theirs, that was all that mattered. That, and the new life that Myra carried. Another boy like David? Or a girl? They had already decided a girl would be called Sara. Yes, God willing, a Sara to give them fulfilment of the dream they had dreamed. He looked at Myra and David, reluctant to move and let this moment pass.

Most of the monsters rested quietly now, inert. They lay dormant and harmless in a thousand storage caverns across the world. Theirs was a peaceful quiet, disturbed only by the soft throb of a conditioning plant, the occasional plump of rubber soles as an attendant acolyte moved among them. They were pampered monsters, these, supplied with an atmosphere constantly checked for correctness of temperature and humidity, ministered to by expert technicians who ensured that though they slept it was a sleep in which they would lose none of their efficiency. No urgency to be rid of them now, men agreed, now that war was impossible and had been made impossible by their existence. As for their final disposal, men must confer, establish small points. It would take time, but no matter, now there was peace on earth. Let them lie then, impotent as very old men after a debauch, until a time in the future when they could safely be emasculated and buried and forgotten. So most of them lay quietly.

But not all.

Along Fifth Avenue the crowds moved slowly past the tempting window displays. David rode high in Bernard's arms, his face flushed as much with excitement as with the cold bite of the air. Myra rested her hand lightly on Bernard's arm. She would have liked to look closer at some of the stores, window-shop a little. Only window-shop though; their budget was stretched tight. She would have liked it, but she looked at David's glowing face, sensed Bernard's pride in carrying their boy beside her, and glanced down quickly at the swelling she could no longer conceal, nor wanted to conceal. Then she smiled the small, hidden smile of a woman who knows she is life, and pressed tighter on Bernard's arm.

*Nine miles above New York, out of sight and sound of the peo-
ple in the crowded streets, a B-52 headed north. It was one of the
force always kept airborne, even in these times of peace on earth,
to deter surprise attack. There was a cloudless sky, and the crew
saw clearly the lights of the great city, the octopus shape, with the
body that was Manhattan and the long, light-suckered tentacles that
laced through Brooklyn and Queens and the Bronx. The pilot had
been born on the lower East Side. He looked down at the city, and
he thought of the long, empty hours over the Arctic wastes. "Jesus
Christ," he said to the crew in general, "what a hell of a way to
spend Christmas!"*

They had reached their destination. For David's Christmas gift,
only one store was thinkable. Bernard and Myra, when they were
children, had been taken by their families, near-neighbors in the
Bronx, to F.A.O. Schwarz. They had continued the tradition, and
always they had taken David to Schwarz for his Christmas gift. The
first year it had been a plastic ball that gave out musical notes when
he shook it in his small fist. The second year, a large furry monkey
that endured countless indignities, including the frequent removal of
its eyes, and that still shared David's bed. Last year, a police car, of
which now only the battered, wheelless body remained. And now, this
Christmas, it was to be a locomotive. Myra had already taken David
for a preliminary reconnaissance. As soon as he saw the locomotive,
she knew that was what he wanted. The price was eighteen-fifty, three
and a half dollars more than they had budgeted for. But she saw the
shining joy in his eyes as he bent over the red, glossy toy, and she
immediately paid a five-dollar deposit on the gift. It would be
wrapped now, and waiting for them.

*Manuel Chavez padded quietly along West 84th Street. Halfway
along a block he swung neatly over a low wall into the darkness
of a derelict lot. He moved slowly to the corner where it was dark-
est, sat down, and lit a cigarette. He knew he was early, but he
preferred it that way, because while he waited for Consuela
he could think of her tender warmth, and her beauty, and all the
youthful, joyous things that made her his Consuela. He took
the small box from his pocket, opened it, and held the glowing butt
close so that the small ruby on the ring shone, as he knew her eyes*

would shine when he slipped it on to her finger. Then suddenly he became aware of them. They loomed out of a darkness no longer loving but hostile. One of them spoke. He said softly, caressingly, "We been waiting for you, Spick." He was trapped in a corner with walls to left and right of him. He opened his mouth to plead with them, and at the same time he felt the impact of a blade in his belly. The box dropped from his hand, and again he felt a blade, and again. As he went down, his dying mind registered only the grinning whiteness of teeth in what had become one face, a face that was black.

The family went up the winding stairs of the store, moving slowly in the press of people. Everywhere children held gaily wrapped parcels, and competed with the adults for space to view the marvels on display. David was not yet tall enough to look over some of the counters, so Bernard had to lift him for him to see the electric railways, the racing autos, the ingenious mechanical toys. Myra stayed close to them while they toured the store, a little tired now, but uncomplaining as she saw their obvious pleasure. Soon enough, she thought, it will be over, this time of delight for children. Let them enjoy it while they can. She checked her bag again to make sure she had brought the receipt for the deposit she had paid on the locomotive.

At Strategic Air Command Headquarters, located below ground at Offutt, near Omaha, the shifts were changing. Men handed over the duty to their reliefs, briefed them carefully on the happenings of the previous eight hours, and gratefully left in their hands, this Christmas Eve, control of a deterrent force whose power was measured now in the thousands of megatons. Looking down on the main floor from behind glass partitions, officers watched the ever-changing display boards, noting each minor change and correlating it to the main pattern. This was done through all the hours of the day and all the days of the year. The Russians knew it.

They were coming out of the store now, David proudly clutching his wrapped locomotive. Outside, the crowds were thicker than before, but Bernard, seeing the tiredness Myra could no longer conceal, achieved the miracle, at this time and on this day, of a taxi. Although there was heavy traffic, they made it to their small apartment in the

East Eighties within ten minutes. The taxi driver was polite and cheerful, and wished them a Merry Christmas. Bernard paid him, and hurried up after Myra and David to the apartment.

The Tibetan girl did not know how long she had been walking, how long it was since she last ate. Her senses were almost numbed now with cold and hunger. But when she saw them appear suddenly in front of her out of the mist, recognized their thick quilted uniforms and the star on their caps, she reacted with the pulsing quickness of awful fear. The invaders were quicker. They carried her to their small outpost hut, jabbering excitedly as they saw that she was young and well formed. Later, just before they finished her, their faces had already blurred into one leering face that hung over her. The face was yellow.

They had finished the complicated ritual of the bath, the hair-drying, the story, the search for the monkey, without whom sleep was not endurable, and at last David was in bed. Bernard sipped a brandy from a bottle that had been given to them by Myra's father. The spirit slipped warmly and fragrantly down his throat, and he relaxed contented while the clatter of dishes came from the kitchen and the bell on the small Christmas tree tinkled in a slight movement of air. The locomotive, still wrapped, lay under the tree with other gifts. Bernard smiled. It would not be wrapped when morning came, he thought. David shared with all small children the ability to wake long before their parents on Christmas morning.

At Soviet Strike Headquarters, located below ground at Tutaev, near Yaroslavl, the shifts were changing. Men handed over the duty to their reliefs, briefed them carefully on the happenings of the previous ten hours, and gratefully left in their hands, this twenty-fifth of December, control of a deterrent force whose power was measured now in the thousands of megatons. Looking down on the main floor from behind glass partitions, officers watched the ever-changing display boards, noting each minor change and correlating it to the main pattern. This was done through all the hours of the day and all the days of the year. The Americans knew it.

Not long after midnight David stirred, rolled over in bed, and was suddenly awake. In the distance he heard the wail of a police siren, and he thought of the police car he had been given last year. And that led to this year, and the knowledge that his locomotive would be lying under the tree in the living room, waiting for him. He slipped out of bed and cautiously opened the door into the corridor. Opposite was his parents' room. He listened for a moment to their deep, regular breathing, then gleefully hurried on into the living room. A dim, reflected glow from the street lights showed him the tree. He hurried across to it. The wrappings around the locomotive were difficult for his small hands, but finally they yielded. The last paper fell away, and he held it close to him, hugging it, as he drank in the ecstasy of the new-paint smell, the rumble of wheels as he spun them, the whole polished smoothness and cleanness of it. If only he could see the beautiful red and silver. . . . Switch on the light perhaps? No, too dangerous. But it was wonderful to hold it, to smell it, to be content with the dim outline shape that tomorrow would flash across the floor of the room. But still . . . if only he could see it now. He made a wish. And he saw his locomotive.

For one, bright, unholy millisecond.

INTERLUDE: Nanyang, Honan Province, October, 1964

The villa was large and spacious. It was not built in traditional Chinese style, but looked more like a big house you might see in a suburb of Minneapolis. Ironically, it was the creation of an American missionary who had obtained the necessary money by an appeal in his native State of Illinois. The missionary had used the villa as a home for some of the many destitute and abandoned Chinese children in the area. Therefore it had seven large bedrooms upstairs, each of which at one time had accommodated three or four children. But that was back in the thirties before first the Japanese, and then the victorious Chinese revolutionary army had fought over the country. The missionary had died in a Japanese prison camp in Shanghai.

On the ground floor, in addition to several rooms where children had once played and eaten their meals—food that was also provided by the generous people of Illinois—there was one very large room, which had been used as a chapel. All religious symbols had been removed from this room, and it contained now only a large circular table, ornately carved and inlaid with mother-of-pearl. Around the table were three chairs, and in one of these Comrade Li sat waiting for the arrival of the two men who had been summoned to this most important meeting.

Li was a man of middle height, slightly built, and with a thin ascetic face. Although he was nearly sixty years old, his smooth hair was still dark. He was in excellent health, except for an occasional twinge of rheumatism, which he had found could easily be alleviated by a simple process of acupuncture. His own personal physician occupied one of the bedrooms in the villa, and when Li experienced a twinge of rheumatic pain the cure was speedily effected. His was a mind of extremely high quality, and no less high was his status in the Party. He was not known at all outside China, and to only a few people inside the country. He never appeared in public, but in private he was an intimate friend and close confidant of the Prime Minister, and more important than that, of the Chairman of the Party. It was, in fact, the Chairman who had delegated to him the enormous power and responsibility that his present task entailed.

Li glanced at his wrist watch (the most accurate Swiss watch obtainable, and imported, of course, through Hong Kong) and saw he had twenty minutes before the other two arrived. This pleased him, because always before an important conference he liked to summarize the characteristics of the men he was meeting. As he thought, his long fingers delicately stroked the three-inch hairs that sprouted from a small mole on the right side of his chin, hairs that no true Chinese would dream of removing. He pressed a button on the table and almost immediately a servant appeared and placed before him a glass of warm, fragrant tea. Li sipped it, nodded in appreciation, and the servant left the room as quickly and quietly as he had entered it.

Li sipped the tea again, and began to think about the two men who would form, with him, the operational planning committee. He thought first about Comrade Professor Chen. A brilliant mind, of course, but only when concerned with atomic physics. A son of one of Chiang's officers who had been taken to Taiwan when Chiang's rabble were finally driven out of China. From Taiwan, at a suitable age, had been selected by the Americans for a scholarship at Georgia Tech. Followed that by two years' research at Yale. Was present at one of the American atomic tests. Returned to Taiwan, then after two years suddenly disappeared from Taiwan and arrived in the real China, where he was made very welcome when the extent of his knowledge about atomic physics had become clear. Appointed Assistant Director of Research on production of a Chinese atomic weapon, succeeded brilliantly, and was largely responsible for the explosion of the first Chinese atomic weapon in October, 1964.

But, was a man who had once defected completely reliable? It would be a point to remember, and also something of which he could remind Chen at some time, and thus establish moral as well as practical superiority. On the whole, Li thought, Chen would be reliable, but there was no point in missing any chance to establish his own position.

Li dismissed Chen from his mind and turned his thoughts to Marshal Chuang. He would not be so easy to deal with. Recognized as the most brilliant soldier in China, it was the Marshal who had defeated the American program of interdiction in Korea by organizing over fifty thousand laborers who each night humped anything up to one hundred pounds of supplies to the forward troops. It was he also to whom the Chairman turned for all advice on military matters. Marshal Chuang would take very clever handling. There was also, of course, his ridiculous attitude in pretending not to speak the national language. He was a Cantonese, and insisted that he had no time to learn another dialect. He spoke a few words occasionally, it was true, but then with an accent and with a complete disregard for tones that always made Li feel almost physical pain. That was one of the reasons the meeting would be conducted in English.

Li sipped his tea again and smiled gently as he thought how Chen had learned his English in America, while Marshal Chuang had been educated in an American school in Canton. He himself, of course, was a graduate of Oxford, where he had obtained a first in Politics, Philosophy, and Economics. He had not greatly enjoyed his time at Oxford. The British were kind, but in a manner that Li had always found slightly condescending, and therefore irritating, because as a Chinese he had been conscious from an early age that his race was superior to any other in the world.

He smiled briefly again as he thought that when it came, the British would be the first to go. Geographic distance made that certain and, as he was well aware, there were several air bases near Oxford that would certainly be prime targets. He found a great deal of satisfaction in that thought.

He looked at his wrist watch once more. In ten minutes the other two would be at the villa. They had already been fully briefed on the purpose of the meeting. Now it was time to consider a code name for the project.

Necessarily it would have to be in English, because a second reason for holding the meeting in English was the need for absolute security. Li had selected his staff of servants with extreme care. Not one of them could speak a word of any language other than Chinese. Not one of them could read or write. But even so, there would be no written notes recorded at the

meeting. Everything would be verbal, and since the details
would be relatively simple there was no reason to suppose that
two men like Chen and Chuang would forget, or fail to carry out
any of the requisite actions that the plan would entail.

He murmured a few phrases, and finally settled on one of
them. It seemed fitting, because it could easily be put into English form, while at the same time preserving a Chinese flavor in
the implication. Yes, that was it, the plan would be known as
the S-Day Plan. He smiled again as he wondered whether
Chuang had ever heard the phrase from which he had evolved
the English equivalent. He guessed that Chuang would probably
mutter something about literary nonsense, but that would not
matter. The S-Day Plan it was to be; and if he had to insist on
the name—well, he had the authority, as the other two men
would both realize.

He was satisfied now that he was ready to meet his co-
planners. He had five minutes left to think, but he did not think
about S-Day or about Chen or Chuang. Instead, he composed in
his mind a small poem in the classical style. He considered it
very good, and made a mental note to put it in writing after the
meeting was concluded.

The big door of the room that had once been a chapel swung
open, and Chen and Chuang were bowed in by one of the
servants. Li did not rise from his seat. He inclined his head very
slightly, and at the same time with a brief motion of his hands
indicated the two vacant chairs. Chen sat down at once. He was
a man nearly six feet tall, extremely thin, with a worried expression on his face. But Li knew this was perfectly normal.
Chen always had a worried expression, even at moments of
success. He was, Li considered, a neurotic, an introvert, as so
many of his colleagues were. But that did not matter. If Chen
could produce what was required, that was all Li was interested
in.

Marshal Chuang did not sit down immediately. He walked
round the room, deliberately ignoring Li's gesture that he
should sit. He was a short man, heavily built, with a broad,
seemingly stupid peasant's face. His hair was cropped close, and
he was dressed in the full uniform of a Chinese marshal. After
completing a circuit of the room, he turned abruptly and sat in
the one remaining chair.

Li pushed a button to summon a servant, and immediately three glasses of tea were brought. Li waited until the servant had left the room, then said, "You will have read your instructions, gentlemen, and you will realize that for security reasons we will conduct our discussion in English, and that nothing must be committed to writing. Not at any time. I believe"—he smiled briefly at Chuang—"that will suit the Marshal very well." But though he smiled, there was a veiled insult in the way he spoke.

Chuang looked directly at him. He said, "Well, we all understand English, and I agree we should conduct the meeting in English." He paused while he considered just what annoying remark he could make in return for Li's insult. Then he said, "Anyway, we won't have to waste time on Mandarin platitudes and meaningless four-character phrases." His voice was deep and thick, with just a trace of an American accent.

Chen said quickly and nervously, "I agree, I agree. That is, I mean I agree it would be better for security reasons to talk in English."

Li placed his fingertips together and said pleasantly, "Excellent, then we are agreed. But before we start our discussion I'm afraid I'll have to introduce a four-character phrase, though it is so common that no doubt the Marshal will forgive it."

He looked at Chuang, but Chuang remained completely impassive.

"The phrase I have in mind," Li said, "is *Syh hae ney way*. In view of the ultimate purpose of our planning I feel this is completely appropriate. As you both know"—he paused and smiled again briefly at Chuang—"the literal translation of this is 'Within and outside the four seas.' 'Within the four seas' means, of course, inside China; but the inclusion of the last character, which can be translated as 'outside,' indicates the whole phrase has the meaning, 'the world.' Now, if we take the first romanized word and use its roman initial—that is, S—to represent the world, then I am going to propose that we call this committee the S-Day Committee; and similarly the plan we shall evolve will be known as the S-Day Plan."

Chen said immediately, "I agree."

Chuang said, "Call it what you like, we all know what we're here for."

Li sipped a little tea before saying, "I am extremely glad we are in harmony. Then the S-Day Plan can now be formally introduced. Basically, gentlemen, it is a question of time and logistics. From you, Comrade Professor Chen, I shall expect the time factor. From you, Marshal Chuang, I shall expect the logistic answer. Now, before we discuss these vital aspects I expect you will wish to study the whole matter thoroughly. But remember this, we have—or rather, perhaps I should say *I* have"—he stressed the word "I" emphatically—"been given a maximum of two years by our Comrade Chairman of the Party, not only to produce a working plan but to implement it."

Chuang started to speak, but Li interrupted him smoothly and quietly. "*I* have been given that responsibility, and before we talk about the few technicalities that will be necessary at this time, let me point out to you that since I first approached you with a verbal briefing on the objective, a most important thing has happened. Khrushchev has been deposed. And this, gentlemen, has given us the chance we needed to take a certain step without losing face before the world."

Again he paused and sipped his tea. Chen drummed nervously on the table with his fingers. Chuang sat completely immobile. His face was impassive, as always.

Li continued, "And that, gentlemen, is a step that a year ago would have been unthinkable. I refer, of course, to an apparent rapprochement with our Soviet allies. The removal of Khrushchev and the detonation of our own atomic weapon have enabled us to do this without, as I said, losing face before the world. We can afford now to appear conciliatory, though not, of course, too conciliatory. Consequently I have to inform you that a delegation will be leaving for Moscow within the next few days. It is even possible that our Prime Minister will lead this delegation. But gentlemen, we must not lose sight of our ultimate objective. Now let us discuss the preliminary details."

The meeting lasted approximately two hours.

WAR: DECEMBER 25, 1965

In the past decade the Pentagon had been photographed more often than any other building in the world. More than St. Mark's, more than the Lincoln Memorial, more than the Houses of Parliament and the river that flows beside them. That river, the Thames, had been described as liquid history. But the Pentagon was living history. The highest policy decisions were shaped in the White House. Here, at the Pentagon, they were implemented. History was written in other places; here it was made. This was a building of supreme importance to the national security, and its physical stature was in keeping with that importance. Yet though the building appeared massive enough from street level, few knew that deep below ground was an even more elaborate structure; for, like an iceberg, the Pentagon showed only a small portion of itself above surface.

It was easy to assess the tension of the world situation in terms of the number of lights burning at night in the Pentagon. On this Christmas Eve there were few, and that in itself indicated a world at peace, a world free from major crisis or tension. But that was above the surface. Eight floors below ground level, deep down inside the concrete vitals of the building, purposeful activity continued, as it did through all the hours of every day and night of the year. Tonight was no exception.

Brigadier General Barry Kingston looked at his watch as he rode the last escalator down to his place of duty, and frowned. He estimated he would be three minutes late taking over the duty from Dixon. And Dixon was a major general. To a newly promoted brigadier this was an important distinction in rank, and though Kingston knew that Dixon was a tolerant, easy-going sort of person, he knew also that Dixon would certainly make a joke about his lateness. Kingston hurried on through the maze of corridors. He made a final turn to the right, and came to a stop facing a green metal door. Set in the top half of the door was a two-way mirror. Kingston pushed a buzzer, and although he could not see inside, he knew that the guard would be identifying him through the treated glass. He waited fifteen seconds, which was normal procedure, then spoke a sentence into a microphone set in the mirror.

The human voice has infinitely more varieties and patterns in its tones than the differing characteristics of fingerprints. A total of thirty officers and civilians were cleared for entrance to this room, which was designated simply BD927. The speech patterns of each had been recorded and fed into an electronic device set beside the door inside the room, which would immediately detect any discrepancy between the voice pattern of the officer who had spoken, and the original speech recording.

This system was foolproof. But it had been known to cause minor irritations. Such as the time, for example, when a general was suffering from a heavy cold, and the machine refused to identify him because of the discrepancy in speech pattern. And there was another occasion when an officer with toothache and a swollen jaw had been similarly refused.

But tonight there was no discrepancy, and the door swung open. Kingston stepped into the room and nodded to the A.P. sergeant guarding the door. They exchanged Christmas greetings, and Kingston heard the door close behind him as he walked across toward Dixon.

Dixon was on his feet. He glanced briefly at Kingston, and checked the displays once more. Then he turned to Kingston. "Well, hi there, Barry. Too much sack time?" His voice was deep and pleasant.

Kingston said quickly, "I'm sorry, sir. One of the kids playing around with the car left the headlights on. My battery was kind of tired. It took me a while to get the car started."

Dixon grinned. "Forget it. It's Christmas. And I'm going right on home to enjoy it. Eight hours from now, that is." He switched crisply from social to professional talk. "Everything normal, Barry. Situation is DEFCON FIVE. NORAD had a little excitement earlier, but it turned out to be electrical interference at one of the radar posts. So look forward to a quiet night, and a Merry Christmas to you." He bent and signed off, then turned and walked to the door.

Kingston signed the operations log. He meticulously noted the time he had taken over the duty as three minutes past midnight, and then, as was his normal practice, went over to look carefully at the displays on the main floor. The room in which he was could perhaps better be described as a balcony. It was long, and along its entire length a plate-glass window, slightly tilted, enabled him to see all the activity on the main floor. His personal exec, Major Schmidt, handed him the current Intelligence Report, and Kingston sank into one of the upholstered beige chairs that were scattered about the room. "Anything new?" he asked Schmidt.

"Not a thing. Everything as peaceful as it could be. Even our little yellow brothers continue to be cordial with the Russians. Could be it's Christmas."

"Now, that just could be," Kingston said. He riffled rapidly through the sheaf of reports, laid them on his desk, and said, "Wonder what the Chinese are doing? That's a hell of a big delegation they have in Moscow. Maybe we have them both lined up against us again. Okay, Smitty, make the checks. Looks as though it's going to be a quiet night."

"I can use it," Schmidt said, and he moved away to start procedural checks with SAC, NORAD, and the other major commands.

Kingston moved over to the window, and looked down on the floor. Whenever he was in charge of the Command Post, it gave him a feeling that he supposed was like the feeling the captain of a big ship would have as he stood on his bridge. He looked first at the screens, which displayed in a variety of colors the vital information that was fundamental to any decisions that might be made in this room.

As always—again like the captain of a big ship—his immediate concern was for the safety of his command. But the NORAD display showed no threat. Intelligence from intercepted enemy signals indicated that a comparatively large force of Russian bombers was active over northern Siberia. But it had been known for some days that the Russians were pulling a major air exercise. So there was nothing to worry about in those reports. The usual seven or eight Russian submarines were indicated about two hundred miles off the Atlantic and Pacific coasts of the United States. Also a few trawlers, electronic spies whose presence had to be tolerated, since they were in interna-

tional waters. All this was completely normal. And of course the
NUDETS (which stood for Nuclear Detection System) was completely blank.

Kingston next looked at the offensive forces he had available to
him at this time. First, of course, because he was a SAC man at heart,
he checked the display indicating bombers on airborne alert, and on
ground stand-by at various degrees of readiness. Forty B-52's, fully
loaded, were airborne and on patrol, mostly over the Arctic Circle.
Another hundred were on five-minute stand-by, and a further hundred at fifteen minutes. Also, of the force of ninety B-58 supersonic
bombers available, thirty were at five minutes. The twenty-five Atlas
intercontinental ballistic missiles were at ten minutes. These were all
that were left from the original Atlas force. The others had been
gradually phased out as they were replaced by the Titans and Minutemen in their hardened bases. But the Atlas bases were not hardened.
Therefore the Atlas missiles were kept at the highest state of readiness, since if anything happened—though there seemed little chance
of that these days of peace on earth—they would be the first to go to
escape destruction by an enemy first strike. Kingston noted also that
there were twenty Polaris submarines at sea, each with a load of
sixteen missiles.

For a brief moment, which yet encompassed the twenty-seven
hours he had spent with the combat crewmen, he thought about his
experience in a Minuteman Silo. This had been part of his indoctrination before he assumed his assignment in the Pentagon C.P. First, a
helicopter flight from the H.Q. of the 341st Strategic Missile Wing to
the site of one of the underground capsules scattered across twenty
thousand square miles of central Montana; and the towns over which
the helicopter had passed, small towns with names like Geyser and
Coffee Creek. Then the site itself, with the missiles sitting under
eighty-ton concrete lids, which would be blasted off by high explosive
once the order to launch was given. The checks, double checks, and
triple checks, required before he could join the two white-overalled,
shock-helmeted missile crewmen in their journey down the elevator to
the capsule itself. He himself had been similarly clad in white overalls
and shock helmet. He thought about the way in which the missile

crew on duty below, after the appropriate checks, unfastened the two-inch steel bolts that locked the eight-ton door of the capsule.

He recalled how the crewmen who were on duty handed over the keys that would enable the replacement crew to launch the missiles, and how he then settled into the self-contained capsule floating on its shock-proof cushion of compressed air, sitting on a specially installed pilot's chair from a Boeing KC 135. There were two other such chairs in the capsule, but this one had been installed especially for him, as was the custom when the higher brass visited a launch capsule where comparatively junior officers exercised a responsibility unequaled in the history of warfare.

But, he recalled, though these officers exercised this unequaled responsibility, there were still precautions against individual actions of bigots or plain madmen. Only after the President had issued the order—and the order had to be in voice coded of course—could the officers direct the missiles to be launched. This required an insertion of two keys on the right side of the control panel; and further, the two keys would have to be inserted within two seconds of each other. It had been physically established that this was impossible for one man to do, even if he had put his companion out of action.

Even so, the launching could be negated if it had not been received and authenticated by officers in the linked capsules of the complex. Such was the realization of the awfulness they might let loose upon the world.

But if the inhibitor switches were not thrown prior to thirty-two seconds of a launching, the missiles would go, and then it might be a very different world into which the combat crewmen emerged.

They did not know their targets, and for that matter neither did Kingston. But a certain colonel who had once commanded the 341st had stated that Minutemen in Alpha flight were exactly 4,432.3 miles from the Kremlin.

Kingston put all this away from his mind and turned to the displays again to make his final checks. These were on state of readiness of NATO forces and the SAC bases overseas, from the United Kingdom to Okinawa. The NATO forces, of course, included not only that tactical fighter bomber and strike aircraft on the continent of Europe, but also R.A.F. Bomber Command. He noted with a wry smile that

Bomber Command had available six V-bombers at four minutes'
readiness, and twelve at ten minutes. Kingston thought neither figure
mattered very much. In his opinion there was little chance of any of
them getting off the ground in the event of a sudden strike. The
United Kingdom simply did not have the depth to absorb a surprise
attack, especially if it did not come from the expected direction.
From the north or east, maybe there would be four minutes' warning.
But if the threat came from the south or west he doubted if there
would be any warning at all. But naturally, commanders everywhere
always based their plans on the doctrine of the preferred attack. It
made everything simpler and easier to plan for. Without it, war games
were impossible. Therefore the preferred attack it had to be, so the
commanders could show satisfactory—if highly and improbably
theoretical—figures of enemy forces destroyed in a war game. Thus
they justified their continued existence.

From the displays, Kingston turned his attention to the people on
the main floor. Most important of these were the seven officers who
occupied the central command position, five of them in constant
communication with the major U.S.A.F. commands, two in communication with NATO and Navy. The seven officers sat at a long
bench, each position well equipped with telephones and other communications apparatus. If the balcony was the brain center of the
Combat Post, then the floor represented the main nervous system by
which the brain's intention could be transmitted to the operative arms
of the worldwide body.

Two of the officers wore keys around their necks, each affixed to a
plastic tag. If the word should ever be given, if the Presidential
klaxon should announce DEFCON ONE, the order to go to war,
these officers would make use of their keys.

Two more men sat at each side of the bench and slightly behind it.
Both of them wore holstered .38-caliber Smith and Wesson revolvers.
Their sole function was to shoot any member of the team who might
crumble when the pressure was on, and who might attempt to start a
war on his own, because of some illness, or mental unbalance, or
even deliberate intent. No precaution had been overlooked. But that
situation was unlikely ever to arise until DEFCON TWO had been
ordered. So the officer and sergeant with the holstered weapons

though there had been a time when a reporter had picked up a stray piece of conversation and considered calling it in to his paper. But fortunately the reporter was a man both of loyalty and discretion, and before calling in the item he had checked with a friend of his who actually worked in the War Room. And so the information was never published, and a captain found himself abruptly separated from the Air Force.

Similarly, on a fatal November day when a man of great and good heart had been struck down by a murderer's bullets, there had been speculation, worry even, about what would have happened if the Russians had hit between the time of the assassination and the swearing in of a new President. Nothing was revealed, even in the pressure of that awful time, but in fact the speculations and worries were unnecessary.

McConnell and his seven colleagues were a team of carefully selected, highly trained men who directly represented the President. They knew his thoughts and intentions. They knew the innermost secrets of military procedures and orders. They had been told quite bluntly that it was probable their services would never be needed, except in conditions which would require the exercise of absolute power normally and constitutionally belonging to the President alone. They had accepted these conditions. They had been granted this power.

And so it was that on that November day one of the team—not McConnell, but a man called Pulaski—had stood here for hours until a new President was sworn in and was in executive control. Only when that had happened could Pulaski sigh with relief and return to obscurity in the aides' duty room.

Of the eight men in the team, six were on call at any time. Two were on leave from duty, and it was insisted that this leave should always be taken a long distance from Washington. The six who were not on leave worked twelve-hour shifts, spending most of the time in the comfortably appointed room set aside for them at the end of the balcony. After their twelve hours they would be relieved and would be free for sixty hours. But during this sixty hours they were required to be within easy distance of the Pentagon, and capable of being reached by telephone at any time. Always before their turn of duty they were exhaustively briefed on the latest military and political intelligence.

They were faceless men, and so far as the general public was concerned, men without names also. In their job there was no prospect of advancement, no chance of glory or distinction. When they reached the age of fifty they would be quietly replaced by younger men who had undergone the same intensive training and briefing. They would retire, unheard of, unknown, to some place of their choice, and they would forget all about the War Room and what happened there. At least they would forget it consciously, but in their subconscious would always be the memory that, given certain circumstances, they were the most powerful men in the world; and more important than that, the men who might have to make a terrible decision. They all understood this, and accepted it, and it was because their acceptance and understanding had been proved by exhaustive tests that they were selected in the first place.

So on this Christmas Day McConnell stood on the balcony. Behind him he could hear Kingston talking to NORAD. In front of him on the NUDETS a small red dot appeared on New York City. He made a decision, and turned to Kingston. "Civil Defense," he said quietly, "full alert, Barry."

Kingston reached for a phone and gave a brief code-word order. Then he looked at McConnell. "Is that all?"

Schmidt broke into the conversation. He said, "Sir, it just isn't possible to reach the President. They've tried everything. But if they can make contact they'll get back to us immediately." He replaced the gold phone on its cradle.

McConnell and Kingston were thinking together, though both of them were probably unconscious of that; and their thoughts were perhaps divergent, slanting away from each other though they emanated from the same starting point.

McConnell was thinking of the chaos that would inevitably be caused by ordering a civilian alert. By this time the sirens were wailing in New York—if there was anything left of New York—and in a thousand other places too. People would be rushing to shelter, though McConnell knew that if this was a big strike the shelter wouldn't be much use to them. Not in the large towns anyway. But there would be chaos on the roads, chaos everywhere as people sought refuge. The Vice-President was in Helsinki, the Secretary of State in Washington. The Secretary of Defense was in North Carolina with the President. But the absence of these officials did not mean anything to McConnell. At this moment, lacking any communication with the President, he must make the decision. He thought for a moment about his own children, and was glad they were thirty miles out of Washington. He had already assessed the wind direction and strength from the displays. With any luck the fallout might not hit them. With any luck . . .

The clock recorded fifteen minutes past midnight. The clock was absolutely accurate, or at least as accurate as modern science could make it. It would gain or lose one second about every twenty thousand years.

Kingston was thinking more about the strictly military implications. He could not understand why they had not so far gone for **NORAD** and **SAC** and Washington. He marshaled the thoughts in his mind. Clear was out. This could be a bluff, but the bomb that had hit New York was no bluff, and neither was the explosion in North Carolina. In little pieces, he thought angrily, they're going to knock us out. So far, the damage wasn't great. But Clear was *out*. So that could mean the big missiles would be striking inside fifteen minutes, or it could mean thirty-plus minutes if they were trying for the end run over the South Pole. He glanced briefly at the displays and saw that now there were over two hundred B-52's at combat readiness, and twenty of the missiles on the non-hardened bases had started their countdown. He ordered the B-52's off, as he had the right to under **DEFCON TWO**, and let the missile countdown proceed. It could be checked at any time up to two minutes before blast-off. He had a feeling that this was it. But somehow he also felt that McConnell did not realize this. . . .

All over the country people heard the sirens wail. But not in certain areas of New York. The center of the explosion had been near the Central Park Zoo.

The apartment where Bernard and Myra and David had lived no longer existed. Three human beings, and the new life that one of them contained within herself, had ceased at midnight. Without pain, it is true, but also without trace, without volition, without even the human dignity of knowledge. They were not alone in this. . . .

McConnell turned to Kingston. "Where in hell is Dixon?" he asked. "What's taking him so long?"

Kingston shrugged. "Could be he was taking a shower when I gave you the three-bell alarm." He heard a sound from the identivox apparatus, and a few seconds later the door swung open and Dixon came quickly into the room. The same alarm that had summoned McConnell had brought Dixon down from the comfortable suite where each general going off C.P. duty was required to pass the next eight hours. This ensured that two generals were always available, one actually in the C.P., one on call in the suite on the third floor.

Dixon said briskly, "Mac, Barry, just what in hell's going on around here?"

Kingston said, "Smitty, clue the General in on what's happened." Schmidt moved over to the displays and began talking rapidly to Dixon.

McConnell felt a sense of inward relief. Now, if necessary, he could act. Without the presence of two generals he was powerless, and the reason for this went a long way back. A few years previously a book had been published hypothecating the situation in which one general, in the right place at the right time, could on his own initiative order an attack on the Russians. McConnell did not know whether this was true or not at that time. He did know that there had been a lot of comment and speculation, and that certainly it was true no longer. This held good even if the President himself gave the order to go to war. It still required the presence of two generals to confirm the enemy threat before the order could be implemented, in the same way that it required simultaneous action by two men in each of four Minuteman Silos to act in concert. This additional safety precaution had not generally been made public, but in the usual Washington way there had been a few inspired leaks hinting at the existence of the system. But now Dixon was here with Kingston, the necessary order could be given if circumstances should require it. McConnell looked at the displays again and wondered if the order would have to be given.

Major Schmidt finished his explanation to Dixon. The latter nodded, and said, "Okay, Barry, I'll take over now as senior operations controller. You'll act as deputy."

"Yes, sir," Kingston replied. He too felt a sense of relief. From now on he was third in the chain of command. The order to go would have to come from McConnell, but in giving that order he would of course be influenced by the advice of the two generals. The two generals would also have to concur in the necessity for the order. But with the displays before them showing clearly the threat against the country, it was unlikely there would be disagreement.

McConnell looked at Dixon. "What do you think of it, Joe?"

Dixon paused for a moment before replying. When he spoke his voice was heavier, without the jovial bantering tone he had used earlier. He glanced at the wall clock. "The way I see it, it's eight minutes now since the launchings. If they're trying for an end run I'd say that gives us up to thirty minutes before they start hitting. But if they're faking, if they're really coming in through the Clear segment, I'd say we have about six minutes, maybe a little more."

Kingston spoke urgently, "General, I'd like to get those thirty B-58's off the ground. SAC has plenty of tankers to refuel them, and I'd sure hate for them to be caught on the ground if the Russians are coming in from the west."

"Get them off, Barry," Dixon said crisply. "Bring as many more to stand by as you can. And as fast as they come to stand-by, get them off too. Same with the fifty-twos."

Kingston turned to Schmidt. "Get that out to SAC."

Schmidt picked up the red phone to SAC and gave the coded order. The hands of the clock moved onto eighteen minutes after midnight.

The gold phone buzzed. Kingston picked it up, listened, then replaced it. "Positively no contact with the President. No contact at all."

McConnell said, "How long do we have before we have to hold the countdown on the Atlases?"

"About a minute."

McConnell thought quickly and made a decision, in which he was influenced by another possibility that had occurred to him.

He gave his executive decision first. "Hold the countdown at the last possible moment." Then he went on, speaking fast. "I'm puzzled, gentlemen. Why haven't they hit NORAD? Or SAC? Or Washington, come to that? Why just the President and Clear and New York?"

Kingston started to speak, but McConnell interrupted him. "Hold it, Barry." His voice was authoritative. "Have you fellows thought of this? We know we have effective systems of command and control. We know we have safeguards. But maybe their system isn't as sophisticated as ours. Maybe one of *their* commanders could take things into his own hands, order off some of his missiles before he could be stopped. That would account for only three missiles. And even if the President is wiped out, don't forget the teleprinter link,"—he smiled faintly—"what the papers call the 'hot line,' runs through here. I'm going to talk to them myself. Set it up, Kingston."

Kingston picked up the phone that connected with the teleprinter room, where no less than three teleprinters were linked with Moscow. It was unlikely one would not function, almost impossible that two would not. And completely impossible that all three would go out simultaneously, the experts agreed, since each of them was checked every hour. As Kingston spoke into the phone, the hands of the clock moved on to twenty after midnight.

Dixon said, "Mac, I can't go along with you. New York, yes. Maybe a lunatic would do that. But Clear, no. What's his purpose? The President, no. Again, what's his purpose?"

McConnell shrugged. "Who can say what a lunatic will do?"

"Or a genius," Dixon said softly. "Don't forget these people are the greatest chess players in the world. I've studied the games some of their masters have played, and they're great, and I'm telling you I think this is a gambit. You play chess?"

"No, I don't."

"Well, never mind. I've thought this thing through, and I see it differently from you. Forget New York—that's part of the gambit. It's a fake, a trap, and you're about to walk right into it. Forget Clear, if you like—I don't think they'll be coming that way for a while yet. But think of the President. As far as they know, he's the only one can authorize reprisal. They *don't* know you and the seven others have immediate executive control. Oh, I know it's been published that there's an established pecking order, but the way I see it they figure that in the confusion of the President's death there will be an interim period before the next in line can take over. I'd guess they'd figure on at least an hour. And I'll go further and say that the first launchings were an end run." He looked at the clock. "That means they'll start hitting in about twenty plus a few minutes. And then they use Clear, pump in their main missile force through that segment with a scheduled time on target to coincide with the missiles coming the long way round by the South Pole." He looked steadily at McConnell.

Kingston replaced his phone. When he spoke to them his voice was calm, but beneath the calm was an undertone of strain. He said, "They're getting no response from the Russians. They've checked the lines, and there are no faults on our side. But the Russians aren't answering."

"Well, now—" McConnell began, but broke off as the NORAD line buzzed.

Schmidt grabbed the phone. He listened to the message. His voice was steady as he said, "Roger, I will repeat. MIDAS reports more launchings in Bodaybo region. Multiple." He had heard Dixon's argument, and though his voice had been steady, his face was white.

Dixon said, "Mac, this has to be it. This has to be their plan, as I said. And naturally they pick tonight. Remember the Luftwaffe attack at dawn on January first in 1945? Their last desperate gamble for air superiority?"

"Yes, I do. And they did a lot of damage. But it didn't win the war for them."

"No," Kingston said, "but they didn't have megaton, or possibly gigaton, weapons either. I'll go along with General Dixon. Everything fits into the picture. As far as they're concerned, tomorrow's no holiday. But they know it's a holiday with us. They don't know about you and the other seven, but they do know we're at DEFCON FIVE—or were. But what's really important, they don't know about you and the other seven."

"Not seven," McConnell said quietly, "fifteen." He glanced at the clock. "But that doesn't matter for the moment. Joe, if you're right, if the first firings were an end run, not directed through the Clear segment, that means we won't be hit in the next few minutes; correct?"

"Correct. I'd say about twenty minutes from now. But when we are," he continued, "it's going to be with everything they've got. Including one missile for here, probably with a hundred megaton warhead. I know we're pretty deep down, but if they fuse it for ground burst that isn't going to help us any. Our central command will be gone, and without any warning, not even a minute. We'll be in the same state they assume we're in now."

"Not quite," McConnell said. "Not quite. Any link with the Russians yet?"

Kingston picked up the phone. "No contact," he said.

McConnell lit a cigarette. Normally he was a heavy smoker, but this was his first cigarette since he had stepped onto the balcony. He exhaled smoke, and asked, "What's our shape, Joe?"

Dixon looked intently at the displays. Without turning around he said, "Good as it can be. We have two hundred fifty B-52's airborne. Forty B-58's. All twenty-five Atlases now holding at two minutes. Eighty Titans and forty Minutemen at two minutes also. We don't have to worry too much about the Titans and Minutemen. They may get some of them, but certainly not all. And all the Polaris subs are ready to fire. It's pretty good, but it won't be under certain circumstances."

"What circumstances?"

Kingston said, "Let's suppose they've targeted the first of the end-run missiles for Washington. I won't worry about SAC, because they already know we have a flying command post airborne every hour of the day to take over if they clobber Offutt. But *we* could go out just like that." He snapped his fingers. "And then who gives DEFCON ONE? Who's going to be left to give it?"

McConnell stubbed out his cigarette in the heavy glass ashtray. "Three people just like us," he said. "Don't ask me where they are; I don't know, and even if I did I couldn't tell you. All I know is they're somewhere on this continent. But this whole setup here is exactly duplicated there. They're even listening to our conversation now, recording it, watching the same displays we are. If we go out, they'll pass the word to SAC, and with what we now have airborne and ready to go that's the end of Russia. Everything's been thought of. We personally may not live to see it, but I know those boys will." He lit another cigarette. "We can afford to wait."

"And that's your decision?" Kingston asked. His voice was unnaturally loud.

"That's my decision."

"Now I know what fools people can be," Dixon said quietly.

"Fools?" McConnell said. "Hardly fools, Joe. We've taken all precautions against starting a war by accident. That's why there are three of us here. We've also taken all precautions against losing a war because the President or this C.P. is knocked out. Hardly the action of fools."

"I said fools, and I meant fools," Dixon repeated. His voice was definitely angry now.

"I disagree. We've done everything mortal man can do. The rest . . ." He shrugged.

"There's one thing you haven't done. Oh, I don't blame any one individual, but your system isn't as perfect as you may think."

McConnell looked at the clock. "It looks as if your guess was right, Joe," he said. "If they're going to hit us, the first launchings were sent the long way round. You agree?"

"I agree."

"And we're ready for it. So how does that make us fools?"

Dixon said deliberately, "Security mania. We leak the things it isn't important for the enemy to know. We conceal the details he absolutely should know. Don't you see, even if your system is perfect—and I don't agree any man-designed system can be one hundred per cent perfect—it will still fail *if you conceal from the enemy that whatever happens he's going to get clobbered?* And that's what you've done. He may have guessed there'd be someone with direct executive authority to take over here if the President goes. So he plans his attack accordingly to take this place out first. He doesn't know that this C.P. is duplicated. You should have announced it publicly. You could still have concealed exactly where it was—you've done that successfully anyway. So how does he know the deterrent still exists if he manages to get both the President and this place? He doesn't. *And from that moment the deterrent ceases to exist anyway. Because if he doesn't know, how can it deter him?*"

The phone from Combat Intelligence buzzed. Kingston picked it up, listened to the message, and handed it to McConnell.

McConnell said, "I see," and replaced the phone. "Well, Joe, they've monitored a Russian broadcast claiming successful launching of a space platform. What do you think?"

Dixon, his voice normal again, said. "I don't know. All we can do is wait. Maybe they're faking again, maybe not. But if they're really striking, I know where a lot of the blame will be."

No one spoke. McConnell sat quietly, dreamily almost, smoking another cigarette. Dixon paced up and down the balconies. As more airplanes were shown airborne, more missiles at two minutes' hold, he began to calculate the megatonnage represented by the displays. Enough to sink a continent, he thought. Enough to sink the world almost. He was convinced his analysis was correct. Kingston sat quietly. He had his own opinions, but as a very junior brigadier he did not feel this was the time or place to voice them, especially now that he knew every word said here was being recorded in another place where an exactly duplicated group of a civilian executive, a major general, and a brigadier were waiting to take over as soon as the Pentagon C.P. went out.

Eight minutes went by. None of the three felt inclined to speak. There was an electric tension between them, Kingston felt, the same tension that spreads through the death row of a state penitentiary when a prisoner is only a few minutes away from the searing flash that will remove him from the world forever, and yet there is also hope of a last-minute reprieve. Once the prisoner was executed, it would not matter whether he was guilty or innocent—not to the prisoner anyway. But to the last moment, until they strapped him into the chair, he would hope for reprieve.

Kingston's thoughts were abruptly interrupted by the NORAD phone. And suddenly he knew. There would be no reprieve.

He spoke slowly and clearly, "Roger, I repeat. Cape Charles reports eight missiles, probably fired from submarines, heading in from the east. Matagordo reports eight-plus missiles heading in from southeast. Mendobino reports ten missiles heading in from west." He covered the mouthpiece and looked at McConnell.

McConnell held up one finger.

Kingston uncovered the mouthpiece, and said, "All NORAD units DEFCON ONE. I repeat, DEFCON ONE."

McConnell snapped into action. So Joe had been right. He calculated swiftly. The Atlases first. He began to give orders.

On the main floor the klaxon sounded. The two officers who wore keys around their necks simultaneously unlocked padlocks on a red, flat box two feet long and eight inches wide. From it they removed seven plastic bags and handed the appropriate bag to each of the officers at the command bench. Inside the bags were the orders for each major command. The orders were coded, but they all had the same meaning. *Go to war.*

But the system was not quite so inevitable as that. McConnell had been thoroughly trained in the necessity of avoiding a spasm response to what had so far been proved a *comparatively* minor threat. The response had to be graduated in relation to the weight of enemy attack. He was secure in the knowledge that the back-up C.P. could and would act on the major threat when it was proved. Now he gave certain amending orders. Two minutes later twenty-five Atlas missiles lifted off their pads and pointed their ugly heads, first to the sky, and then, as they curved gracefully into ballistic trajectory, toward Russia. They were followed thirty seconds later by fifteen Titans. All these missiles were targeted for missile complexes and major bomber bases. . . .

The launchings were detected by a Russian satellite—the Soviet equivalent of MIDAS. Intelligence had, of course, known for a long time that the Russians had developed a MIDAS type of satellite. What they did not know was how sophisticated its instrumentation was, compared with the American system. In fact, it was slightly cruder, but it was still efficient enough to detect the launchings of the Atlas and Titan missiles and report them back to Russian Air Defense Headquarters in Omsk. The message reached there only seconds after the missiles had blasted off. It was instantly relayed to Strike Headquarters at Tutaev. . . .

McConnell, with a glance at the clock, said, "The big ones haven't hit us yet."

Dixon shook his head. "Could be any time in the next few minutes. We don't know exactly how fast their strike missiles travel."

Major Schmidt broke in. "All Russian radio stations are broadcasting full civilian alert. The Intelligence boys have just intercepted the first broadcast." He listened again as a voice crackled in the receiver of the phone. Then he continued, "All stations except Radio Moscow, that is. For some reason they've picked this exact moment to go off the air. The boys on monitoring say they can't even pick up a carrier wave."

Dixon said loudly and positively. "It has to be an all-out strike. They're obviously—" He was interrupted by the insistent buzzing of the NORAD phone.

Kingston seized the phone. He listened to the brief message, then said, "Okay, I'll hold the line open." He covered the mouthpiece and spoke rapidly to Dixon and McConnell. "MIDAS report further multiple launchings. No positive identification on numbers, but more numerous than previous launchings." He continued to listen for any further news from NORAD, the receiver pressed to his ear.

McConnell drummed his fingers on the table. Then he rose from his chair and paced up and down the balcony.

Dixon noted that another forty B-52's were airborne, and while he watched the displays the figure for Hustlers rose to fifty. They've failed, he thought grimly; whatever happens now they've failed. There was enough megatonnage airborne to sink Russia without trace. More than enough. He knew it was the SAC system of reserve crews that had enabled so many bombers to get off the ground so fast.

Kingston spoke sharply. "Roger, I repeat." His voice was deliberately loud so that Dixon and McConnell could hear. "Fylingdales report ballistic missile trajectories definitely tracked. Thirty-plus. I'll hold."

McConnell looked at Dixon.

Dixon said, "The rest of the Titans and Minutemen. You have to do it."

McConnell nodded curtly. He turned to Kingston. "You agree, Barry?"

Kingston, the NORAD phone still pressed to his ear, said, "Concur."

McConnell nodded again. Dixon picked up a phone and began to give orders. On the displays a number of points began to appear as the trajectories of the missiles and their probable striking points were computed.

The remaining Titans and Minutemen were one minute from blast-off when Kingston spoke again. "Roger, I repeat, Thule reports thirty-plus missile tracks. Trajectories not yet established, but definitely ballistic missiles. I'll continue to hold."

Dixon said, "Sixty at least, plus what they've got coming through Clear segment. This is it."

"I agree," McConnell said. "Total response." He looked first at Dixon, then at Kingston. Both nodded their agreement. "All right, let's get it out. The Polaris subs first."

Again Dixon picked up a phone and talked with the naval officer on the floor. He said only one word. The Navy man checked with his coded sheet, and reached for his telephone.

"Now the manned bombers," McConnell ordered. "Global."

"Roger," Dixon said. Within seconds the war orders had been passed to all SAC bombers, whether based in the continental United States or overseas. Also to NATO and all other major commands.

One last formality remained. It had in the past been hypothecated that a runaway bomber might in itself start a thermonuclear war. But this hypothesis took no account of the sophistication of modern weaponry. Before the weapons in the planes could be armed, a signal had to be sent to them from transmitters sited about fifty miles from Washington, and connected by deep cables with the Pentagon. Until this signal was received, the crew of the bomber simply could not arm their bombs. It was yet another precaution taken to prevent war by accident or madness. Further, the signal could only be sent by the simultaneous activation of three trigger switches. One of these was situated in the aide's room, two on the balcony.

McConnell looked at the wall clock. The sweep second hand was vertical. He said calmly, "At thirty seconds past the minute, gentlemen," and went across the balcony into his room.

Dixon and Kingston moved to their switches. As the second hand reached thirty, each of them pushed the switch button and held it in for exactly ten seconds. Only five seconds was actually necessary, but the drill called for ten seconds in case one of the officers was a little late in pressing his button. Again, by a procedure similar to that adopted for the Minutemen, it had been established that it was physically impossible for one man, or even for two men acting in concert, to press all three buttons within the requisite time. This was another safeguard, another indication and proof of the national determination to prevent war by accident or madness.

McConnell came out of his room. He lit a cigarette, sank into one of the chairs. "Well," he said, "that's it. Now we can only wait."

Dixon and Kingston took chairs near him. They waited together.

It was eleven minutes later that command transferred automatically to the duplicate C.P.

INTERLUDE: Nanyang, Honan Province, December, 1964

The three men sat around the ornate table in the same room in which they had sat before and, as before, tea was brought for them. Li, after murmuring a few conventional phrases of greeting, took the opportunity of the few minutes in which the tea was being served to study, though not noticeably, the demeanors of Marshal Chuang and Professor Chen. Chuang, he thought, was as imperturbable as ever. In a moment he intended to do a little to shake that imperturbability. Chen was obviously nervous. He would not have liked the urgent message he had received, Li thought. No matter, that would encourage him to work all the harder. If a scientist could not sleep, he tended to spend more time at his work. Li decided that he would not relieve Chen's anxiety. After the project was finished Chen would be disposable anyway. There were plenty of younger and perhaps even more brilliant minds coming along to replace Chen in the New World.

Chuang broke in on Li's thoughts. He said, in that thick, cultureless voice that Li always found so jarring, "I don't want tea, I want beer. A cold bottle of beer."

Li pressed the bell to summon a servant. He said quietly, "You shall have it, Marshal. Though of course it is a habit that . . ." He let the sentence trail off unfinished, as indeed he had intended to, though ostensibly the reason was the entry of a servant into the room.

Chuang shrugged his thick shoulders. What Li said mattered little to him. His part of the preliminary planning was almost complete, and he knew it. Let Li be as offensive as he wanted. After the day—he could not help thinking of it now as S-Day—there would be more need for men of action than for dreamy intellectuals. The servant returned with a large bottle of San Miguel beer, brewed in Hong Kong, and brought to Nanyang by one of the many devious ways Li used for importing merchandise.

Li watched with disgust while Chuang poured a glass of the beer from the moisture-glistening bottle and swallowed half of it in one gulp. He said, "Since Marshal Chuang is occupied for the moment, we will begin by hearing your report, Comrade Professor Chen."

Chuang ignored Li's barbed remark. He refilled his glass as Chen began to speak. Chen said rapidly and nervously, "All is well, Comrade Li. In fact, it is better than well; our progress has been faster than I anticipated."

Li said quietly, "So you made a mistake in your estimate?"

"No, not that," Chen replied hastily. "It's just that we made what the Americans would call a breakthrough, and the devices will be ready much sooner than we thought."

"How many?" Li asked. "What size? Are they acceptable to Marshal Chuang?"

Chen said, "They are. Last week I visited the Marshal and gave him the exact details of size, shape, and weight."

Chuang smacked his glass on to the table. He looked first at Chen and then at Li. "That's right, he did exactly that. And if his figures are accurate, I can pull it." He picked up his glass again and drained the rest of the beer.

Now, Li thought, now is the time to bring in the shock, to teach these two—admittedly skilled but nevertheless ignorant peasants—exactly who is master. He said, "Your news gives me much pleasure. It will also, I know, give great pleasure to our beloved Comrade Chairman. I was talking with him last night, and he specifically asked me to report to him on the results of today's meeting. He stressed how important this project would be, and also how much he depended upon me to carry it through to a successful conclusion." He stressed the word "me" very slightly, but with just enough emphasis to ensure that both Chuang and Chen got the message.

Li smiled benignly at them both, then continued, "We talked for a long time. You are aware how conscious our Chairman is of our past glories. Let us remember, gentlemen, that we Chinese were civilized when the rest of the world thought a mud hut or a cave was luxury. Even in those days we had our poets and philosophers. Our beloved Chairman looks forward to the day when again we shall be supreme, and I do not think it will be very long now. Our rapprochement with the Russians has been successful. Very successful, if you consider that we have re-established full diplomatic relations without concessions and without losing face in the eyes of the world. The next step, of course, will be to arrange a trade fair in Moscow. It is true that the products we send along will probably not be competitive in design or price. But a trade fair there must be."

He broke off abruptly, sipped his tea, then looked directly at Marshal Chuang. "Would that help your logistic problem, Marshal?"

Chuang thought for a moment before he answered. He knew that he himself could easily persuade the Chairman to talk to him. But he was beginning to have an uneasy feeling that Li had got there first, that Li was closer to the seats of power than he was. And certainly the idea of a trade fair was attractive. It would also solve his remaining problem. He said shortly, "It would help."

Li smiled again. "I thought it might, Marshal." Then suddenly his mood changed. His voice was sharp as he looked away from Chuang, and toward Chen. "Comrade Professor, let us have the details of the devices, and more important, let me know immediately just how soon you can have them ready."

Chuang broke in. His voice was gruff and impatient. "I already have the details. I don't see any need for Chen to lengthen this meeting." He poured the remainder of the beer into his glass and stared at Li defiantly. If it came to a test of strength between them, Chuang thought, at least nobody could say that his services to the Peoples Republic had been in any way at fault in the past. What Li had done he did not know, but certainly nothing so spectacular as what he himself had accomplished. He gulped some more beer and waited for Li to resume.

Li, in a characteristic gesture, placed the tips of his fingers together. Then he said, quietly and moderately, "Of course, Marshal, you have heard them, but I have not. And since I am the head of this committee, I think that I should be aware of all the facts and figures that my two very expert advisers have decided upon. Take your own time, Comrade Professor, but let me have the details, and particularly the exact date these toys will be available for Marshal Chuang to play with."

Chen said quickly, "Comrade, the facts are very simple. Each device will be approximately two meters in length, and something less, a little less, than one meter wide. They will weigh approximately eight hundred kilos."

He paused, and for the first time Li permitted himself to show outward impatience. "And the time? And how many? Just when are you going to be ready with what?"

Chen still hesitated, while Li stroked the hairs that grew from the wart on his face. Then Chen said, "You must understand I cannot guarantee this. But if all goes well, we should have at least six of the devices ready by August next year."

Li looked sharply at Chuang. "This will be suitable?"

"Very suitable," Chuang said. "It will fit my timetable adequately."

Li responded quickly, "Not *your* timetable, Marshal, but the timetable our Chairman agrees to. However, if we are all agreed that the devices will surely be ready in September next year it will give me something concrete to report to the Chairman when I call him immediately after this meeting."

The inference was not lost on Chuang. For a moment Li detected a scowl on Chuang's usually impassive face. Very good, he thought, he's beginning to realize who is master here. No need to press the spur in harder now; a worried general differed from a worried scientist. The scientist would perhaps work harder and longer, the military man would almost certainly brood and sulk. So it was time to take the pressure off Chuang and put it on Chen.

Li said, "Comrade Professor, I am a little disturbed by the thought that these devices might not be ready in time if—as I think you said—all does not go well. I should like to report in my call that September next year is a definite date."

Chen looked at Li, at his impassive bland face, and said, "Of course, I can assure you, Comrade Li, that they will be ready." He hesitated, while Li continued to watch him, and then went on, "As a scientist, you must understand that I am careful about giving actual dates on a project as complex as this."

"Of course," Li said. His voice was no more than a murmur. "One understands the scientific dilemma. But I must have facts. I will have to report them in my call to Peking. Now"—and his voice suddenly became harsher—"Will they or will they not be ready? I want an answer. Now!"

"In that case," Chen said, "they will."

Li smiled at him briefly, with approval. Chen had been shaken, he thought, and the necessary incentive had been given to ensure that the schedule would be met. Now it was time to get Chuang to speak.

Li said, "Marshal Chuang, can you be sure you will be ready when our distinguished scientist Comrade here has the devices for you?"

"I will be ready," Chuang said.

"Excellent. And the details of your plan?"

Chuang looked at Li. At that moment he really hated him. But he also realized that Li was a person whom it might be dangerous to hate. Far better to wait for the right time before expressing open antagonism. He said simply, "The actual operational details I cannot work out until I have the exact date of the S-Day project. But I have a plan that I consider almost foolproof. It is based on the principle of the fulcrum." He permitted himself a slight, malicious grin as he continued. "But perhaps you haven't heard of that?"

Li himself smiled. "On the contrary, Marshal, I too have read about Archimedes, though of course in the original Greek. He discovered nothing new, you know. There are references in our literature, dating at least five hundred years before that, that lead me to suppose that the principle you mention was not unknown to us even then. But what is more important, please tell me just what you will need to apply the lever utilizing this, ah, fulcrum."

"I shall need resources that do not come under me," Chuang said. "In particular, I shall need full co-operation from our Ministry of Marine."

Li bowed slightly. "They will be available. The Chairman has given me"—again he lightly stressed the word "me"—"unlimited powers to ensure co-operation and co-ordination. Now let me have a rough outline of your plan."

Chuang began to speak. He was well briefed in his subject, and Li listened with increasing fascination. A dolt, he thought Chuang might be; a moron, a person incapable of understanding the infinite variety and finesse of language. But certainly as a soldier he knew what he was talking about. Li listened with admiration as Chuang explained his strategic plan. He caressed the wisps of hair lovingly as Chuang explained just how he proposed to restore China to its proper place as the leading nation of the world.

Altogether, Chuang spoke for about forty minutes. When he had finished Li murmured a few conventional phrases, and both Chuang and Chen departed.

Li reviewed in his mind exactly what they had said. Then he went out of the room into a soundproof communications room, picked up a telephone, and asked for a certain number in Peking. Five minutes later he was giving a highly satisfactory report to the Chairman of the Party.

THE NUCLEAR SUBMARINE: DECEMBER, 1965—JUNE, 1966

Extract from the Journal of
Commander James William Geraghty, U.S. Navy.

Dec. 24

Nearly a month now under the ice, and I can't say the time has gone quickly. For the six human guinea pigs I suppose it's even worse; they can't move around the way I do. But the prospect of seven more months like this doesn't exactly thrill me. Here it is the eve of Christmas, and the endless days stretch ahead. This morning I heard one of the crew talking about it. He said: "Come tomorrow night and we can start saying we'll be home for Christmas." He said it jokingly, it's true, but it looks to me I'm going to have a morale problem before we're through. Could even be my own morale. That's why I think this journal is a good thing. I can record my thoughts, not Navy thoughts, though of course I hasten to say there's nothing wrong with Navy thoughts. But these are personal thoughts, not the thoughts of a naval officer with a nuclear sub and over a hundred and twenty lives depending on him. It will give me a chance to let off steam a little, and I can see already I'm going to need that. Also, it uses up time, and it's working fine. I record my thoughts first on a tape recorder. Then later I write down exactly what I've recorded, no alterations at all, and I *write* it, not type it. This uses up more time. Of the twenty-four hours in each day I've set myself a working day of ten hours. I sleep about seven. That gives me seven hours of leisure, though I suppose you could say that theoretically I'm on duty all through the twenty-four. Well, I suppose I am, actually as well as theoretically.

But anyway, this journal helps me fill those seven hours, and I've been surprised to discover how long it takes to get it down on paper. I mean, just the mechanical side of it, the starting and stopping of the recorder when I'm writing down what I've said takes a lot of time. And that's good.

Dec. 25

So here it is, Christmas Day. I just came back from eating turkey dinner with the men off watch. I think there were a few there not strictly off watch, but on this day I am not going to say anything about that. The essential of a good Commander is he overlooks things on a special day of the year. The men know it and they appreciate it, I'm sure. It was a good dinner but spoiled a bit for me by those goddam psychiatrists. Or psychologists or whatever they call themselves. I have never been able to understand the difference, but I know that the head man is a psychiatrist and the others are psychologists. I suppose they have to be along to keep an eye on the guinea pigs but that doesn't mean I have to enjoy their company. Still, they've been ordered along, it was a Navy order, and in this Navy orders are to be obeyed. Orders are orders are orders—that's pretty literary, isn't it? The people on top know what they're doing, no one can question that.

A new paragraph here. Looking back through the journal—I like to think of it as Geraghty's Journal now—I have been horrified by the pages running on with never a break for paragraphs. How did I do this? I read a lot, and at Annapolis I was considered pretty much of a hot-shot on my literature course. So how did I run on like this? There must be paragraphs, and from here on in there will be. One idea or thought to a paragraph—isn't this the rule? Well, it's going to be my rule anyway, Geraghty's rule. And so that ends the paragraph.

One other little thing is disturbing me. We haven't today received the batch of messages I thought we would receive. We found a suitable place to push the aerial up through the ice, but nothing came through, and there was very heavy static. I guess some freak conditions are operating and the messages will come through tomorrow. I'll give it until tomorrow anyway, but if the freak conditions continue I'll have to move away because we're having difficulty in holding at exactly this position. The currents here are very tricky.

Dec. 26

I know now why we did not receive any messages yesterday and I can guess at the reason for the very heavy interference. It is simply this it means also I am faced with a further problem. This is, do I tell *that means we are in a major shooting war.* Now I have some very tricky decisions to make and while I am thinking about them I find it relaxes me to describe how we got the message.

As I recorded yesterday, the currents were very difficult and I had to move away from the gap where we had pushed up the aerial. But theoretically there are two ways in which we are able to receive messages, even below the ice. The first is by ultra-low frequency radio signals. The second is by sonic explosions that are guided in our direction. It was from the second of these that I received the message.

I have the following factors to consider. First, I am under absolute orders not to break radio silence at any time during this mission. It seems to me therefore that in the absence of any further orders from base I have to observe this order and continue as before. But if I do this it means also I am faced with a further problem. This is do I tell the crew we are at war? Also, do I tell the guinea pigs? I feel reasonably sure about the answer to one of these questions. I feel it is my duty to tell the crew. About telling the guinea pigs I am not so sure. In any case I do not intend to do anything until I have slept on it and had time to consider at length the courses of action open to me.

I should add that since we are not carrying any Polaris missiles, because of the highly specialized nature of our mission, it would not be physically possible for me to take any active part in the war except to return to base on my own initiative and arm for the mopping-up operations which I am sure will be all that are required by the time I

get there. Because I am certain of one thing—if there has been a war
we have already won it. I know enough about the respective strengths
of both sides to be sure of this.

Dec. 27

Today is going to be a long passage, because there are several
things I feel it my duty to record for posterity. After sleeping on the
decision whether to tell the crew (I should mention that I am the only
person in possession of the code book, which enabled me to tell that
the message was DEFCON ONE, and therefore there isn't the usual
scuttlebutt about it), I decided to call in my exec, Lt. Commander
Brennan, and also Dr. Barnard, who is in charge of the guinea
pigs.

My discussion with them was quite brief. I first informed them
both that we were at war, and second, that I was quite certain we had
already won it. I then put before them a number of queries and proposals to obtain their reactions.

First, I felt the crew should definitely be informed. It seems to me
that in a Navy as democratic as ours it is the duty of the Commander
to ensure that his crew receives the fullest possible information
consonant with security. Brennan completely agreed with me, and
Barnard also. So I informed them that I would address all members
of the crew at 1100 hours G.M.T. I should add that though it is
perhaps an anachronism, we operate always on Greenwich Mean
Time, mainly because all nautical tables are based on G.M.T. I shall
be saying later in this entry just what I told the crew. I am rather
proud of it.

Next, there was the question of whether to tell the guinea pigs.
Here I must record that Barnard disagreed with me though I must
admit in a very reasonable and polite way. My decision was not to
tell them, and to my mind for a very good reason. The experiment we
are engaged on is of extreme importance, otherwise the Navy would
certainly not have allocated a nuclear submarine that cost God knows
how many million dollars, plus a Commander of my experience, to
the project. Therefore Barnard had to agree that the experiment must

continue, though reluctantly I thought, and that it would definitely interfere with the progress of the experiment if the guinea pigs were told at this stage.

I said to him flatly that was my decision and one I intended to maintain. I pointed out to him that I *knew* we had already won the war, that I was under absolute orders not to break radio silence whatever the circumstances, and that since I had received the message telling me we were at war I would certainly receive a message by the same means of communication if there was any change in those orders.

He muttered something which I could not quite catch, but when I asked him to repeat it he said it was nothing. I do not altogether believe this, but one thing is certain, we are going to continue. I repeat that I *know,* that is I am morally certain, we have won the war and therefore I see no reason why we should not continue the experiment, which is obviously considered to be of great value to projects we envisage for the future. These projects may be delayed a little, because we are bound to have suffered a certain amount of damage. But I am confident we will soon recover and I am confident also that my decision to continue according to my orders is the correct one, and indeed the only one I could possibly make. If I am needed they will inform me. If I am not, then I shall continue.

I now include the exact text of what I told the crew. It did not take me long because it was simple, though I feel at the same time dignified and worthy of the occasion. It follows:

Men, this is your Commanding Officer. I have a message of the greatest importance to pass on to you. On Christmas Day, and I think you will agree this is typical of our enemy that he should choose that day, our country became involved in a major war. I have no details yet of how things have been going, but I should think you know me well enough to trust me when I assure you that we have already won it. As you all probably know, I recently attended a course of instruction concerned with this very possibility. From this I learned exactly what the score was, and I can assure you our enemy has already virtually ceased to exist.

Now naturally you will be concerned about the fate of your relatives at home. I completely understand this, though of course it helps us all that none of us are married. Let me assure you that though in any case it is S.O.P., I have ordered the strictest possible round-the-clock watch to be kept on all our communication facilities. Let me assure you also that as soon as I receive any news I will immediately pass this on to you. Let us at least remember that we have certainly prevailed, and we shall return to a country—our country—which though it may be damaged will be in its rightful place as the unquestioned leader of the world.

"He means well," Barnard said. "I don't for one moment doubt his sincerity, but I do doubt his facts." He sank gratefully into a chair, a large man whose heavy muscles had succumbed to the fatty degeneration that the age of fifty brings. His hair had suffered also, for he was completely bald, and his eyesight had deteriorated to the point where his rimless bifocals showed clearly he needed assistance.

One of his two assistants, Frank Jones—the other assistant was on duty observing the guinea pigs—merely grunted. Barnard expected nothing else. He knew Jones as a phlegmatic man, interested in his chosen science to the point of obsession, but completely uncommunicative about his conclusions. For Jones, men were stupid people who did stupid things to each other, but he was interested only in how they did them and why they did them. Barnard did not believe Jones could ever bring himself to communicate his beliefs, even to his own colleagues.

Barnard looked at him and sighed. If Herman Goldfinch, his other assistant, had been there Barnard was sure he would have participated eagerly in a discussion about Commander Geraghty, the war, the reactions of the crew, and the decision not to inform the six guinea pigs that there had been a war. And there was another question too, one that was actively engaging Barnard's mind. Later he would go along to the observation chamber and talk with Herman.

But before that he wanted to refer again to a book that he had brought along with him among a hundred other books to relieve the tedium of the long voyage. It was a book called *The Fallen Sky,* and Barnard, who had only glanced briefly through it, felt he ought to read it in more detail. It was a theoretical study, true, but he was sure there were facts in it he ought to know, if only to present clearly to Geraghty the half-formed doubt he had felt when Geraghty had spoken of the necessity for continuing the experiment.

He rose to his feet, said good-bye politely to Jones, received a grunt in reply, and then, moving heavily and ponderously as always, left the cabin, which was at the same time the office and the meeting room of the research team, and went to his own personal cabin to locate the book.

Dec. 29

Looking back through the journal I have detected another fault. I suppose it's because I am not yet an accomplished writer, but it has occurred to me that I should have described myself, or at least given some details that will enable a future reader to visualize the kind of man I am.

Well, first off, I am exactly six feet tall and my weight varies between a hundred seventy-eight and a hundred eighty-two. It has remained that way for the past ten years, and at all physical check-ups the doctors always tell me I am in fine shape. I have dark hair and brown eyes, and while I certainly can't claim to be handsome I do not have too much trouble getting myself dates when we are in port. But so far I have formed no serious attachments, though there is a girl who lives near San Diego I often think I might get round to approaching when I judge the right time has come. She is the daughter of a retired admiral.

As regards my personal habits, I am a great believer in physical fitness and try to manage a workout for at least half an hour each morning. I smoke moderately, about fifteen cigarettes a day I suppose, and when I am in port I enjoy an occasional drink of liquor. But I don't like getting drunk, perhaps because the first time I ever did it was the night after the graduation ceremony at Annapolis and it made me pretty sick. I am proud to say that since then I have always stopped at the third cocktail.

I guess that's about all, except that I enjoy football and baseball—

in fact, one of my big regrets was that I was never quite good enough to make the Navy squad at Annapolis. I used to play halfback, but unluckily for me they had two halfbacks while I was there who were both, I have to admit, a little bigger and a little better than I was.

I enjoy reading and I have honestly tried to read as widely as possible. But some writers I just can't get on with. For example, I once started to read a book by some immigrant called Kafka. The reading course I was following said he was a great writer but to me he didn't seem to say anything. He seemed to be lost and wandering around in the emptiness all the time. I did not finish the book, because obviously my mind is too logical for that kind of nonsense. I do enjoy some of Shakespeare though, especially when he is being funny, though I must admit I do not understand some of his jokes.

Well, all the above is the sort of self-portrait I suppose should be included in this journal, and I have done it. On reading this entry through, I see I have forgotten one of the most important things of all, and that is my age. I am thirty-eight, and I made Commander when I was thirty-two. This is considered pretty good.

Jan. 1

Still no real radio reception, but Skinner, my communications officer, tells me he has picked up a message from home base. He couldn't understand it. He said he recognized their station identification but the static interference was too much for him to understand what they were saying. Also I have reports that the water alongside the ship is showing a high degree of radioactivity. As I said before, I'm no expert, but I do know a little about these things and this indicates to me maybe there's been an explosion somewhere near us.

I'm going to a movie now, so I'll break off. I don't know whether I'll like it, but the crew appreciate it when I attend the movies with them. We have three hundred complete movies in cans and the theatre repeats them during the day so the men coming off watch can have the chance of seeing them.

But before I go to see the movie I've got to say this. I don't feel happy. The crew doesn't feel happy either, and you know how it is when the men don't get a message at Christmas. But morale still stays reasonably good and I'm hoping to keep it that way.

Jan. 4

This should be a happy day for me, because it is my mother's birthday. Normally I would have sent her a message, but on this cruise I was strictly instructed to maintain absolute radio silence. This was given to me as a definite order, and of course I can't break it. It's amazing what the enemy can tell by intercepting messages. Before I leave on a cruise like this I always make arrangements for some flowers to be delivered to her on this day. So she will have got those because she lives in a country area that is remote from any possible target, and she will understand—she was always very under-standing, especially since my father died—that I am some place where I cannot send a direct message to her.

I am not what you would call a superstitious man, but I keep getting a feeling things are wrong somewhere. Also the crew are upset because they haven't received any messages. But they understand we are constantly trying to receive, and so far it has been impossible. And I think it is important for morale when the men know they are in the same boat as the officers. I guess that's a pretty funny thought!

Jan. 5

Sometimes I wonder about this experiment. But it must be impor-tant, I know that. These people, three men and three women, are in a capsule, I suppose you would call it, inside the sub. Attached to the capsule is an observation chamber where they can be seen on a TV screen. Also their conversation is recorded, and presumably this is then analyzed. I haven't yet been to the observation chamber myself since the guinea pigs were first sealed into their capsule, but I am told everything is going well.

Well, I only know what the Navy told me and that's enough for me. Also the chief psychiatrist, Dr. Barnard—he's quite a nice guy really, I didn't realize this before—tells me they can reasonably endure the time they have to go without any alterations in plan.

"All right," Herman Goldfinch said, "I agree with you." He put the book that Barnard had given him on the table. "But listen to me, Ernest. I don't want to offend a medical man, but there's maybe more in this than you read into it."

Barnard looked at him closely. Usually Goldfinch was punctilious in addressing him as Doctor, though Goldfinch himself was a Ph.D. from Columbia. Perhaps, Barnard thought, it was because Goldfinch had dragged himself up from the slums of Chicago to his present position that he was so punctilious in these matters. It was a kind of inverse snobbery, which made him aware of the gulf that separated a doctor qualified in medicine and also qualified in psychiatric medicine from a psychologist, even though Goldfinch himself was one of the acknowledged experts in his field.

Barnard said quickly, "You have something on your mind, Herman; get it off."

Herman Goldfinch spoke quietly. "I have, Ernest, and don't interrupt what I say, because I'm going to say it. I don't pretend to be a great expert. Oh yes, I've read Herman Kahn, Thomas Schelling, Amron Katz, Albert Wohlstetter—all the real experts you like to name, but I didn't realize before what you told me. Maybe they were writing under government restriction."

"No," Barnard said, "I don't think any of them would have tolerated restriction of any kind."

"Would have? You mean they aren't there to tolerate it any more?"

"You've read the report. What would you say?"

Goldfinch said slowly, "That's just the point. I don't exactly know what to estimate. What I do know is that in a closely detailed summary it has been established that in an attack on the state of Massachusetts with something like sixty megatons—and you and I know that's only a fraction of what it would have really received; probably it would have been more than six hundred—there would be only about eight thousand beds from an available seventy thousand still left in hospitals. I know that there would be only one physician left to about two thousand patients who were seriously injured. I can work out all the implications for myself, and I know if there had been a nuclear attack I wouldn't have wanted to survive it as an injured person, seriously injured or not."

Barnard said, "You see my problem?"

"Of course I do. But it's easily resolved, isn't it?"

Barnard said nothing, and Goldfinch continued.

"All you have to do is tell this man we have to get back there as fast as possible. All you have to do is tell him that just one more doctor might help to save a lot of lives that wouldn't be saved otherwise."

"And if the doctor dies?"

"Who said he would?"

Barnard said, "No, Herman. How long do you think we'd last if we went back now? And another thing, don't forget that in a few months' time you and Jones are going to be worth as much as I am, because we'll have to deal with people who have tremendous psychological disturbances, even if they've survived the original radioactivity. I'll be able to do what I'm best qualified to do, and so will you."

"It's your duty to go back," Goldfinch said. His voice was flat and definite. "It's your duty to save life wherever possible, Ernest, and you know it as well as I do. You have to tell this man Geraghty, and you have to tell him now."

Barnard leaned back in his chair. He pushed his glasses up on to his forehead and said calmly, "Herman, I didn't want to tell you this, but I have to. Don't you understand I've already asked him? You don't have to tell me what my duty is, even though in this case doing it was futile. But I asked him."

"And?"

"He absolutely refused," Barnard said. "The experiment continues, Herman, though in God's name I cannot think why, because I'm sure we won't be sending anyone to the planets in this century. But the experiment continues, that's the decision. There is nothing, absolutely nothing, you or I can do to alter it. But at least it serves one useful purpose."

"What purpose?"

Barnard said quietly, "It will give us something to do. Maybe it will keep us sane." He paused, looked away from Goldfinch, and said even more quietly, "Maybe."

Jan. 8

A disturbing report today. The radioactivity in the water passing by the ship continues to rise. Fortunately we are well shielded against this and there is no immediate danger to my crew. But I am assured by some of my officers who are expert in these matters, and of course naturally we carry several of them, since our own propulsion plant is nuclear-powered, that this indicates a war that was perhaps bigger than I first envisaged. Strange thing, today I have been feeling a little like the man in the book I was talking about. I am beginning to feel I just don't know, and how long it's going to be before I do know is something about which I can't help speculating.

I find myself nervous, and find too it's very difficult for me to go to sleep even after putting in a full day of work and of writing up my journal. If this doesn't improve and if I don't come back to my normal healthy self very soon, I suppose I shall have to ask Barnard for some tablets or something that may help. I could of course approach my own Medical Officer about this, but I don't think it's a good thing—though he's a very excellent man and I'm sure a good doctor—to take a member of my own crew into my confidence on a matter like this. Barnard is slightly different. I suppose theoretically he is my subordinate, and certainly while he's on this ship he is exactly that because I am in command, but I've a feeling it might be wiser to approach him. After all, he's supposed to know about everything like this, and I'm quite sure he can very easily prescribe something that will enable me to rest better at nights.

Jan. 11

I had that talk with Barnard. I must admit I was wrong in my estimate of him. I think it's essential for a good Commander to realize when he is wrong and to admit it. Barnard was very sympathetic, and assured me my worries—I suppose you could call them that—were completely natural. He went away and came back about twenty minutes later with some tablets, one of which I take each night when I go to bed. They certainly seem to work. I've slept much better and feel fully fit when I awake to undertake the routine work demanded of me each day.

Radioactivity of water appears to have leveled off, but the level is very high. And I have had no communication from base since the original message, DEFCON ONE. I just don't know.

Jan. 16

I feel a new man. Maybe this is a cliché but I don't feel ashamed of using it. I don't need Barnard's tablets any more, because the last two nights I've been able to sleep perfectly normally without any artificial aids. So today, because I am absolutely *sure* now that this journal will be published in the future, I'm going to work off some of my excess energy by describing exactly what this submarine is like.

I have noticed that this kind of break is often introduced into journals, so maybe it is a good thing if I do it too. I think I am learning literary tricks quite fast since I started writing.

Well, to begin with, this is a big ship by any standards. I suppose I had better not give the actual details but she is just about four hundred feet long from bow to stern and a little over thirty feet in diameter. She is of course powered by a nuclear reactor, which in turn supplies heat for steam condensers that actually drive her along. There is more to it than that, one of the things being that because she is nuclear-powered there does not have to be vast storage space for diesel fuel as on conventional submarines, and so there is more space for accommodations and amenities.

I do not want to be too technical, because this journal is intended for general reading, but we have some interesting items of equipment. One of them, for example, is a CO_2 scrubber. This is necessary to remove poisonous gases from the atmosphere, and as the gases are removed oxygen is fed into the ship to maintain a pure air supply. Also we have very advanced radar, radio, and sonar equipment, but I'm not going to say too much about them because the details I could give are far too technical.

Another interesting item of equipment is the air-conditioner. Actually there are four units, two operative and two on stand-by. In fact, we run them alternately each day. These are very necessary because we may have to operate anywhere from the equator to the Arctic Circle, and therefore built into the conditioners are both heating and cooling devices. We aim to keep the temperature somewhere about 70 degrees, and a relative humidity of about 50. This makes for comfortable living in whatever latitude we find ourselves.

In fact, all through the ship the standards of comfort are very high. Each man has his own bunk, which is not so on conventional subs, and they have access to such amenities as an ice-cream and Coke machine, and other things like that. There is also an automatic laundry where they can wash and dry their clothes quickly and efficiently. Actually, when we are on a cruise, we do not bother too much about smartness, but I do like to see the men clean and dressed in clean clothes. They much prefer it that way themselves. We have lots of other things—for example, a library with over a thousand volumes, but I won't mention any more details except one. This is the movie theatre, which doubles as the main Mess. Since we are carrying a smaller crew than usual, we could if necessary feed everyone at the same time, but in practice this is not necessary since some men are always on watch. At times when the Mess is not being used for eating it operates as a theatre. I also find it very useful when I want to speak to a large number of the crew.

As regards what I might call the operational side of the ship, I suppose it is pretty difficult to describe to someone who has never seen it in action. All I will say now is that under water she handles more like an airplane than a ship. There are bow planes, stern planes, and a rudder control. These require separate operation by three men working together as a very highly trained team.

There are of course also the things you will find in a normal sub, like a bridge, a periscope room, and an attack center. And I guess that's about all I need to say, except that we also carry very sensitive navigation devices that enable us to pinpoint the exact position of the ship at any time, even when we are under the water. This is obviously necessary for accurate aiming of our missiles.

Normally there are sixteen of these, but on this cruise we are not carrying any. They are located in a big area aft of the engine room, but as I say on this cruise we are not carrying any.

Jan. 17

Today I am completely fit, and I had my usual workout, which I admit I have been rather slack on in the past couple of weeks, and as a result no doubt I will be a bit stiff tomorrow, but that's a good thing. It's a wonderful thing how one can relax in a hot salt-water bath and the stiffness after exercise gives one a kind of good feeling.

I've realized that so far I haven't given any full indication of just what the purpose of this cruise is. Perhaps it is because I have been subconsciously worried about the lack of news from base. But I must put this firmly aside, because they have communicated with me and I know that they will communicate with me again as soon as there is anything they need to tell me. I have complete faith in the people at the top and I think I have always shown this faith by my actions. They know what they are doing, and no one is going to argue with me about this.

Anyway, what I have to record now is that I'm not too happy about my present role, though I know it is my duty to continue. I would have liked to be in the fight, even though it was probably of very short duration. It is what I was trained for, and what I have spent my whole active career anticipating and preparing for. But in the end I find myself relegated to a subordinate role, though of course it must naturally be very important, while many friends of mine have been in the fight and are probably now continuing it. Though I don't think they'll have much left to do after this passage of time.

We continue to poke the aerial up whenever we can, but there is tremendously high static, and despite all our efforts we receive nothing that is intelligible. Today I was called by my communications officer, Lieutenant Skinner, as he thought he had something about to come through. We waited about an hour, but although there was a message from someone somewhere it was not decipherable because it was submerged in the high static interference. I don't pretend to be an expert on these things, but Skinner tells me that the transmission was simply not powerful enough to break through the static. Naturally I accept this since he is one of my specialist officers, and a Commander must rely on his specialist officers because in this day and age it is obviously impossible for him to know everything himself.

I break off here to record a literary thought. I find as I continue the journal I am relying more and more on the very fine books I have read in the past, and drawing on their knowledge and also their technique. But I think it fit to record here that I do remember that the last man who was supposed to have comprehended all human knowledge was in about the fourteenth century. I do not recall his name, but he was some European.

Jan. 21

I don't know why, but for some reason I'm depressed again today. Perhaps the reason is that my officers, each of whom I try to speak to each day if possible, tell me that crew morale is becoming low. Now, I don't think I'm a man who lacks understanding, and while of course I must be completely on top of the situation—which means that I sometimes have to be rough—I can understand quite well how the crew are feeling. I am going to think about this, because I'm quite sure there must be some way I can boost crew morale, though since this is a private journal I must confess my own morale is definitely sinking. I'm wondering whether my mother received my flowers on her birthday. I see no reason why not, because where she lives is a country area remote from any big town, but somehow I have this niggling feeling at the back of my mind that maybe she did not and is thinking I have forgotten her.

Why haven't I heard anything more? They got to me once, surely they can get to me again. Is it just possible I should break orders and try to communicate with them? I must think about this, but all my training tells me I must not do it.

Jan. 22

This question of morale has made me think a great deal. This is not a normal situation, and therefore I feel I am entitled to try remedies that are not perhaps strictly in accordance with Navy Regs. I was thinking very hard about this whole question, when it suddenly occurred to me that I had expert advice immediately available.

Now, it is true that Barnard made a pretty stupid suggestion to me when I informed him there had been a war. I do not think I recorded this in the journal, but what he said was that I ought to return immediately because the services of every doctor would be required at this time. I quashed this instantly, because though he quoted me some figures out of some book he had read, I was of course aware exactly what my orders were. But on the whole he seems quite reasonable, and I thought it was a good thing to consult him about the best way in which to keep morale of the crew high through the long months we have ahead.

He was very co-operative, once I had explained the problem to him. He said it was perfectly natural the crew should be worried about the total absence of communication with home base, and that what was required was something quite out of the ordinary to divert them from their thoughts about what might have happened. He did not know it, but I was eagerly awaiting his suggestion because I felt that perhaps I needed some diversion myself. He pointed out that such things as movies and books were normal amenities, and what was needed was something different, something if possible that had never been done on a Navy ship before, but he could not suggest exactly what it should be. Tomorrow I shall call a conference of all officers to ask for suggestions. I think Barnard has been very helpful in this matter and certainly I regard him more highly than I did when we started on this cruise.

Jan. 23

Today I held a conference of all my officers who could be spared from duty. I told them that I thought we were going to have a problem with morale. I also told them that though I had no positive evidence, I was certain we had won the war. One or two of them seemed dubious about this, but I emphasized to them that I was in a position to know more than they did. I think I convinced them, indeed I am confident I did. I had asked Barnard to be present at the conference, but for some reason he was not able to be there.

I then asked all officers to pass on to their appropriate sections my feelings about the war. I felt sure, I said, that we had certainly won the war and sure also that confirmation of the victory would be received very soon.

Then I asked for the comments of all officers on how the crew were reacting. The main issue that emerged was crew morale. I have been so busy I haven't really had time to assess this, but the others are in daily contact with the men and they all agree something needs to be done to avert their minds from the possible consequences of what might have happened to their homes. Because although they are all single men, most of them do have parents and homes to worry about, and naturally they're concerned. Several suggestions were made by the officers and one of them immediately hit a responsive chord in me.

I remember when I was at Annapolis reading about a destroyer Commander who stimulated morale among his crew by clipping his hair in a different way each week. Soon the whole crew were following his example, and then he fooled them all when they got back to port in a way I can't quite remember, but which was pretty damn funny. So when this officer—Lieutenant Perkins—made this suggestion I thought it was a very good one.

Perkins suggested that everyone from myself down should start growing beards, and there should be a weekly competition to decide whose beard was the most promising. It sounds childish, I know, but little things like that can help morale out of all proportion to their true significance. Now, of course in our Navy the growing of beards is forbidden. I know the British Navy allow it, but they allow liquor on their ships too—and this is a thing I would never tolerate. But we have got to stay under the ice for a few months yet, and I don't feel I will be doing any harm in bending Navy Regulations a little, at least until we reach the island. After that we will go back to normal routine.

So I gave my permission.

Jan. 24

I was right! Today I received a message by the same means as before—by wave-guided detonation—that we have won the war. So I immediately called another conference of my officers and addressed them.

This is a wonderful, wonderful day. We have clobbered them, but good, and that's what matters. I never really had any doubts about this, though I must admit that some of Barnard's pessimistic remarks about the situation in the United States made me wonder at times if perhaps we were suffering badly. But now I know. The message—in code—was perfectly clear, and it interpreted as "Complete victory assured." So I went to address my officers and give them the wonderful news.

I explained to them my interpretation of everything that had happened and asked them to pass on the news personally to every sailor in their sections. There are certain things that cannot be passed on because they are classified for anyone below commissioned rank. But my officers know these rules quite well. I think what I had to tell them came as a considerable surprise, except of course to my exec, who had to be in the picture all the time in case something happened to me. I mean, a man can die of a heart attack as easily at sea as on shore, though that wasn't likely in my case, since I had a thorough physical check-up just before we sailed. But the Navy doesn't take any chances.

Now, the first thing is that we have won. The second is that the reason we won is the Air Force did it. Believe me, this caused a lot of consternation among my officers. Then they saw I was smiling, and the buzz of exclamations that had started immediately died away because they knew me well enough to know I had something up my sleeve. And it was this. The reason the Air Force won it is because the Navy had already won it for them! I explained it to them.

In the same way we fooled the enemy about the range of our Polaris missiles (and did they kid themselves when they used to read openly published reports about the range), we also fooled them about the targets assigned to the nuclear submarines. I have mentioned previously that each sub carries sixteen missiles. The enemy assumed, and we let them assume, these were the immediate deterrent. That is, that they were targeted primarily for centers of population. But they weren't. We have long known that there are twelve important Sector Defense Control Headquarters in Russia. Also that there was one main center, Omsk, which I suppose would be the equivalent of our NORAD. There was also, we knew, an alternative center near Karaganda.

Now, the facts of the situation we have to consider are these. Once we get warning they are about to hit us, we have to hit them immediately, not just where it hurts, but where we can make sure it's going to hurt a lot more later. So, of the twenty subs on constant patrol the entire missiles of two were allocated to the main center at Omsk, and the missiles of another two to its alternative at Karaganda. Each of the other subs had been allocated one of the Sector Headquarters as a target for eight of its missiles. The other eight would go to air bases and missile bases that we have located with pretty fair accuracy, to ensure that even if the first wave of missiles had gone, as probably they would, there would be no follow-up.

It is further likely that they could have hit us only with their immediate first strike capacity of missiles, and we have good reason for thinking that this force would not be sufficient to knock us out. *But* by hitting their Sector Headquarters we could give the Air Force a free run to their targets, because the defense would be so disrupted there would be no effective communication and control of the defensive forces. Of course, in local areas where a bomber just happened to be detected on a radar screen, maybe they would knock him down, but communication and control is the absolute essential in modern warfare, and without it I don't think they would have been able to knock down more than at the most ten per cent of our attacking forces.

This would mean that we hit them with something like forty thousand megatons. That means forty billion tons' equivalent of high explosive. And even a country the size of Russia cannot absorb that amount, but the important thing is it would be the Navy made it possible, and for one simple reason. However efficient our Minuteman and Titan missiles might be, *they take ten minutes longer to get to their targets than the Polaris missiles our nuclear submarines carry.* And that's why I say that though the Air Force won the war, the Navy had already won it for them.

When I had finished telling them all this there was, as I expected, a very excited buzz of conversation. I let them continue for a minute or so, and then told them I knew they were disappointed they had not themselves been in the fight, but I was sure there would be work for us all to do later on. I then asked if any of them had any questions to ask me about my deductions, and I emphasized to them they were only deductions.

The only question asked was by Perkins. I might have expected this, because already I have noted him as one of the sharpest and most intelligent of my officers. He told me first that he had studied a lot of the facts about nuclear explosives, and then he asked whether the application of forty thousand megatons to a target, even when the target was as big as Russia, was not a contradiction of the principle of economy of effort in war.

This was a good and intelligent question, but I had the answer to it. I know a lot of civilians think of us military (I suppose I should say naval) officers as morons, but in fact we have to study pretty hard to get to any reasonable rank. And I had studied in particular that great advocate of sea power, Admiral Mahan, and that great theorist, Karl von Clausewitz. So I replied to Perkins in this way.

I told him first that Russia was the main enemy. No other country in the world, including our allies, had the power to hurt us. I did not tell him that in my opinion our allies do not exist any more, because I do not want to cause any feeling of depression. Then I quoted him von Clausewitz's dictum: *"War is an act of force, and to the application of that force there is no limit."*

There were no more questions, and I knew they were all very excited by the news, so I dismissed them to pass it on to the sailors in their sections.

Jan. 30

I have had no further communication with home base, but in the absence of this I feel all is well and that they would certainly have communicated with me if my presence was necessary.

Therefore I feel all the happier that we are continuing our cruise and that the men have entered wholeheartedly into the spirit of the beard contest. It's a little early to tell yet and I don't propose to have the first judging until at least fourteen days after the start. But already I see several of the crew have sprouted healthy growths, though I must record mine is well behind some of theirs. Perhaps I can fool them in the end by appearing completely clean-shaven. This seems a very exciting prospect, the equivalent of what Admiral Arleigh Burke did to his crew in a different way. This will keep morale high, and a week from now we'll be able to tell who is in the lead. It's amazing to me how some men with black hair have fair beards, and some with fair hair have ginger beards. I put this down to some miscegenation in the past, shown in the growth of a beard rather than in any other way. For this reason alone I'm glad we had the contest. And of course I must record my appreciation of Perkins for suggesting it.

Again today I heard from Skinner that there was an attempt to get a message to us, and I listened in the Communications Center for upwards of an hour. But nothing came through. I suppose it is only natural that a major nuclear war would disrupt communication with the enemy and therefore with us also. But I still cannot understand why base have not communicated with us by proved wave-guided detonation system.

There must be a good reason for this, and therefore it's my duty to stick to my orders and not to attempt communication with base.

Feb. 6

Today we had the first judging for beards. From now on we will hold them each week, but it had been agreed the first would not be held until about two weeks after the contest started. All the men, and the officers too, including myself, have entered the contest without exception. I refer of course to the Navy men. Barnard and his team do not seem inclined to participate. But after all they are civilians, and we are not greatly interested in whether they participate or not.

Anyway, by unanimous vote, the prize for the healthiest growth went to a sailor called Petersen. He is one with fair hair and a beard that's ginger-colored. I looked up his records and I see he is a farmboy from Kansas. I made a joking remark that maybe growing all that corn out there had given him an unfair advantage, and he was maybe using fertiliser. The crew loved this, and I am convinced now that Perkins had a great idea when he suggested this contest. I have written my appreciation of him and his idea into the official log.

I should also add that for the past few days I have been watching the checks on the radiation level of the water. It is declining. It is true the rate of decline is very small, almost infinitesimal, but it *is* a decline. Now, this has great significance. It means no more nuclear weapons are being employed—and that means the war's over. And we know who's won. Our readings merely confirm this, because of course we have already had a message from home base telling us exactly this. I am more than ever convinced that I must continue on my mission. The morale of the crew has risen appreciably since we started the beard-growing contest, and I am sure that by this and other devices I will succeed in maintaining a happy ship until our mission is completed.

But I myself am not happy. I do not like being left without knowledge of exactly what has happened. Of course I know in general terms that we have annihilated the enemy and that we ourselves survive, but I think—though of course there may be a good official reason for this—they should have given me more information about exactly what is going on.

But Perkins' idea was a good one and I feel more than ever he is one of my most brilliant officers, certain to reach high rank in the future.

"All right," Barnard said, "how are they doing?"

"Doing well," Jones said.

Goldfinch and Barnard looked at him in amazement. It was rare for Jones to offer the first opinion on a question Barnard asked. "Maybe too well," he added, and relapsed into the gloomy silence to which they were accustomed.

"How do you mean, doing too well?" Barnard asked gently.

Jones said, "You've seen as much of them as I have—what would you think?"

Goldfinch burst out angrily, "Goddamit, how do you expect them to behave! You seem to forget they were picked on a basis of mutual empathy from the N.A.S.A. enclave after a year there. They know each other well, they like each other, maybe they love each other. Wasn't that the idea? To test exactly how empathetic people would react in confined quarters where they were under constant observation, where their every word is recorded? Wasn't that the idea?"

Jones said, "It's not my idea of a scientific experiment."

Goldfinch started to speak, but Barnard interrupted him. "Now listen both of you, and listen good, because neither of you is in charge of this experiment—I am. All right, Herman"—he broke off as Goldfinch stood up in anger—"sit down, and *listen*. Frank is as entitled to his opinion as you are, Herman. But let me put this to you both. We have created an unnatural environment, in which three selected pairs of men and women are put together in a situation that deliberately frustrates their normal feelings. This was done intentionally, and we all knew it when we took on this experiment. But just imagine the problems that would arise in the next experiment—if there ever is one—when they put in three antipathetic pairs. Now let's cool down and assess the facts. All right, there's evidence of great affection between Evans and Nichols. Have you noticed a similar feeling between Levin and Girard, and Anderson and Dimarco?"

"No," Jones answered.

Goldfinch said, "Well, I think so, but I'm not sure."

"I am," Barnard said calmly. "Of course there is. It's perfectly natural and perfectly inevitable, considering the basis on which they were selected. But we don't have to consider that, it's not our concern. What we *are* concerned with is whether this state of"—he paused again and smiled briefly for a moment—"harmony continues, not only through this experiment, but into the future. On the basis of our observations thus far, I'd conclude it will. Is there any disagreement?"

Goldfinch said, "I agree."

Jones thought for a moment, then he said tentatively, "I agree. But they haven't been told there's been a war. And both you master minds tend to forget that." He picked up his notebook and pencil and walked out of the cabin.

Feb. 10

Today I received a most disturbing report from my exec concerning the behavior of two of the crew. By my orders they have been relieved of all their duties and placed under arrest. But I must give considerable thought to the way I will deal with them. There are numerous possibilities open to me. Of course, strictly, I should abide by Navy Regs, but perhaps this would be a little inhuman considering the length of the cruise we are undertaking. Therefore, I have to consider just what alternatives I have, and just what it might mean to me and my career if it was found that a Commander had gone over his authority in this way. I think I have an idea, but again I feel it is the wisest course of action to sleep on it and make my decision tomorrow.

Feb. 12

Of all the nerve, Barnard called on me today and asked me what I proposed to do about the two men I referred to earlier. I don't think I have gone into details about these two men, but let me only say they were found in a very compromising situation. Perkins has completed his investigation into this matter and I am quite satisfied there has been a gross case of indecency. Therefore I resented Barnard's interference, especially since his gloomy feelings about the outcome of the war have been proved wrong. I informed him very coldly that though the six people in the capsule might be his business, this was a disciplinary matter that was Navy business. And that meant me. I am the Commander, and I don't intend to have anything unnatural like that on my ship.

He tried to argue with me about it, and said that under certain circumstances unnatural was the wrong way of describing it. Then he started to talk in the sort of jargon those guys always use, but I cut him off and asked him to leave. This he did.

Well, this afternoon I had the two offenders brought before me. I had decided there were only two courses of action open to me. I could of course convene a General Court right here on the ship, have them arrested, sentenced in accordance with regulations, and held under arrest until we return to base, where they could be transferred to a shore prison. But there is an alternative. I am a great believer in the effect of sudden shock—and this applies to human relationships as much as to war. So I told them what the alternative was, then offered them the choice between a General Court and accepting my punishment.

I am not going to deface this journal—as Boswell and Pepys did theirs—by going into sordid details. So I will only record here that the defense they put forward was that they were "wrestling." Then, to my surprise, they accepted immediately the alternative I had given them to a General Court. I had statements to this effect typed up, and these statements were then signed by them and witnessed by Perkins.

I informed them they would remain under arrest until 10.00 hours the next day, when the sentence would be carried out. After saying this, I told them I would certainly record the facts of the case in their confidential jackets, and this would be the last time they would have the honor of serving in a nuclear submarine. Then I told them to get out of my cabin fast, because I could not stand looking at them much more, and to keep the hell out of my way for the rest of the cruise if they knew what was good for them.

After they had gone I discussed my solution with Perkins. He completely agreed with me, and made another suggestion, and I think it's a good one, because it will give them no leisure time to get in trouble again.

Feb. 13

At exactly 09.50 this morning every sailor and officer who was not on vital duty paraded into the movie theatre, which we use when I want to talk to large numbers of men. At one end of the theatre is a small raised platform, and on this two chairs had been placed.

At 09.55 the two prisoners were brought in, and stood to attention under guard facing the crew. I allowed a full five minutes to pass before I entered myself, because I wanted this to be a really impressive moment. All the men present rose and stood at attention, and I let them stand while I read out the offenses of which the two prisoners had been accused, the sections of Naval Regulations under which they had been charged, and their pleas of guilty.

I announced they had agreed to my method of dealing with the matter, thus avoiding a General Court, which could only bring disgrace on the reputation of the ship and all who sail in her. I then announced the punishment I was awarding them, which was in two parts.

First, though they would continue to be allowed their normal eight hours' sleep, in addition to their normal eight-hour duty period they would also remain on duty throughout what would usually be their eight-hour leisure period. I added they would be under constant supervision during all this time.

I then told all except the prisoners to stand at ease, and outlined the second part of my decision. The two prisoners, I explained, had forfeited the right to be treated as sailors and as men. I felt they should be set aside from the rest of the crew. I had therefore ordered that their beards should be shaved off, and they were specifically forbidden to be other than clean-shaven throughout the cruise.

I then stood back while my exec ordered the two prisoners to sit at attention on the chairs, and they were publicly shaved by the two sailors who act as ship's barbers.

After the ceremony was over, and I have to record it was most impressive, I released the two men from arrest and ordered them to return immediately to duty under supervision. I then said a few brief words to the other men, and dismissed them also.

I feel that everyone has learned a great moral lesson from this, and the reputation of the ship and my own position have been upheld.

Feb. 16

A wonderful, wonderful day. At 15.31 Greenwich Mean Time (I suppose I had better repeat that for navigation purposes we always use G.M.T. when at sea) Skinner called me to say he was in contact with another sub passing close to us and the skipper wanted to speak with me personally. I ran to the Communication Center and found that the sub was "Stingray," commanded by an old friend of mine, Bob Driscoll. Skinner quickly told me that "Stingray" was passing just south of the polar icecap heading east, and I was able to talk with Bob loud and clear for about a minute.

Naturally I asked him immediately what had happened. What were the details? Bob replied—and I recognized his voice in spite of the distortion—we had clobbered them real good. He told me he was now heading back on enemy coastal reconnaissance. I asked him for details, and he repeated they were beaten, and then he faded and we were not able to pick up any more.

When Barnard entered Geraghty's cabin he did so quietly and with complete formality. He said, "Good morning, Commander. I believe you wished to see me."

Geraghty stubbed out a half-smoked cigarette in the ashtray on his desk. Aside from the ashtray and a folder he had been perusing, the desk-top was clear. He said, "You're right, Doctor. Will you please sit down?"

Barnard said, "And exactly what is it, Commander, that you wished to see me about?"

Geraghty looked at him without speaking for at least thirty seconds. He had found this extremely effective in the past when dealing with any malefactors who were brought before him. Finally he said slowly, "I am not happy with your attitude, Barnard." He deliberately omitted the "Doctor."

Barnard said, pleasantly but at the same time firmly, "I can't pretend, Geraghty, I am particularly happy with yours."

"All right," Geraghty said. He was speaking more quickly now and his anger was beginning to show. "But what you have to understand is this. This is a Navy ship and I am the Commander. I suppose you already know I went and took a look at two of your people in the capsule yesterday afternoon."

"Yes," Barnard said. "Jones told me about it."

"Just what the hell do you think this is? In case you don't know it, I have a certain duty, and when I see two people who are obviously— let me put it this way—flirting with each other, just where the hell does the purpose of a scientific experiment go? Is this supposed to be a holiday cruise ship or something?"

Barnard said, "I don't think the behavior of the two people in the capsule is your business. It's my business, and my responsibility. I am completely satisfied with the progress of the experiment, though as you well know, if I had my way the experiment would no longer be continuing. But you insisted on it, and therefore I have to insist you allow me to run the experiment in my own way and to make the proper decisions. I'm completely satisfied with the results so far, and I refuse to be dictated to by you regarding their outcome. Let me also add that I consider your behavior in the case of the two sailors whom you punished recently was the act of an irresponsible man, and it's only because I don't know you well enough and haven't observed you sufficiently that I don't add, the act of a psychopath. . . . Was there anything else?"

Though he found difficulty in restraining himself, Geraghty made allowances for Barnard before he replied. After all, he thought, Barnard couldn't really know too much about it. He had never had experience of command over men. So he merely said, "I am the Commander, this is my ship, and what I say goes."

Barnard stood up. He said, "Not perhaps so much as you might think. If you will permit me, inside five minutes I will bring you back a certain document signed by the Secretary of the Navy. And perhaps this may convince you that while this ship is your responsibility, those people in the capsule are mine."

Without saying any more he left the cabin. He was gone only a few minutes, during which Geraghty considered smoking a cigarette, but decided not to. Then Barnard returned, closed the door quietly behind him, and handed a letter to Geraghty.

"Here it is," he said. Geraghty looked at the letter. It was signed by the Secretary of the Navy. Geraghty read it through twice, but what it said was quite clear at first reading. Barnard had absolute authority over the people in the capsule, and the Commander was required to assist Barnard in his enquiries and research.

After Geraghty had finished reading the letter, he placed it on the table. Barnard picked it up, folded it, and replaced it in its official envelope. Geraghty said nothing as Barnard turned and left the cabin.

Feb. 20

Barnard called on me today at my request, though I must confess I don't particularly wish to talk about anything with him. Nevertheless I feel that as Commander it is my duty to do all I can to ensure the satisfactory completion of this cruise. And therefore we had a long talk together. I felt perhaps he did not altogether understand the reasons for the decisions I had made, so I again explained them to him. Further, I told him, which I should perhaps not have done, because he is a civilian, that I know I have made the right decisions, and that, very simply, the reason is because I know the Admiral thinks a great deal of me and trusts me to do the right thing.

I must admit Barnard was extremely polite. But he asked me how I knew the Admiral thought so much of me and I told him just what happened when the Admiral interviewed me before I was given this command. But I have an urgent matter to attend to now and the rest of our conversation will have to wait until tomorrow.

Feb. 21

The reason I had to wait until today before writing down exactly what I told Barnard is, I had another message from Skinner that he thought something more was coming through. But it didn't.

Anyway, Barnard didn't know too much about the Admiral, although of course he'd heard of him, as I guess everyone back home has heard of him. So I was able to tell him this.

It is no secret, because I think it's been published somewhere, but the Admiral had a habit—no, I guess the more literary thing would be to say a *penchant* for asking tricky questions when he interviewed potential commanders of his nuclear sub force. For example, I did hear he once asked an officer he was interviewing this question:

"Suppose you have a choice. Imagine there is a choice between your death and the death of a streetcleaner. Imagine this is inevitable —one of you must die. The choice is yours. Who would you choose to die? You? Or the streetcleaner?"

Well, what do you think the idiot said? He said he would choose to die himself. Now, can you imagine anyone as stupid as that? I'll tell you he didn't get his command! It takes ten minutes to train a streetcleaner. What the hell do you have to do—you pick up a broom and push it. But it takes a lot longer than that to train a sub Commander. So he didn't get the job. And I'm glad, because I knew him, and he wouldn't have been suitable.

But when I went there, went to see the Admiral, that is, he didn't ask me any of those tricky questions, but he didn't give me command of an operational sub either. I can't figure this out.

I'm stuck here, and some of the officers who were classmates of mine are in the real fight. I can't understand this, but it was the duty the Navy gave me, and it's the duty I have to accept.

Feb. 28

Now I have a few hours for myself, and I can get round to explaining what the guinea pigs are doing. I had better explain first that the capsule they're in simulates the kind of restricted quarters you might get if they fired you off to one of the planets. I would not know which one, but the guess among the better-informed of my officers seems to be Venus.

The point of it is this. Human beings react in different ways, and obviously the scientists do not feel happy about firing people off until they know just how they are going to react to claustrophobic conditions. And also they can't assume that three men and three women are going to be able to make it without terrible disharmony.

The guinea pigs will spend approximately six months on the island, to represent the time that would be required before Venus would be in the most favorable orbital position for the return flight. Then they will be picked up from the island, brought back up here under the ice for a further period approximating the time required for the return trip to Earth, and finally will be returned to the States.

Before we became on what I can only call unfriendly terms, Barnard told me they would then be subjected to continuous pyschological and medical tests over a period of maybe up to six months. This will give the scientists the information they require regarding the psychological influences of close proximity during such a planned flight. He also let slip—obviously he is not too bright security-wise, because I picked it up right away—that the flight could not take place until at least fifteen years from now, but that with such a delicate operation it was essential that all the necessary information should be collected well in advance and preparations made according to the data obtained.

But though I have to accept that the Secretary of the Navy has given Barnard responsibility for the subjects *while they are in the capsule,* I do have to have the material to report in the official log how they are progressing. I mentioned this to him and he agreed. What I said was this. I asked him for an exact report in terms that I can understand, because I don't intend to use a medical dictionary every time I get a report from someone who, despite the Secretary of the Navy's letter—and I am still not very happy about that—I regard as responsible to me. I haven't yet seen a detailed report except in the kind of medical jargon these guys use, and I want to know in simple terms just exactly what the guinea pigs' physical and mental condition is.

The reason for this is not that I am trying to interfere with Barnard and his team. Obviously if the guinea pigs are all fine we will continue normally. But I like to think that I would not allow any people in my ship, even though they may not be directly under my command, to suffer in any way. They cannot help their environment; and of course there is no reason they should not feel happy, because they do not yet know there has been a war. But I would like to make sure of this, and I have therefore asked Barnard and his two assistants to join me in the next few days at a time to be arranged when we can discuss this matter. And I don't think it's quite right they should feel *too* happy.

Mar. 1

Barnard informed me in a very polite note—we don't talk a great deal any more—that it would take a few days to collate all the information they have gathered about the state of the guinea pigs. I accept this, which seems to me only reasonable, as he is obviously recognizing my authority.

Mar. 5

I received another note from Barnard today and he tells me we should be able to confer in two days' time. But today I feel restless, perhaps because I am still waiting for a definite message from home base about what has happened.

So I am going to explain, because after all I think this journal could be of importance in the future—indeed I know so now, because it is the first time anyone has tried to stay under the ice this long. So I feel it could be important that I explain just how we do things.

There is this matter of reception. I guess everyone knows even radio waves won't penetrate everything, and they certainly won't penetrate fifty feet of ice. But occasionally you can find places in the ice where there is what we call a polynia. Without being too technical, this means a place where there is a small break in the icecap and it is possible to penetrate the ice from below, not perhaps with the whole sub, but certainly with an aerial. It is difficult to find these places, because usually you don't see them until you're underneath them. But when you do see them, if you can maneuver the sub into the right position and poke up the extensible aerial, you can receive pretty well. This is what we have been trying to do.

We do have a system operating on very low frequency that was supposed to penetrate through the water right under the icecap. But it doesn't. Also they have been developing a sonic system of transmitting messages by wave-guided detonations, which reach the sub and can be interpreted according to the values that have been placed on them before we set out on patrol. This we know works, and I am just wondering why they haven't given me more information about what has happened. More and more I am wondering just what is the situation back there and why they haven't made contact with me. But I know they can, and that is the important thing.

For some days now I have been wondering whether I am justified in asking base for information. But I deferred any decision on this and now I am glad, because an hour ago Skinner informed me there had been a message from them instructing us to maintain complete radio silence until the mission has been completed. I take this to mean until I have landed the guinea pigs on the island. Naturally I will comply with this order, but it has certain implications that make me feel just a little uneasy.

Another thing that also makes me a little uneasy is that we haven't heard from "Stingray" again. I have been carefully calculating the amount of time she would have spent on patrol, and I would have expected her to begin her return some time during the last week. I know Bob would not pass up the chance of talking with me as he returned. But we have not heard anything. Maybe he also has received orders to maintain radio silence. But I can be sure of this: there is some very good reason for the precaution, and since I know now that efficient command still exists, I am quite happy to go along with it.

Mar. 6

I was horrified and disgusted today when Perkins reported to me twelve of my crew had shaved off their beards. I take this as a deliberate personal affront to me, and though I can of course take no official action about it, I have instructed Perkins to annotate their records with comments that will ensure their disloyalty is not overlooked in the future. I am glad to say, however, that the rest of the crew and, of course, all the officers remain loyal and their beards are flourishing. So I can safely assume the majority of the crew are definitely on my side and giving me their support.

But this has seriously weakened the effect of the second part of my punishment of those two . . . well, I just don't like to use the words. I will just say those two *criminals,* and I will make sure that this action, which I regard as a deliberate act of subversion, with all the word subversion implies, is brought immediately to the attention of the Commander in Chief when I return from the island.

Mar. 7

Barnard informed me today he was ready to discuss with me the state of the people in the capsule. But I must confess, although I don't believe personal opinions should enter into a matter like this, I was so horrified by the news Perkins gave me yesterday that I didn't feel inclined to meet Barnard and his two associates. I suppose I should really call them his subordinates, but they don't seem to have any system of demarcation between them and therefore I suppose I can only call them his associates.

But my orders clearly lay down that I must check the documents and progress of these six people before the end of March. Therefore I must do this as quickly as possible.

But I am the Commander of this ship, and everything that happens on it is of tremendous importance to me. For example, I notice that though the radioactive level of the water passing alongside us continues to decline, it is still very high. I don't feel it's important if I keep Barnard waiting a few days, and I shall record this fact in the official log. I have told Barnard provisionally—by sending him a note—that I will see him in three days' time at 14.00 G.M.T. and I expect his assistants Jones and Goldfinch to be along with him, and to give me a complete physiological and I guess you would call it a psychological breakdown on the people in the capsule. I am not looking forward to this but it's a thing I have to do, and meanwhile I am wondering more and more why I haven't heard anything further from my base. But certainly I shall stick to my orders and as I think I said before in the journal, this is the sort of thing that takes you to the top.

And where I said before, orders are orders are orders, similarly the top is the top is the top. I like this conception. I am coming along pretty well.

Mar. 10

I thought today before seeing Barnard's team—that's about the best description I can give of them—I would first check through the documents concerning the six guinea pigs. These documentary summaries give a very realistic picture of the life of the guinea pigs, but since I intend this journal to be of interest for future readers I think it would be more stylish to connect the details in a kind of narrative, I guess you would call it, not just a bare list of statistics.

Well, the first thing I notice is that they are all college graduates —except one of them, that is, who is a nurse, but I guess that's just about the same thing. So I am going to go through their documents in alphabetical order selecting what I think will be of interest in the future.

Here we go. First is John Anderson, graduate of Harvard in soci-
ology. He was born at Englewood Cliffs, New Jersey, and is now
thirty. He is pretty big, six feet and weighing one hundred eighty-five.
I don't see any religion listed for him, and this is obviously an
omission on the part of some clerk. But I do see he is a reservist in
the United States Navy, and obviously he is the best of the six. He did
not serve very long, only the time his selective service required, but I
feel he is extremely reliable. His Navy service will have ensured this.
I intend in due course to make him the leader of the group when we
reach the island. I haven't yet been able to observe him in the
capsule, because he and Dimarco were sleeping when I visited the
observation room, but I feel certain he is doing his duties in accordance with the briefing he was given before we sailed.

Next, Helen Dimarco. Twenty-six, medium height and slim build.
She was born in Minneapolis and had experience as a nurse at the
Hospital of the Good Samaritan, Los Angeles. She is described as
Roman Catholic, which I suppose you would expect with a name like
Dimarco.

Now, there is someone I am not at all sure about. His name is
given as William Evans. Apparently he went from the University of
Wales to Yale University, under some exchange scheme that operated
between the British and American universities. Age thirty-three, five
feet nine, weight one hundred seventy. I have to break here to comment that there must be a mistake. They say that his hair is very
dark, but his eyes are described as blue. He was born in a place called
Treorchy, wherever the hell that is. I presume it must be in Wales.
What he is doing on this trip I wouldn't like to say. He is a U.K.
citizen, and therefore he must have been included to please the U.K.
government. This must be another of those exchange deals. His religion is stated as Methodist.

Now for the next one, and again I would not have thought her a
very good security risk. Her name is Mary Girard. I suppose I should
add that I might be unfair in saying this, because if they are going to
allow foreigners in on the experiment anyway, it must be because
they can't learn much from it that they can betray later. Anyway, she
was born in Hawaii and her father was a U.S. citizen, a staff correspondent on one of the news agencies there. I guess that explains a

lot, because her mother is described vaguely as Eurasian. She is only five feet three inches tall, and of slight build. She studied languages at the University of Southern California, and I see that she speaks Russian, French, and Chinese. I don't somehow feel the Russian is going to be much use to her any more. Again there is no religion stated.

I have looked at my watch, and suddenly realize it is only two hours before I meet Barnard and his team. Therefore I must describe very quickly the two guinea pigs I have not yet mentioned. First, there is Arnold Levin, born in the Bronx and now twenty-nine. Five feet eight, one hundred forty-eight, graduated from Columbia, and is a physicist. The documents don't specify what kind of physicist, but I suppose not nuclear or they would not have released him for this experiment. He has dark curly hair and brown eyes. He is Jewish, which I suppose you would expect with a name like Levin.

Last, Jane Nichols. She is the biggest of the girls, five feet seven, and medium build, with fair hair and blue eyes. Born in Chicago and later majored at the University of Chicago in psychology. I suppose that would make her Barnard's blue-eyed girl. Literally.

Incidentally, I have decided that another officer should be present with me during the interview. It does not call for this in the orders, but I feel I would like to have a witness to everything that is said. I have asked Perkins if he will do this, and he instantly agreed even though I stressed to him it was purely a voluntary matter and in no sense an order.

It was precisely 14.00 G.M.T. when Barnard tapped at the door of Geraghty's cabin. Lieutenant Perkins opened the door and asked the three observers to come in. He indicated three chairs that had been placed in front of Geraghty's desk. Barnard sat in the middle chair, with Goldfinch on his right and Jones on his left. Perkins moved behind the desk and sat down in a chair placed to the right of, and slightly behind, Geraghty's.

Geraghty said politely, but formally, "Good afternoon, gentlemen." The three observers returned his greeting. Geraghty went on, "I have just been going through the documents of the six people you have in the capsule, and I think I'm pretty well acquainted with their backgrounds. However, at this stage I must receive a report from you on the physiological and psychological condition of each of them, and record it in the official log. Therefore I have called this meeting. Doctor Barnard?"

Barnard looked at Geraghty steadily. He could observe no signs of nervous degeneration in the man, yet he had a strange feeling that there was tension building up in him. It was nothing he could put his finger on and say precisely, this is hypertension or this is something else, but definitely he felt that Geraghty was under some stress. He said quietly, "Well, Commander, we have of course prepared a written report, which we will leave with you, but I expect you would prefer to hear in simple nonmedical terms a general summary of that report."

"I think that would be a good idea. Let's have it."

Barnard said, "Let us deal first with their physical condition. I think Doctor Jones is best qualified to give that to you. He is our expert in physiology."

"Why Jones?" Geraghty broke in. "You're all doctors, aren't you?"

Barnard smiled. "Yes, but not in quite the same way. Jones is a doctor of medicine. Goldfinch is a Ph.D. in psychology. I am also a doctor of medicine who later specialized in psychiatry. So I suppose you could call Jones a physician, Goldfinch a psychologist, and myself a psychiatrist."

"I had the impression you were all psychologists of some kind."

"Then you had the wrong impression," Barnard said. "Except, of course, that every doctor who has practiced for ten years, as Doctor Jones has, is bound to be something of a psychologist even though he may have no formal qualifications."

"All right," Geraghty said, "all right. I've got the picture now. Let's get on with it. Doctor Jones?"

Jones spoke slowly, as he always did. "Their physical condition is excellent. You know their routine. Eight hours' sleep, eight hours' relaxation, and eight hours performing simple repetitive tasks that would be necessary if they were actually in a space ship. These tasks, incidentally, have been so designed that they exercise the whole body, and this has helped in maintaining their good physical shape. Also, they're living in a completely germ-free environment, and therefore they haven't picked up any minor virus infections such as the common cold. Taken as a group, their individual weights have dropped by an average of four pounds. I won't bother to give you the individual details, as they're all in the report. But I will say that the maximum drop has been recorded at four and a half pounds and the minimum at three and a half. This is what we anticipated. Every three days I check the pulse rate of each pair. They have remained completely constant."

"Hold on just a minute," Geraghty said. "Exactly how do you take their pulse rates? You mean you go into the capsule?"

"Certainly not," Jones said precisely. "On the inner wall of the capsule is a projecting rod to which is attached a stethoscopic head. The subject has merely to place his wrist against the head—which is extremely sensitive—and we can record their pulses from outside the capsule."

Geraghty said, "I see. So all in all they're in good shape?"

"Physically, yes." Jones hesitated, and for a moment Geraghty thought he was going to qualify his statement, but Jones merely added, "I can guarantee they're in good shape physically."

Lieutenant Perkins said, "Pardon me, Commander."

Geraghty turned toward him. "What is it, Perky?"

"Well, I wanted to ask Doctor Jones a question. It's something that interests me and that I can't quite understand. Have I your permission?"

"Certainly," Geraghty replied. He had a very high respect for Perkins' intelligence, and no doubt the question and the reply would be most informative.

Jones asked, "What is your question, Lieutenant?"

"One thing I don't understand. You say they've lost weight. How come? We find that our crewmen tend to put on weight on a long cruise despite the fact they have regular calisthenics to keep them in shape. So I'm a little puzzled why these people should have lost weight."

"The answer is quite simple. Although the people in the capsule receive a diet that is perfectly balanced as regards vitamins, proteins, and so on, they're not getting as many calories per day as your sailors. This, you understand, is because to make the experiment as realistic as possible they're not fed the type of bulky food your men receive. Therefore, although they eat regularly and spend only eight hours of the day doing anything active, they would naturally tend to lose weight. All this was carefully calculated at N.A.S.A. before the experiment started."

"All right," Geraghty said. He thought Perkins' question a good one, and certainly it was something he had not thought of. But now he was anxious to get on with the rest of the items they had to discuss.

Barnard said, "Do you have any questions on the physiological aspect, Commander?"

"No, everything seems to be fine. I'm quite happy with Doctor Jones's report. Now, how about the psychological aspect?"

Barnard turned his head and said quietly, "Doctor Goldfinch?"

Goldfinch was holding a sheaf of notes, but he did not refer to them while he spoke. He said, "Unlike Doctor Jones, I'm afraid I'll have to deal with each of them individually. But I'll try to make it as brief as I can."

"I'm taking them in pairs, as they have been selected. Anderson and Dimarco first. Both of them are extremely stable. They carry out their tasks with efficiency, they sleep well, and they appear to me to be in excellent psychological shape. I won't go into a lot of technical detail as it's all in the report, but we don't have to worry at all about those two.

"Next, Levin and Girard. Here we must remember that Levin is by nature extrovert, while Girard is rather shy and introvert. Levin appears to have thrived on the experience. He is constantly making funny remarks, and this seems to have greatly assisted in drawing Girard a little out of her shell, if I can put it that way. As regards their efficiency, it is one hundred per cent. We have no worries about them.

"Finally, Evans and Nichols. Evans appears to me to be quite stable, though undoubtedly emotional, but I wouldn't go so far as to say he is neurotic. Indeed, I'd say he is a great support to Nichols, who is the only one of the group about whom we have the slightest reservation. She has undoubtedly exhibited signs of stress during the period, but we had anticipated this from observations at N.A.S.A. before the group ever entered the capsule. In spite of her stress, however, both she and Evans perform their tasks with as much efficiency as any of the others. I myself think she finds great comfort in Evans' company, and this to a large degree has helped her to withstand the feelings of stress she has from time to time exhibited. I should add that of all the group she is the only one who appears to have any difficulty in sleeping normally. But this is not necessarily indicative of any serious disorder of the mind. We know there are many people, especially among those with high I.Q.'s, who have the same trouble. But generally speaking, they get by, and I'm pretty confident she will get by too. And I think that about summarizes what I have to say."

Geraghty looked at Barnard. "And from you, Doctor Barnard?"

Barnard shrugged. "I think that's about it, Commander. You will, of course, continue to receive my monthly reports. But for the purpose of this meeting, I think you've heard a concise summary of what is in our report. Do you have any questions yourself?"

"Well," Geraghty said, "there is just one small question. You may remember a talk we had a little while back about the way the people were behaving when I observed them?"

"Yes, I do."

"I'm still not satisfied about that," Geraghty said flatly. "Are you?"

Barnard said quietly (he always spoke quietly when he felt a mounting anger in himself), "I'm perfectly satisfied."

Geraghty slammed his fist on the desk. "Well, I'm not. What the hell do you think this ship is, a floating brothel or something?"

Barnard said nothing for a few moments. His face was white. He started to speak, but Goldfinch cut in on him abruptly. He knew that Barnard was extremely angry, and he knew the reasons for his anger.

"I don't think you have quite the right idea, Commander," Goldfinch said. "Those people in the capsule are being observed all the time—except when all three of us are required to see you together. There is simply no question of any what I suppose you would call *misconduct* between them." He glanced quickly at Barnard, saw that he was regaining his composure, then went on. "I repeat, Com-

mander, there is simply no question of misconduct. You must understand that this experiment was deliberately planned to test the reactions of six people, men and women, similar to the men and women
who might in ten, twenty, thirty years from now be required to travel
to one of the planets." He paused, again glanced at Barnard, and
continued quickly, "Maybe to the stars, how the hell should I know?
But I'm sure Doctor Barnard can explain it much better than I can."

Geraghty said, "Okay, Barnard, so explain."

Barnard's voice was again very quiet. "Listen, Geraghty—"

Again Geraghty crashed his fist on the table. "To you," he said,
"Commander Geraghty."

Goldfinch looked anxiously at Barnard, but he was completely
calm. "Very well. Listen to me, Commander. I want you to realize
that in my opinion this experiment should have been discontinued
when we first heard there had been a war."

"Yes," Geraghty said, "and maybe I was wrong to tell you there
had been. But I decided the experiment would continue in accordance
with my orders."

Barnard said, "You decided it, and since we can't control this ship
we had to go along with your decision. But let me try to explain to
you exactly what we are trying to do. First, you must realize that
these six people were picked from a hundred or more who were
subjected to intense psychological tests at the N.A.S.A. experimental
station. Second, they were picked for two reasons. One of these was
because in the year—and I emphasize it was a full year—they were
under observation, all three individual pairs demonstrated affection.
And further, the three pairs seemed to us to have a mutual empathy.
They appeared to us to show that as a group they would be suitable
subjects for the kind of group that is envisaged for future coloniza-
tion of one of the planets. It would have been quite useless, though
we could easily have done it, to have picked six people who were
mutually antipathetic. Obviously such a group would disintegrate,
and all hopes of founding a new civilization would be wrecked.
Therefore we selected men and women we considered most likely to
maintain empathy. Once they were selected on this basis, we would
be able to study their reactions to living in confined quarters, with
verbal and visual contact only between the six of them. Obviously the

man and woman in each pair have been drawn together in these circumstances. This confirms our theories, and I would repeat that the purpose of our experiment has been achieved. Wait a moment, I'll qualify that. I'll say almost achieved, because we can't be certain of anything until the experiment has run its full course, but I'm pretty sure of the outcome. Now do you understand why these people appear mutually attracted?"

"All right, all right," Geraghty replied. "It's a great experiment, but I've already told you I won't have anything peculiar going on in my ship."

"I wouldn't call it peculiar, I'd call it natural."

"You can call it what the hell you like, but I don't want any physical contact between them while they're in the capsule." Geraghty lit a cigarette. He did not offer one to the three doctors or to Perkins. It made no difference anyway, as neither the doctors nor Perkins smoked.

Barnard said, rising to his feet, "Well, if that's all?"

"I suppose so," Geraghty said.

Barnard placed an envelope on Geraghty's desk. "In this envelope you will find details of our observations to this date. You will still receive my monthly report."

Goldfinch had also stood up, but Jones was still seated. Now he said, his slow voice unreasonably loud in the small cabin, "Hold it a minute. I think the Commander has a point."

Barnard turned to him. "Indeed? And what point, Doctor Jones?"

"A good point. I can't put an exact word to it, but somehow this whole experiment seems to me to be, well, unhealthy."

"The whole experiment," Barnard said, "is now quite useless." He looked directly at Geraghty. "We've been going through the motions, more to fill in time than anything else, and maybe in a couple of hundred years' time the notes we made will be useful to whoever follows us, if anybody does. But as I told you, we should have returned right away. The services of even one or two doctors could have been invaluable in the few weeks after the war."

Geraghty stubbed out his cigarette. "I had my orders." he said. "I made my decision. And the experiment continues."

Barnard said, "Very well, but don't think you'll be going back to a land flowing with milk and honey. You won't, and maybe when we get there you'll realize what I mean."

Geraghty lit another cigarette. He was getting near his daily quota, he thought, but he felt he needed a few moments to concentrate, to shatter Barnard once and for all. He said calmly, "You have, perhaps, the gift of second sight?"

"I don't claim to have it."

"Then explain how the hell you know what we'll be going back to."

"I *don't* know. But I know what the predictions were, and I know that the devastating effect on the minds of those who survived would produce traumas that could lead to their destroying each other."

"I suppose you're quoting that damned book again?"

"I have drawn inferences from it, naturally. It was a responsible book with contributions from responsible doctors and scientists. It postulated the minimum possible concentration against one state. Certainly I'm using it, but I'm not quoting it."

"I'm not particularly interested in your theoretical conclusions." Geraghty swung round in his chair. "But I am interested in what Doctor Jones said. Why do you think it's an unhealthy kind of experiment?"

Jones said, "I don't have the advantage of being a psychologist." His tone indicated he thought "psychologist" was a slightly dirty word. "I agree with my colleagues that these people were selected on a basis of mutual empathy. I don't agree they should have been selected this way. And personally I must dissociate myself from the opinions of my colleagues. From my observations I feel they have acted in an irresponsible manner, they're altogether too intimate, and I think the idea of putting three men and three women together, pairing off one man with one woman, was itself completely irresponsible. There must be order and discipline in these matters, and I'm not referring to military discipline, simply to the accepted code of conduct in our everyday life."

Herman Goldfinch began, "Why, you goddam" but Barnard interrupted him. "Doctor Jones is entitled to his opinion. I can only say I disagree."

"Concur," Goldfinch said quickly.

"Well now," Geraghty said, "personally I'd say Doctor Jones is talking a lot of sense."

Barnard looked at Goldfinch. They turned together and were moving toward the door of the cabin when Geraghty spoke. "Wait."

Barnard did not turn to look at him. "I see no purpose," he said. He opened the door of the cabin and he and Goldfinch left together.

Jones had remained in his chair, but Geraghty did not speak to him at once. He turned to Perkins. "How about it, Perky? How do you feel about it?"

Perkins said, "I think, sir, Doctor Jones was the only one of the three observers who said anything that made sense. Barnard—well, I think his intentions are good, but he's talking about military matters, he's assessing probable damage without any knowledge, all on the basis of some book he's read that I feel fairly sure was compiled by a group of civilians. I think we can disregard his conclusions. But I think we must agree with Doctor Jones that the method of selection for this experiment was wrong. We don't want any more problems than we have, and the way Barnard is running things it looks like we will have."

"Yes," Geraghty said, "additional problems we don't need." He turned to Jones. "Now, Doctor Jones," he said, "let me ask you this."

He asked his question and Jones replied. The discussion continued for about an hour.

Goldfinch and Barnard returned to Barnard's cabin. They did not speak until they arrived there. When they had sat down Goldfinch said, "I always knew there was something funny about Jones."

Barnard was sitting behind his desk. "Forget it, Herman," he said quietly. "You have to get back on observation duty. I'm older than you, and I've seen a lot more, had more experience, if you like to put it that way. Right now we just have to continue. There's no other way of doing things."

Goldfinch said, "I'll get right back on observation."

"No," Barnard said, "it won't hurt anyone if we take time out for a little while. You need a cup of coffee and so do I." He lifted a telephone and spoke briefly into it.

Their coffee arrived and they drank it together. Strangely, they did not discuss Jones or Geraghty at all. When he had finished his coffee Goldfinch went back to observation duty.

Apr. 1

I had to see Barnard today to receive his monthly report on the people in the capsule. It was much the same as before, which I must confess I didn't like. I was very stiff with him, and I would describe his manner as being distant, but, I must admit, polite.

It so happened Perkins was with me at the time. My exec is so busy supervising the preliminary details—and there are a thousand and one of them—concerning the voyage to the island and the unloading of stores there, that I have appointed Perkins assistant exec, and consequently rely upon him a great deal for the normal running of the ship.

When Barnard had left, Perkins told me he thought Barnard didn't like me too well. I replied that that was fine by me, and we both laughed.

Apr. 10

I do not have time for very many entries in the journal now because I am getting set for the start of our voyage to the island. In accordance with my orders, this voyage will be made submerged, but of course as soon as I have arrived at the island and successfully landed the six subjects of the experiment, and seen the stores ashore, then I shall immediately contact base to establish whether I should return submerged or on the surface.

We will have to spend two or three days off the island, and I shall try to ensure that most of the crew get a run ashore, and a chance to stretch their legs, swim in the lagoon—incidentally it's a nice island; they are pretty damn lucky—and get plenty of fresh air. I have asked Perkins to work out a rotation system for this, and he made a suggestion that I agree with. He pointed out that priority should be given to those members of the crew who had demonstrated their loyalty to me personally and to Naval Regulations as enforced by me, in that they had not shaved off their beards.

So fourteen sailors are going to find that they do not have as much time to relax as the rest of the crew. And maybe that will teach them a very effective lesson.

One final thought for today. I can't help laughing about the way we must have fooled the enemy into thinking that if he knocked out our major naval bases our subs would not be able to refuel and rearm with missiles. What he didn't know was that we never intended to rearm at the bases. I cannot reveal more than that at this moment, but I can say that the places the subs have been rearming are nowhere near any of our major bases.

Apr. 15

I have been busy in the last few days with my navigation officer, charting our course to the island. We have decided we will need to sail on June 3, and maintain a moderate cruising speed of about twenty knots submerged. We have to pass through several pieces of ocean where the currents are not exactly known, but this sailing date gives us a comfortable reserve, and we should arrive off the island about June 16 as planned.

Last night I was thinking about what will happen when I have completed the mission and returned to whatever base they assign me to. I think I can make an informed guess about this.

After the crew has been rested—or maybe they will have a replacement crew for me, and they are certainly going to *have* to replace the fourteen sailors I have mentioned—I figure that I will take on sixteen missiles and then sail on a long cruise to patrol off the coast of our beaten enemy. And this is something else that even well-informed people never imagine. You don't need to occupy ground any more, and you could not occupy it anyway because it would be dangerous to your troops. All you have to do is have missile submarines constantly on patrol off the coast, and if aerial reconnaissance shows any sign of military activity that the enemy has somehow managed to conceal from us, then the nearest sub lobs in a missile at the particular point where the activity is concentrated and thus effectively preserves the status.

Anyway, this is the role I envisage and I anticipate it with eagerness, because even if I missed the actual fight, at least I can take part in ensuring that any attempts on our national security, any kind of sneak attack by previously concealed weapons, can be blotted out before it has time to get on the road.

I have informed Barnard of the sailing date. I should perhaps say my exec informed him; and the six people in the capsule will be brought out two days before we reach the island. But somehow I am not very interested in them any more. I am more interested in getting back into whatever action is still going on.

Preparations for the voyage to the island are going well. All equipment in the ship has now been checked and everything is in good shape.

Except, of course, for the radio. We still do not receive anything intelligible, though occasionally we do pick up a brief message, or part of a message, in a code we cannot decipher. But this is to be expected. I have sent a note to Barnard informing him that when the six people are released from the capsule they are to be taken at once to the quarters set aside for them, without communication with anyone on the ship. And that includes him. He is not going to like it, but this time I have got my orders to show him. As soon as they step through that door they are under my command, and what I say goes. I shall brief them personally on their life during the time they are on the island.

Apr. 19

The navigation officer and I have now decided on our charted course to the island. I will not go into technical details here except to say we shall be steering on a heading of roughly two hundred and fifteen degrees. This seems to us the most economical cruising route to the island, but of course we can adjust it if necessary.

There are several more things I have to do, but they will all be done during the next month, and I am sure our cruise to the island will be accomplished as smoothly as the rest of the cruise has been.

I am going to be very busy in the next few weeks checking all necessary details, so I don't think I will be able to make many entries in my journal until we have actually sailed and everything is going well. Then I may have a little time to record my thoughts again.

May 15

A very short entry, but this is because everything has to be ready for sailing, and I guess it would surprise quite a few people if they knew just how complicated it is to prepare for a voyage of this nature. But all goes well and I am confident we will reach our destination in accordance with the date and time given me on my first briefing by the Navy.

May 29

Barnard called on me today—this is very unusual because we have been communicating only by note. But he came and asked as a personal favor to be allowed to talk to the guinea pigs before we land them on the island.

I could not see any necessity for this, and told him so. If I may break off for a moment to record my feelings, I would say all right, so he is a psychiatrist and he knows a lot about people. But so do I. You do not hold as many commands as I have in the last ten years and not get to know and understand men. I told him this.

He agreed—though I could see he didn't want to—but suggested the circumstances were different. He asked if I was going to tell them there had been a nuclear war.

I replied very stiffly, but I hope correctly, that what I told them was entirely up to me as Commander. However, I did add that I would naturally give them whatever information I thought fitting to enable them to adjust to their new environment.

He then asked me again as a personal favor to allow him to talk with them before they were left alone on the island.

I refused his request. I cannot deny it gave me a certain amount of satisfaction. After Barnard left I reflected for a while on the way these civilians seem to think they know everything. Well, they may know a lot, but I know *this:* once those people step out from the capsule everyone on this ship is under my command, and I have both Navy Regulations and my own secret orders to back me. They are under my command, and that's how it's going to be.

June 3

Well, we have sailed, and from now on I am going to be pretty busy. During the time we have been under the ice I have left a lot of the running of the ship to my exec, but while we are cruising I like to feel in control of the situation all the time, except when I sleep, of course.

A lot of people who will one day, I hope, read this journal, will wonder just how we manage to find our way under the ice. Especially since we do not have radio to help us. The answer to this is the S.I.N.S., which is a pretty wonderful thing that was dreamed up to help submarines locate exactly their position anywhere in the world, even after the length of time we have been submerged. The initials stand for Ships Inertial Navigation System, and without being too technical I will just say it consists of an incredibly complex system of gyros, which detect and record every movement of the ship in any direction and pass this information on to an automatic log—I guess you could almost call it a computer—which then alters readings of the ship's position according to the information it has received. One of the things we have constantly had to do while under the ice was to make sure this system was working perfectly. I am glad to say it is.

June 5

We are clear of the polar ice, having passed through the Bering Strait. Our sonar detectors are working perfectly, and though they are picking up a few isolated patches of ice ahead, we are clear of the main icepack. These sonar detectors are invaluable to us, and so sensitive they can pick up objects like dolphins swimming ahead of the ship. We have noticed in the past that dolphins seem to be greatly attracted by subs, and when we are submerged there are often some of them around. What is more, they can move even faster under water than we can, and that's something. I have now brought the ship up to periscope height and we are steadily on course for the island. From the latest check on our position, the navigation officer and I have agreed we shall make it easily by June 14, and we have adjusted the cruising speed accordingly.

One thing I didn't record previously—six of the sailors who had shaved off their beards have started growing them again. I take this as a mark of renewed loyalty to me, and a recognition that they were wrong. Now, it is difficult for a man to admit he was wrong, but they have done this. Therefore I have ordered that the entries in their documents be deleted.

June 13

The island is in periscope sight. It is not very distinct in outline yet, because there is a heat haze that tends to distort vision. But it is certainly the correct island. I have been looking closely at my charts and I find there is plenty of water for us to go quite close to the narrow entrance of the reef that runs along the north side of the island, forming a natural lagoon. Once we arrive at that position the procedure is quite simple, and I do not anticipate any trouble in being able to leave on June 17, as planned. When we arrive and have secured our position, we will then make sure the crew have some fresh air and sunshine. Perkins is in charge of this.

June 14

We have surfaced just outside the lagoon, and I have had a chance to observe the island at close quarters through my binoculars.

The lagoon itself is about two miles long and five or six hundred yards wide. The entrance to it is very narrow, and inside the lagoon the natural movement of waves is greatly restricted by the walls of coral that form this natural harbor. The beach seems to be a kind of silver sand, and coming down to the beach there is the usual tropical vegetation and trees you would expect in a Pacific island at these latitudes. There are palm trees, of course, and other trees that one of my officers who is a keen botanist in his recreation time identified as banana plants and breadfruit trees, and some plants that I thought were trees because of their height, but which he tells me are tree ferns. All in all, I think it must be a pretty nice island.

I have also been able to pick up through the binoculars the clearing made for the accommodation huts, and the huts themselves. These are set about twenty yards back from the beach.

The first reconnaissance party returned two hours ago. They reported that it was quite easy water through the entrance to the lagoon, and beaching the boat was simple, as the sand slopes very gently. They also reported all the accommodation huts were in perfect condition, but that the three naval officers who were supposed to be waiting on the island for our arrival were not there. This is disturbing news. I have therefore ordered another party ashore to make a thorough search of the whole island. It is just possible the three of them may be on the other side of the island, but they should not be because this was my scheduled date of arrival.

The crew are thoroughly enjoying the fresh air and sunshine, and even those who haven't been ashore yet are bathing in the sea directly from the stern of the sub, which has been flooded slightly to let the swimmers climb on and off with ease.

June 15

Today has been a full day, in more ways than one. I suppose I had better deal with the events in sequence as they happened, and I think it is important to do this because I want to have a permanent record for the future.

First, the routine part. Landing of the stores began, and the landing parties have begun to deposit the stores in one of the three Quonset huts provided on the island. We estimate that the landing of supplies, including the gasoline required to run the power unit that will supply electricity, will take about two days. So tomorrow night should see us through.

Second, the guinea pigs were brought out of their capsule. I was not present myself, as I was receiving the disturbing report to which I shall refer later. But they were escorted to comfortable quarters where they will pass the next two days, and I shall brief them personally on the morning before they go ashore.

Now for the disturbing news. The three officers who were supposed to be waiting for us are *not* on the island. I have had parties quartering the island and searching for them, and have also tried to attract their attention by repeated sounding of our klaxon and firing flares. But there is no trace of them.

I am now in a considerable dilemma. My orders stated quite clearly that there were to be supervisors on the island. Primarily, of course, they would be there to continue a limited amount of observation. But they were also to be there for another purpose, which I cannot reveal at this moment. They included a doctor, a communications expert, and a weapons officer who was also to be an engineer. I shall have to sleep on this problem, but the beginnings of a solution do occur to me—at least a solution for the doctor problem. About the rest, I just don't know what to do.

June 16

Another full day, and again I am going to deal with it in two parts—the routine, and a bitter personal argument I had later with Barnard. It was not really personal on my side; I like to think I was reasonable in what I asked. But I regard some of his remarks as highly offensive.

This morning I went ashore myself and inspected the accommodations. It was pleasant to feel the ground under my feet again, though I suppose I have become so used to living on a sub it does not have the same effect on me to be on dry land as it would on most people.

Also I inspected the stores and checked on the fuel tank that has been set up a safe distance from the accommodations. The Navy certainly thinks of everything. Finally I gave in to the temptation and took a short break myself, joining those of the crew who were swimming from the beach. It was highly pleasant, and I am sure they enjoyed having me throw a ball about with them in the water.

When I returned to the ship I had made my decision. I did not wish particularly to speak with Barnard but circumstances left me no alternative, so I sent for him—he has been confined to his quarters since the guinea pigs emerged from their capsule.

My decision was this. If there were no supervisors on the island, then I felt that Barnard and his two assistants should stay behind to carry out this function. Now, it is true they can undertake only the medical part of the task—I am certainly not going to reveal to Barnard the other part—but I feel strongly this action must be taken. Whether Barnard likes it or not, this experiment is being run by the Navy, and since the Navy ordered me to proceed with it as planned, then I feel they must regard supervision of the party on the island as important. Therefore I interpret my orders as meaning that I must leave supervisors behind. I cannot spare any of my officers for this task, and in any case they could hardly carry out the medical side of it. I certainly cannot afford to be without my own medical officer, so that lets him out. And I have an idea every other officer is going to be needed when we get back. So I cannot spare any of them either. It therefore seemed to me logical and reasonable to leave Barnard and his two assistants behind. And let me be quite honest, I would prefer it that way.

So when Barnard arrived I outlined to him my proposal that he and his two assistants would stay behind, pointing out that comfortable accommodation was already available for them in the men's hut.

I cannot unfortunately put down exactly the conversation between us because I did not have an exact record—I wish I had thought at the time to have a tape recorder monitoring the conversation. However, I shall record it in as much detail as I can remember.

To my surprise, and without appearing to give the matter any

consideration, which I think is pretty peculiar, Barnard said he absolutely refused to stay behind, and that went for his assistants also.

I pointed out to him this seemed to me a very irresponsible attitude
to take, and one that I would not have expected from a doctor. How,
I asked, could he contemplate leaving six people behind with no
medical advice?

He replied they would not be altogether without medical advice,
since they included among them a nurse with a considerable amount
of experience. Further, they were all healthy, and in good shape
psychologically. The climate of the island appeared to be ideal for
them, but there was something far more important than that.

I asked him just what could be more important than the continu-
ation of an experiment the Navy regarded as highly important. He
replied, his own conscience and duty as a doctor. I must admit I
smiled a little, because it was so illogical after what I had said to him
about leaving them without proper medical care. I do not consider a
trained nurse, even an experienced one, in that category.

He then said very quietly that he was not referring to the people on
the island, but to the people back home, and again he quoted that
goddam book to me, the one he had mentioned months ago, and
told me the survey undertaken by the book showed quite clearly that
after anything in the nature of a serious attack there would probably
be only one doctor surviving and uninjured for every two thousand
people seriously injured. In addition, by now he felt that one of the
most serious hazards would be the traumatic effect on the people who
had survived, and it was therefore not only his inclination but his
duty as a physician to return with his assistants and give what help he
could to the survivors.

I noticed that he was speaking a little faster, and I thought becoming a little angry. I record this now in view of what follows. I said
nothing in reply, but waited for him to continue.

He did, again quoting facts and figures, and all the time becoming
gradually more heated.

I then asked him on just what sources the people who compiled
this book had relied.

He replied, exactly as I suspected he would, that they were a group of physicians and scientists who had compiled this report from non-military sources.

I told him that was exactly the point; they were, in other words, a group of scientists *who did not really know anything about it.* But I did know something about it. I knew that there was a considerable command operating at home, and I was sure that the authorities had the situation completely under control.

He now became openly angry, and had the insolence to tell me nothing would give him greater pleasure than to leave me and remain on the island; but, he added, that was purely a personal pleasure he must put aside in consideration of his moral and ethical duty as a physician. It was then also that he added a few medical terms that as far as I could tell he was applying to me, but I did not understand them, and this is probably just as well for him.

I then informed him I was sorry he felt that way, but that if necessary I could order him to remain behind. And here again I must record that I feel slighted. He immediately produced his own personal instructions—also signed by the Secretary—saying that he and his team must without fail return immediately, once the landing had been successfully achieved.

In the light of this document there was little I could do, but I made one last appeal to him, telling him flatly that without supervision it was possible the men and women might mingle too freely. And we would look pretty foolish if we had to carry out the second part of the experiment with babies on board. I said that as a psychiatrist he should know and appreciate the point.

He replied that as a psychiatrist he appreciated it very well, and if all I wanted him to do was to stay on the island and prevent the men and the women mingling, it was a good thing he had already decided not to stay, because he would not have been able to do it anyway.

I then brought the interview to a close and told him curtly that he and his two assistants were confined to their quarters from now until I landed them back home. I also informed him that although his orders said I had to take him back, he must realize he was now just a passenger on a ship of which I was the Commander, and that under Navy Regulations he would have to obey my orders, the same as any of my crew. He did not say anything, but turned on his heel and left. I hope I do not have to see him again, but I shall certainly make a report about his attitude when I get back.

June 17

This is the last entry I shall make in my journal for some time. After it is finished I shall seal it in a box, which I shall then lock and have sent ashore with the six people who will be on the last boat to go between here and the island. The box will be kept by Perkins, who will ensure it is placed in safe custody. If I do not myself return to the island I can easily arrange for it to be picked up by whichever Commander does.

I have only a few minutes left now, so I will only record briefly that this morning I talked to the six guinea pigs—let me call them that for the last time—and gave them their instructions. I was pretty blunt about some things, but I know my duty. Additionally, I appointed Anderson leader of the party, and in view of the extraordinary circumstances I commissioned him as a temporary ensign in the U.S. Navy. He seems to me the most reliable of a pretty mixed bunch, and unless I misjudge human character he should prove a reliable leader.

I then wished each of them luck and shook them by the hand.

And now it is time for me to bring this journal to a close. Soon I shall be breaking radio silence and asking for my orders. And then, I feel sure, that after taking on stores and weapons I shall be back into the fight; though as I have said I think it will be more in the nature of patrol duties than an actual fight. But whatever the nature of my tasks, I will try to undertake them in the spirit of the Constitution and of my duties as a naval officer.

I shall sign the journal formally:

JAMES WILLIAM GERAGHTY
Commander, U.S.N.

INTERLUDE: Nanyang, Honan Province, May, 1965

The servant brought only two glasses of tea on the tray. He placed one of these in front of Li and one in front of Chen. For Chuang there was a large bottle of San Miguel beer.

Li looked narrowly at Chuang. It would, he thought, be typical of Chuang to insist that he did not want beer, he wanted tea. But Chuang merely grunted as he poured beer into his glass, then took a long pull at it. So, Li thought, Chuang was beginning to learn a few manners; he was beginning to learn who was master here.

Li had not been idle during the months that had passed since their last meeting. He had quietly and deviously ensured that Chuang would receive a hint from the Chairman himself that he was subordinate to Li in this operation. Obviously the message had got through, and Li felt a mild content that this should have been the case.

He waited while Chuang drained his glass, then said more briskly than he usually spoke, "This will be a short meeting, gentlemen. I wish to hear from you personally your progress reports."

Chuang cleared his throat noisily, but Li ignored him and turned towards Chen. "Comrade Professor?"

"Excellent, Comrade," Chen said. "I can now definitely promise that they will be ready late in July. They will definitely be delivered to Marshal Chuang by the first of August."

"That," Li said, "is very good news. I congratulate you, Comrade Professor."

Chen smiled with pleasure and inclined his head slightly in a polite bow.

The fool, Li thought. He knew far too much to be allowed to remain alive after the operation was completed. But for the present let him continue in a state of blissful ignorance. At their last meeting he had used the stick; now it was time for the carrot, to ensure that Chen continued working as hard as ever. He returned Chen's bow with a slight one of his own, and murmured, "Be assured great things await you when all is successfully done."

Then he turned abruptly from Chen and addressed himself to Chuang. "And you, Marshal?"

Chuang deliberately kept Li waiting while he poured the other half of the bottle into his glass. But he did not drink the beer immediately. He considered that the slight provocation the delay had caused was sufficient. At the moment, he knew, he could not risk provoking Li too much. But after the operation . . .

"I have everything I need," he said, "except one thing, which I'll come back to in a moment. But on the positive side everything is going perfectly. I have my two trawlers—they will of course be registered under a false Japanese registration, though that will only be necessary a few weeks before we go into action. They are crewed entirely by North Koreans, and all of them speak Japanese perfectly. There is little ethnic difference between the appearance of Koreans and Japanese."

Li said gently, "Your point is well taken. But could not the same be said of some of our people in the south?" He did not elaborate, but he knew Chuang understood exactly what he meant.

Chuang did not allow Li the satisfaction of seeing that he was annoyed. He said gruffly, "I couldn't find enough Cantonese who spoke Japanese to the degree I consider necessary." Then he hurried on, "Training is almost complete, and I'd say I will be absolutely ready by the time Chen makes his delivery. But that's not all. The four submarines are making substantial progress, and so is their crew-training. They too will be ready at the same time."

Li looked faintly surprised. "Four?" he asked. "But in your previous outline you suggested that only two would be necessary."

Chuang said, "Now I have decided on four. It is possible that one or two of them will prove defective. It is a military risk I'm not prepared to take."

Li sipped his tea thoughtfully before replying. Then he said, "Correct me if I'm wrong, but surely our entire fleet comprises only six ocean-going submarines?"

"It does."

"So if my figures are correct, that will leave us only two for coastal defense. Surely that is too great a risk, Marshal?"

For the first time Chuang smiled. Now he would prove to Li that it was foolish for a civilian to meddle in military matters. He thought carefully for a moment, then said derisively, "Defense against whom? You think six would be enough if they decided to invade?" He did not specify who "they" were, because it was unnecessary. Both the other men realized quite well he was referring to the aging army on Taiwan. "You'd need more like sixty. You can call it a military risk if you like, but no military plan is without risk. And even if they did land a few divisions, my southern army groups would throw them back in the sea in a couple of days."

Li spoke quietly. "I would think that a risk of that nature would be militarily unacceptable."

Again Chuang smiled briefly. "Yes, you would think so, but it's a risk that has often been taken in the past. I don't know whether you remember when England was facing imminent invasion in 1940?"

"But of course," Li said softly. "One has read history."

Chuang's voice was stronger now, more arrogant. "Did you read this particular piece of history—that at the time when the danger was greatest, Churchill sent a large proportion of the armored forces in England to Egypt? And do you know why he did that? Because he realized that, in spite of the very real danger of invasion, the really decisive battles would be fought in North Africa. Now we are faced with a somewhat similar position. I *need* four of our six submarines for the major operation, and the hell with coastal defense." He sat back in his chair and lifted his glass.

For a few moments there was silence. Li had not been aware of this particular incident, but he could not afford to admit his ignorance. To give himself time to think, he sipped his tea. Then he said suddenly, adroitly switching the subject, "Naturally I would not question your military judgment, Marshal, and the

case you mention is certainly an excellent example, but haven't
we strayed a little from what I think should be the main point in
your report?"

"And what's that?"

"You mentioned the one thing you needed. I am perfectly
satisfied your preparations are proceeding admirably, but I am
definitely disturbed that there should be one thing you still need.
What is it?"

The clever bastard, Chuang thought. He had wriggled out of
that one without admitting his ignorance of the incident, though
Chuang was quite certain he had not known of it. But he merely
said, "The date of the operation. I must have it, and I must
have it at least two months before the operation is scheduled."

"Then there are problems?" Li probed softly.

Chuang snorted. "Of course there are problems! The operation itself is simple, but the time and space problem is not. I
shall need at least two months, and even that will only just be
sufficient."

"No doubt at our next meeting we shall learn exactly why,"
Li said. "But if you assure me you will require two months,
Marshal, I accept it without question. Yes," he continued, with
the benevolent air of a parent promising a small boy a Christmas present, "you shall have your two months. Indeed, when
the Chairman calls me in just"—he glanced at his wrist watch—
"six minutes from now, I will inform him of your, ah, dilemma." Then before Chuang could reply, he went on quickly,
"And now, gentlemen, if there is nothing further to discuss, I
am sure you would not like me to keep my esteemed friend the
Chairman waiting for me."

Chen shook his head. "Nothing more. I shall continue at full
pressure."

Chuang said nothing, but pushed back his chair and turned
away, muttering something that could have been a farewell. He
knew that Li's reference to his "esteemed friend" had been
deliberately meant for him. Well, the time would come . . .

He walked out of the villa, closely followed by Chen and
escorted by two bowing servants, servants who, Chuang
guessed, also doubled as Li's personal bodyguard.

Li himself walked slowly to the communications room.

THE ISLAND

The three men sat on the clean, firm sands of the beach and watched the submarine. They did not speak much, but each of them was busy in his own mind with thoughts about what the Commander had said to them before they came ashore. It was unusual for them to speak so little. In the capsule there had been moments when all three of them, together with the three girls, had laughed and joked during a change-over in the shifts. But those moments were past, those happy moments when they had not known; and though they now had the opportunity for talking freely, without any forced break because one pair had to resume the simple, standard tasks that another pair had just left, they were mostly silent.

John Anderson was thinking about the way in which the Commander had told them of the war. The information they had been given was scanty, almost negligible, but at least the Commander had said a stable form of government existed. He wondered how many people were in the government. And how many people did they govern? He could not answer these questions, and since he could not answer them he dismissed them from his mind. His training, his character, required this. Given the requisite information, he would work patiently at a problem, but without the information he could do nothing. He knew only that something terrible had happened, but in spite of it they had been landed on the island. They were alive and had a certain amount of supplies, and for the moment there was nothing he could do about the situation.

Bill Evans said suddenly, "I think she's moving." His voice was deep, thick, in keeping with his physique. Beneath a veneer of New England accent there was an undertone of Welsh. Like the other two men, he had been shocked by the news the Commander had given them, but he did not realize he had been shocked. Nothing had prepared him for this moment, this realization that they were on their own, and that probably he would never see Wales again. He thought about his years at Yale, and the years before that when he had struggled to get his degree at Cardiff, then endured two years of National Service. And for this—to be left on an island with five other people who might perhaps be the only people he would ever see again in his life. He wondered for a moment about Wales, and what it was like there now, but he put the thought from his mind and watched the movement of the submarine. He realized he must accept the situation, accept the fact that these five were the only companions left to him. He was glad Jane Nichols was among them.

Arnie Levin remarked, "I think you're right, she *is* moving."

In comparison with the other two, Arnie seemed almost frail. It was not something usually noticeable, because his energy, his effervescent wit, took away the impression of physical smallness. But now he too was dejected, perhaps with better reason than Bill Evans or John Anderson. He was a physicist, and knew that if there had been a major war, then there was also a global fallout.

John said, "She's moving all right, but I don't think the girls would be very interested. They all said they wanted to unpack right away."

The men sat silent while the submarine moved away toward the north. When it was about two miles from the island they heard three short blasts from its klaxon, and it began to submerge. The blue waters closed over it, and it was gone.

Arnie said, "So we're on our own."

While Mary Girard and Jane Nichols were preparing the adequate but unappetizing dehydrated food that had been left for them, Helen Dimarco was checking the medical supplies.

The Commander had said so little, she was thinking. He had told them there had been a major war, and apparently America had won it. But what did that mean to the six of them who had been left behind? She herself was far more concerned by his implication that they were in constant danger from fallout. Why hadn't he given them more information, given them the facts and figures?

At least she had the comfort of plentiful medical supplies to deal with any emergency that might arise—physical emergency, that was. But she could not be sure that the emergency would be physical rather than mental. She thought for a moment about the other two girls. Mary would be all right, she was sure. She accepted the fact that they were on their own.

But Jane was different. She was a girl with a fine mind, but also a delicately balanced mind, Helen thought. Of all the group, she probably had the most volatile temperament. And of course it would not be easy for her to adjust to the idea that she could not live a completely natural life.

Helen placed the last of the drugs neatly in the white cupboard, and as she did so she heard the klaxon of the submarine and realized it was leaving.

Jane and Mary also heard the klaxon. Mary hardly seemed to notice it, but Jane said immediately, "The submarine's leaving."

Mary shrugged her slim shoulders and said, "So let it leave. I didn't think much of that Commander character. He gave me, you know, a kind of crawly feeling."

"Yes," Jane said, "I know. Do I have time for a bath before we eat?"

"Oh, sure, about fifteen minutes. It'll be cold anyway, so it doesn't matter too much about time."

"Doesn't it?" Jane said. She left the center hut, turned right, and walked to the hut she shared with Helen and Mary. There was only one bathroom in the hut, so the times they used it would have to be arranged between them. As she relaxed in the bath she thought that at least they were better off than travelers to Venus would have been. She rippled the water with her hands, the way she had always done since she was a child. She was a tall girl, well-built, and although her skin was lighter than Helen's or Mary's, she had been browned by the sunlamp in the capsule. The lamp had also made her hair even lighter than it was before. All the comforts, she thought as she soaped herself, but not the true comfort, the only really important comfort, which was full knowledge of what had happened and what they could expect to happen. She reviewed in her mind exactly what the Commander had said, trying to remember each phrase. But it added up to nothing. There had been a war. There was still a government, or at least he claimed there was. As she got out of the bath and wrapped a soft towel around her, she thought of how they were alone and would continue to be alone, uncertain of the invisible hazard that might be attacking them.

In the kitchen, Mary had put the food out on plates. She carried the plates through to the dining room, then called Helen and walked along the beach to tell the men the food was ready.

The light was still good, though the sun was sinking fast. She saw the three men about two hundred yards away, shucked off her shoes, and began to walk toward them, enjoying the feel of the clean sand between her toes. She could not see any sign of the submarine, and assumed that it had left and was on its way back to the United States. Perhaps it would call in at Pearl Harbor on the way. It would be nice, she thought, if it did. She had been born in a house that overlooked Pearl Harbor; her father a French journalist, her mother the daughter of a rich Chinese storekeeper. She was probably the most attractive of the girls, and in her the best points of French and Chinese breeding had emerged. She walked lightly, provocatively, with a delicacy and grace in her movements that was Oriental. But her eyes were less slanted than those of a full Chinese, her complexion a little lighter. She was an extremely beautiful girl.

She had gone only twenty yards when she saw a turtle emerge from the water and scuttle up the silver sand of the beach into the green overhang of tropical plants. She stopped while it passed her, not afraid at all because she had often seen turtles before, and anyway this was a small one. The turtle ignored her, accepting her presence without feeling any need to be anxious, to be afraid. Mary wondered why people could not be the same way, why they could not accept the presence of others without feeling fear, without feeling the necessity to impress upon the others that they were not afraid, though really they were. She did not know exactly what had happened, but she was quite sure that whatever had happened it was because of this awful fear people had of each other. She waited until the fronds had stopped vibrating after the passage of the turtle, thought briefly and mischievously of the erotic connotation that the turtle, and particularly turtle's head, had in Chinese, and then she began to walk again toward the men.

The three men did not see her approach. They were sitting on the firm sand, and talking about what the Commander had told them.

The water of the lagoon lapped gently on the shore. Beyond the pink and white of the reef, the long, rolling waves pounded against the coral. But inside the lagoon the water was calm and still.

Arnie Levin said, "All right, so maybe he didn't know too much about what had happened in the war. But I still can't figure out why he wouldn't tell us just where we were."

"But he did," Bill Evans said quietly. "He did, Arnie, though he didn't know it."

John Anderson looked at him quickly. "You mean you know? You mean you can tell where we are by something he said? Hell, Bill, I know you're a geography specialist but I don't see how you can figure that out."

Bill Evans scooped a handful of sand, let it slowly trickle through his fingers. He said, "It's easy. Listen now. He told us we were a little south of the equator, right?"

John and Arnie nodded agreement.

"All right then. I'm not going to be able to tell you exactly, but I'm going to assume we're somewhere between the equator and ten degrees South. That's a rough fix on our latitude." He tapped his wrist watch. "And the answer to our longitude is right here. What time do you have, Arnie?"

"Ten after seven." He grinned, and for a moment he was almost like the old Arnie. "Or maybe for the ensign's benefit I'd better say 19.10 hours."

John Anderson said, "Lets forget that ensign crap, Arnie. I don't give a damn what someone with a piece of gold braid says to me. I'm a civilian, we're all civilians, and that's the way it's going to be. Go on, Bill."

Evans said, "You boys set your watches by local time before you left the sub, right? But I didn't. I kept mine at G.M.T. And I have eleven after eight." He smiled suddenly. Or maybe 08.11 if Arnie specially wants it that way. And that means we're about one hundred and seventy-two degrees east of Greenwich. Give or take a few degrees each way, and that puts us somewhere between the Gilbert and the Ellice islands. From what I've seen of the vegetation, that would fit exactly."

"A genius yet," Arnie said with mock admiration. "I thought he told us all to set our watches by local time."

Evans shrugged. "Like John here, I don't take too much notice of what anyone says, just because he has some gold braid to back him. I suppose I'm just a rebel at heart. All the Welsh are."

Anderson asked, "Bill, you're pretty sure about your figuring?"

"Good God, man, of course I'm sure! I know I've spent the last few years learning more and more about less and less, but I still haven't forgotten the basic geography I knew. You know what, come the autumnal equinox, I'll tell you inside two degrees just how far south of the equator we are. Then, *if* we have an atlas among the books they left us, I should be able to tell you just what group of islands we're in."

"Correct me if I'm wrong," Arnie said, "but if we're roughly where you say we are, aren't there a hell of a lot of islands around?"

"Sure, hundreds of them. Most of them you dont see marked on the maps, unless they're very large-scale maps, like ships' navigation charts, that sort of thing. Probably this island wouldn't be—it doesn't have any population, not even a name. It's about five miles long, two miles wide; that wouldn't even be a dot on a map of the Pacific."

Mary came up to them very quietly. "The food's ready."

John Anderson stood up. "I can use it," he said. " What do we have, Mary?"

"Nothing very special, I'm afraid. You realize everything they left us is dehydrated, and dehydrated food is usually almost tasteless."

"But that's better than we'd be having on one of the planets," Arnie said. "There, we'd probably only have a few pills to take each day."

The four of them walked slowly back along the beach to the hut where Jane had been joined by Helen.

After supper there was coffee in the small, comfortable leisure room next to the dining room. But although the leisure room was small, it was still big enough for the six of them to relax in ease because it had originally been planned for nine. They were aware of this, but none of them mentioned it. They drank their coffee, and relaxed in comfort and silence.

"It could be worse," John said. "You've all read the handouts they gave us after we left the capsule. No poisonous reptiles or insects. No mosquitoes, not much wild life of any kind except the birds. The only hazard they mention are the sea snakes, but they are timid creatures; they'll move away fast if anything disturbs them. We have electricity, and gasoline to run the generators. We have reasonable supplies, though I must admit they don't taste too good."

Jane Nichols broke in on him. At first her voice was hesitant, but as she spoke it became firmer. "And if they don't come back? If that's the last we ever see of them, or anyone else? Look, we're kidding ourselves. There may be nobody left alive back there. That submarine could just disappear. You all heard what Geraghty said about difficulty of communication. How are we to know?" Her voice had risen sharply. She stood up abruptly and walked to the window overlooking the beach.

Bill Evans moved quietly up beside her. He touched her gently on the shoulder and said, "Jane, it's something we don't know; but you also heard Geraghty promise he'd try to communicate. Then we'll know." He turned away, feeling that what he had said was inadequate. Jane ignored him.

Arnie spoke up quickly. "Sure, that's right. We have a powerful receiver, we can listen for a message from the sub, and that's not all. You may not know it, but I'm a radio expert myself—well, maybe not an expert, but a few years back I had my own ham outfit and I figure that pretty soon with that receiver they left us we'll be able to hear just what's going on in the world. Meanwhile there's lots we have to do—that right, John?"

Anderson said, "Glad you brought that up, Arnie. There sure is. First—and I've said it to Arnie and Bill already, but now I'm saying it to you three girls—we forget all that ensign crap Geraghty handed out before he put us ashore."

Jane was still staring out of the window. "He said there'd been a war," she said tonelessly. "He said we'd won it. He said that was all he knew. But if we won it, why didn't he know more? How did he know we'd won it?" She swung round to face them. Her face was white. "If they could tell him that, why couldn't they tell him more?" Her voice was trembling now, rising in pitch. "Because they're dead.

And soon whatever killed them will kill him and all his crew, and we'll be alone. Oh my God, don't you see it, we'll be alone!"

She burst into tears. She brushed past Bill and ran out of the room. He moved to follow her.

Helen Dimarco said quickly, "No, Bill. Not right now. You, Mary, go after her. Probably she's gone to her room. I'll fix a sedative."

Mary Girard went swiftly from the room. Helen laid her hand gently on Bill's thick arm. "Don't worry too much," she said quietly. "It's a perfectly natural reaction. I'll fix her something strong, and in the morning she'll be fine. You'll see." Then she turned and went to the small room set aside for the medical supplies. Evans sank into a chair.

"But she was talking a lot of sense; we all know it," Arnie said. "We know it, but we have to live with it, isn't that right?" He looked sympathetically at Evans. "I figure you're more than a little fond of her, Bill?"

"Yes, more than a little. You know, all those months we were so close together, at first I was a little bit shy with her. But soon it was as though we were thinking together, as if everything she thought communicated itself to me, and everything I thought communicated itself to her. Do you understand?"

John Anderson said, "I understand perfectly. I guess much the same sort of thing happened to the rest of us."

Arnie nodded.

"So let's get organized," John said. "Arnie, you're the radio expert, how about you staying here tomorrow and setting up the radio and checking the technical equipment, while Mary takes an inventory on supplies."

"Suits me."

"Bill, you're the geographer, you take Jane, start exploring the island. Okay?"

Bill said, "Okay. Tell you what, John, I've been looking at the sketch map they gave us in the handout. There are two hills, one on the west, one on the east. The one on the west goes up to five hundred feet. We should be able to see everything from there." He paused. "I think it might be good for Jane to go up there, let her look down on the solid land, make her feel part of it."

"I agree," John said. "Now, we know we don't have any natural hazards to fear—I mean no snakes, scorpions, anything like that, but there's always the chance one of us might fall, break a leg or something. I'd like to propose that when any of us leaves the camp we take one of the pistols along. Loaded. If anyone gets into trouble they fire two quick shots. One every two minutes after that. Anyone who hears the shots drops everything, comes running. Also, they've supplied us with whistles. If anyone runs out of ammo before they're found, use the whistles."

"A whistle I can use," Arnie said. "A pistol, I don't know one end from the other. I'm uneducated."

"I'll show you," John said.

"There's just one more thing," Arnie went on. "All right, we don't have any natural hazards to think about. But there's one unnatural hazard I'm thinking about right now."

Bill looked up. "What's that?"

"Well—" Arnie said, then broke off as Helen and Mary came back into the room.

Helen said, "She's easier now. I've given her a strong sedative. She wants to say good night to you, Bill." Her voice became softer. "And be very gentle with her, Bill. I think right now she's feeling a little ashamed . . . feeling she's let us all down, particularly you."

"Which room is she in?"

"Third on the right after the bathroom."

Bill nodded and went out.

Mary Girard moved across the room and sat on the arm of Arnie's chair as Arnie said, "Now *that* the Commander wouldn't like. You remember what he said? Women's quarters strictly off limits to men, and likewise vice versa."

"Screw the Commander," John said.

Arnie looked at him. "Bad language. Now, bad language is something I never use." It was true. None of them had ever heard Arnie use a word stronger than damn. "But," he continued, "all the other vices, you name them I got 'em." . . .

Bill Evans opened the door of Jane's room. She was lying quietly on her back, her blonde hair spread over the two pillows that supported her head. Her face was still pale, but her breathing was regular. He moved to the side of the bed and took her left hand in his.

She said, "I'm sorry, Bill. I'm so sorry."

"What for? You only said what all of us were feeling."

"It's just that suddenly I had a feeling, like a dream, you know, but not a dream."

"I know."

"And I suddenly saw all those people back there, and they were dying."

"Listen, *cariad*," Bill said softly, "we don't know they're dying. We don't know anything much yet, but we will just as soon as Arnie gets that radio working. That isn't what we have to think of, we have to think that we're living. John and Helen, Arnie and Mary, you and me, Jane—you and me, *cariad*."

He felt the grip of her hand relax slightly. Her voice was drowsy now. "What does that word mean?"

"*Cariad?* It's Welsh. It means darling."

Jane sighed. "Darling." Then her eyes closed and she was asleep.

Bill gently took her hand from his and laid it on the bed. She was breathing easily and deeply. He bent and brushed his lips lightly on her forehead, turned off the light, and went quietly from the room.

Mary went to bed and fell asleep immediately. Arnie stayed awake a little longer. He was thinking of all he had read about the global fallout pattern. He wished now he had studied the subject more fully, but somehow there had never been time to fit it in. Also, he was considering the implications of the strange iridescence he had noticed in the northern sky. Perhaps it was natural—he had never been south of the equator before. But perhaps it was not. He tossed and turned fitfully before he slept.

Bill Evans also lay awake for some time. If there had been a major war he was under no illusions about what had probably happened to Britain. One of his friends from M.I.T. had worked it out for him as a theoretical exercise. There would be practically nothing left on the surface, he knew. But he did not think of that so much as of what might have happened to the miners thousands of feet beneath the ground when the bombs exploded. His brother was a miner. He imagined the men feeling the earth tremors, experiencing the sudden failure of power and the descent of a darkness relieved only by their own safety lamps as they groped their way toward the main shaft to wait for the cage that would never come down for them. . . . He thought of Jane. And with this thought came sleep.

Helen Dimarco and John Anderson were quickly asleep, though for different reasons. John had the gift of falling asleep, quickly, a habit acquired during his service in the Navy. Helen, because she was worried about Jane, because during her hospital experience, she had seen many people poised on as fine a knife-edge as Jane, knew that she would not sleep easily without a mild sedative. She took a small Sodium Amytal capsule. Five minutes later she was asleep.

Next morning after they had eaten their tasteless breakfast, Bill Evans eased his belt, which supported the holster of a heavy Colt automatic. He checked that his whistle was safely tucked away in the pocket of his shirt, then looked up at the green slopes of the West hill.

"It's a long climb," Arnie said.

Bill frowned thoughtfully. "Not so long as all that. There won't be any paths, but I don't think the vegetation is too thick. Anyway, we may not try for the top today. We've been cooped up in that submarine so long I think it would be foolish to try too much in one day. You agree, Jane?"

"Yes," Jane said, "I think you're right. Let's go as high as we can today without too much strain, then a little higher tomorrow, and maybe the top the day after that. After all, we've plenty of time."

Helen had been right, Bill thought. Jane was quite different today, with no trace of the hysterical anxiety she had shown the previous night. He said, "All right, let's go. See you, Arnie, Mary."

"Wait a minute, Bill," Arnie said. "There's a question I've been meaning to ask you. When does it rain around here? Is it always like this?" He waved a hand at the cloudless blue sky.

Bill answered slowly, "I'd say you wouldn't see any rain until about next March. Then it'll rain for maybe two months, on and off. Enough to keep the streams flowing and the plant life green. Why?"

"Oh, nothing," Arnie said, "no reason, just curious. See you later on."

Bill and Jane walked across the sand to where the first palm trees fringed the beach. Soon they were lost from sight in the luxuriant green vegetation.

Arnie looked at his watch. It was a little after eleven. "Time for me to set up the radio, tune it to the sub's frequency. You know how to take inventory of the stores?"

"Well," Mary said, "it just so happens I do. My grandpa had a general store in Hawaii. That's where I lived until I was eighteen, you know."

"Yeah, I know. You told me in the sub, remember? Well, do you need my expert advice?"

"Let me tell you, Arnie Levin, every vacation I used to earn a few dollars helping out in the store. The last couple of years before I left for California he let me do his annual stocktaking. And I never made a mistake. At least I don't think so, because he'd have noticed if I had: He was a very smart businessman. Most Chinese are."

"You're darn right," Arnie said. "They can play poker too. I know. Hey, wait a minute. Girard—that's no Chinese name."

"No, but my mother was Chinese. My father was French originally. He was born in New Orleans. A Creole, he called himself." She hesitated, then went on, "I don't know just what that makes me," and smiled at him uncertainly.

Arnie put his hands lightly on her slender shoulders. "It makes you American. Also, I recommend the mixture."

She smiled, then turned away and walked rapidly up the beach toward the supply hut. Arnie checked his watch again and sat down on the clean sand. He had already run a test on the radio this morning. It would take him only a few seconds to adjust the tuning. He had plenty of time to think, and much to think about.

John glanced at his watch and saw it was getting toward noon. Soon Arnie might be getting a message from the sub, and then perhaps they would know something. To know nothing was to exist—he would not call it to live—in a vacuum, in emptiness. It was possible to continue that way for a short time, and fortunately the group appeared to be a happy and self-sufficient unit. But he knew how quickly even a happy, self-sufficient unit could break apart under intolerable stress. And to be without knowledge was just that kind of stress. He tried to put these thoughts out of his mind and concentrate on Helen.

But no message came through. Mary had left her inventory to listen with Arnie. She said, "Would they be heading for Pearl Harbor, do you think? We lived in a house that looked down on it, and they often had submarines there."

"No," Arnie replied slowly, "I don't figure they're heading for Hawaii. San Diego would be more likely." He did not tell her what he was really thinking: that if there had been a major war there would certainly be nothing left of Pearl Harbor, and probably very little of Hawaii. "We'll just have to wait until they tell us."

Well, Arnie thought, I've made the first discovery. A negative discovery, it was true, evidence of nothing except the fact the submarine had not transmitted. But even that was something. Now he would try to discover more. He began a thorough, systematic search through the wave bands, his fingers caressing the tuning controls of the set.

But Arnie was wrong. He had not made the first discovery. That had already been made by Bill and Jane. The discovery was a path that they happened on quite by accident about twenty minutes after leaving the beach. The going had been slow, though the slope of the hill was not steep. Their muscles had become slack during their long stay in confined quarters, and they had to push their way through grass that reached almost to their thighs.

And then, suddenly, they hit the path.

It was obviously man-made. It was about six feet wide and was constructed of some bituminous substance. To their left it sloped down the side of the hill between thick walls of vegetation, and disappeared in a curve a hundred yards from them. To their right it climbed in the same gentle slope to another curve about twice as far away.

Bill Evans opened his knife, knelt down, and pushed the point of the knife into the surface. The knife penetrated an inch, then Bill felt it strike on something hard. He probed again in another spot. Again an inch of penetration, again something hard beneath it. He straightened up.

"Well?" Jane asked.

"Concrete, I'd say. Asphalt laid on concrete."

"By why, on an uninhabited island? Who'd want it? Where does it go?"

Bill said slowly, "I'm not too sure about the uninhabited bit, in the recent past anyway. Who'd want it I wouldn't know. But at least we'll be able to answer your last question. We only have to walk ahead to do that. Then when we've found out where it goes, we'll walk down and see where it ends."

"Suits me," Jane said. "That grass is scratching my legs."

Bill grinned. "You should have worn slacks as I told you."

"But I look awful in slacks. I'm too big for slacks."

Bill looked straight at her. "To me, you'd look good in anything," he said. "Any old thing at all."

Jane moved close to him. She said softly, "You really mean that, don't you? And you really meant what you called me last night?"

"Yes, I did."

As they walked on he said, "What we really need here is a bloody Welsh mountain pony, if there are any left."

She turned away. "You really believe it, then? You believe there's nothing left back there?"

"I don't know, and you don't know, just what's happened. But I know that whatever's happened, whatever's left, I love you, Jane. I've loved you for months, and I—well, I bloody well love you, that's all."

She moved closer to him again. "Why, Bill Evans, you're blushing. How would a Welsh girl ask you why you were blushing?"

"Well," Bill said, "where I come from she'd probably say, 'Why are you blushing, boy? I bloody well love you too.' "

"Just like that?"

"Just like that."

"All right then. I can't imitate the accent—but I bloody well love you too."

Bill laughed. "You're sure?"

"I'm sure." She put her hands round his neck and said quietly,

"Bill, you're all I have left. With you I can forget about what might have happened back there. But if I didn't have you I think I'd go crazy. Don't ever stop loving me, Bill."

The path was mostly straight, with an occasional long sweeping curve. Above them the banyan fig trees, the palms, and the tree ferns towered, forming an almost continuous green roof, pierced here and there by golden shafts of sunlight. Bill saw, too, that there were breadfruit trees and fig trees. At least, he thought, we shan't starve. But he was still disturbed by what he had seen earlier, which he had not mentioned.

After a long curve, they came to a straight section about a hundred yards long, and saw at the end of it a dazzling expanse of white, gleaming in the unobstructed brightness of the sunlight. The path was flat now, and they hurried along it, eager to see what lay at the end.

They stepped onto the white surface. It was circular, and was made of smooth concrete, about a hundred feet across. Around half the circle grew the same kinds of trees as had lined the path. Around the other half was a concrete wall about four feet high. They walked across to it.

Below them the whole of the lagoon was spread out in a panorama of vivid color. They could see the roofs of their huts, the long silver sweep of the sandy beach, and on one side of the reef the blue of the shallow water, paler than the blue of the sea beyond the reef.

Jane rested her hand on Bill's arm as he leaned on the wall. "It's beautiful, isn't it?"

"Yes," he said. But his mind was not registering the beauty. He was thinking back to his British Army days, remembering what he had been taught and what he had seen.

They stood for a while in silence, Jane looking down at the riot of color, Bill examining the plan of the island closely. He was interested in the distribution of vegetation, the contours of the island, and particularly in the slopes of the East hill, where a small patch of white shone from among the surrounding brown of the palm trunks and the green of the foliage. He estimated the white patch to be about fifty feet lower than where they were. But it was still quite high enough for its purpose, if his deductions were correct.

Suddenly he said, "I've seen all I need to from here."

As they left the platform they noticed something they had missed before. Opposite the wall another path, similar to the one they had already traveled, led up from the concrete. They could see along it for about fifty yards before it curved away.

"That must lead to the top," Bill said. "I wonder if——"

"No," Jane said firmly. "Not today. My legs have had it."

They followed the path down, moved through a short stretch of high grass, and arrived back at the huts. On the way Bill had seen two more things he thought unnatural. Jane saw only one, but made no comment on it. Nor did Bill comment on what had seemed strange to him. It had already been agreed between himself, John, and Arnie that each day the three of them would discuss what they had discovered before talking things over with the girls.

Ten minutes later they joined John and Helen beside the lagoon. Mary came too, but Arnie stayed with his radio.

Later in the day while the girls were preparing food, the three men walked along the shore, discussing what they had learned during the day.

John Anderson told them about the inaccessibility of the island by boat unless it approached through the lagoon. Landing anywhere else would be quite impossible. He also reported that the lagoon was literally teeming with fish, and if they wanted to supplement their diet with fresh fish there would be no problem catching them. He had also, he said, seen quite a few turtles, though he was not sure whether they were edible or not.

Bill Evans said quickly, "Yes, I think they would be. I know that in Samoa turtle meat is a delicacy, and if my calculations are correct we can't be too far from Samoa." He paused, then asked, "You want to go next, Arnie? Or shall I?"

Arnie's reply came slowly. "I think I'd rather be last. I want to wait until it gets a bit darker, so I can show you exactly what I mean."

John said, "All right, Bill, let's hear from you."

"First, and possibly most important, I'm beginning to have doubts this island is uninhabited," Bill said.

The other two looked at him in amazement. "But," John said, "we were told definitely it was uninhabited. Geraghty told us that, and the handouts say so too. If you remember, Geraghty stressed there should have been three people here to meet us, but that's all. What gives you the idea it's inhabited?"

"Wait a minute. I'm not saying it's inhabited right now. Certainly I didn't see any signs of life—human life, that is. I'll come to the other kinds of life in a moment. But I found a recently made path—well, I suppose you could almost call it a road. There's no doubt you could drive a jeep along it. It was asphalt laid on concrete, and it looked to me like a gun emplacement."

"How do you know about things like that?" Arnie asked.

"When I graduated from the university they hauled me into the army. It was what we called National Service in Britain. They let you finish your university course first, then you had to do two years' service. I was in the Royal Artillery, so I got to know a bit about gun positions. After what John said about the mouth of the lagoon being the only possible way of access to the island, I'm more sure than ever that's what it was."

"Why?"

"Two reasons. I've seen gun emplacements with approach roads exactly like that. And second—here's where John's point is important —the position is on a natural ledge that gives a perfect field of fire through a hundred-and-eighty-degree arc including the mouth of the lagoon. I was also able to see a similar position on the East Hill. It was slightly lower in altitude, otherwise I wouldn't have seen it, but it's there all right. Those two positions could seal this island off against a landing party without any trouble at all."

"Yeah," Arnie said, "maybe. I'll take your word for that, Bill, but who'd want to seal this island off? And who from? What's a piece of real estate like this worth to anyone?"

"It could be an old position," John said slowly. "Something left over from the Pacific campaign in World War Two."

"No," Bill said, "I'm quite sure this construction isn't so old. You know how concrete gets discolored after a few years. Well, this isn't, it's fresh. I'd guess it's not more than two years old at most. I can also tell you our diet won't be restricted to John's fish. There are more coconuts than we could ever get round to using if we stayed here a million years. Also figs from banyan fig trees, and breadfruit. But most important are the bananas."

"I don't get you," Arnie said.

"It's quite simple. The first three things I mentioned—that is, the coconuts, the figs, and the breadfruit—you'd expect to find on an island of this type. They're indigenous to this kind of island. But not bananas. Bananas have to be cultivated in plantations, and I saw at least four separate plantations. They're overgrown in parts, but they're still bearing fruit. So that means they have been cultivated in the not too distant past. Question: where are the people who cultivated them?"

"It's a point," John said, "but there could be an easy explanation. Maybe there were people here who were evacuated when the U.S. government decided they wanted this island for the experiment."

"Could be, but if you remember, the handouts definitely said there was no wild life except birds. But I saw monkeys and pigs. I only got a brief glimpse of one monkey, but we saw three pigs. As a matter of fact, they walked across the path about fifty yards ahead of us. Jane saw the pigs as clearly as I did, but she didn't see the monkey."

"Maybe John's right. Maybe the government did decide to evacuate the people who were here. But that doesn't explain the pigs and the monkey. And it doesn't explain the gun positions."

"Where exactly does the road finish?"

"About fifty yards from our huts. Also, I forgot to mention that there's a road leading from the concrete emplacement toward the top of the hill. We didn't follow it today because Jane said she was feeling tired. But I'm betting there'll be a similar road up to the emplacement on the other hill. I guess that's about all, except that there are streams in about the same places the plan shows."

"Well," John said, "there may be a simple explanation for all these things. Let's assume there were people here. Let's assume they were evacuated by the government. Perhaps they kept pigs. Perhaps they rounded up the pigs but didn't get them all, and some were left behind. Then the monkeys, or the monkey, escaped from the supply ship that brought our stores here. I don't mean the stores they landed from the sub for us, but there must have been a ship that brought the huts and the parts for the fuel and water tanks. Maybe the monkey

Bill saw was a ship's pet. Some sailor could have brought it ashore, and maybe it decided it liked the island. Oh hell, there could be a lot of explanations."

"But not," Bill said, "for the gun emplacements and the approach roads."

"If they *are* gun emplacements. I know that's how they looked to you, Bill, but we don't know definitely."

He turned to Arnie. "Now can you fill us in, Arnie?"

Arnie shook his head. "I'm a physicist, and I should know everything about fallout. But I don't, damn it. Lots of surveys were made, but somehow there always seemed to be something more important to do. I know all the basic principles, but I'm not too sure how to apply them to our position." He shook his head again.

"But you weren't a nuclear physicist, Arnie," Bill said. "A man can't specialize in every field of his chosen science. In any case, you've no more reason to be ashamed than any of us. We should all have known it. The whole bloody world should have known it, but somehow all those reports and surveys never seemed to reach a very wide public."

Arnie said, "Well, to continue: I spent most of the day searching through the frequencies, but the results were negative except for one item. I'll come back to that later. It's quite possible people were broadcasting somewhere, but I couldn't pick up any transmissions. Very strong interference, and that could have been masking transmissions, but I'm afraid it's a negative report."

"And the transmission you did pick up?" Bill said.

"It was in a language I couldn't understand. It began faintly, then it seemed to grow in signal strength, then it faded again. Anyway, I stayed tuned to the same frequency and called Mary just in case it was a language she could understand. Nothing came through for about an hour and a half, then we heard it again, but much weaker this time. It lasted about three minutes altogether—that is, one minute for transmission, then about a minute with no transmission, then a third minute when we heard it again. After that it faded."

"Did Mary understand the message?"

"Yes," Arnie said. "She didn't get it all the first time, but she did the second. It was in Russian, and was the same message repeated. It went like this: *The peace-loving people of the United Socialist Soviet Republic declare before all men the horrible crime perpetrated by the Fascist American aggressors who have attacked our peace-loving people without provocation and who must now pay the penalty for their inhuman and terrible action. They will not escape the consequences.* Mary has it written out, but that's about it." He paused. "You make sense out of it, I can't."

"I think I can make sense out of the time interval," Bill said. "Also I think I know why you picked up that transmission but no others. I don't know much about radio, but I assume it's easier to pick up transmissions close by you."

"Well, yes," Arnie said.

"All right, then, let's say the thing that transmitted was passing pretty close to you."

John Anderson shook his head. "I'm not with you, Bill. What the hell is all this about?"

"I think the two messages came from a Sputnik. It's the time interval, you see, and the repetition of the message. I think the first time Arnie heard it the Sputnik was passing quite close, maybe overhead. The second time would be after it made another orbit of the world, but this time it would be passing some distance away, because its orbital path would be different by as much as two hundred miles. And therefore the message was weaker."

"Yes," Arnie agreed, "I'll go for that. It's easy to rig a voice transmitter and the storage batteries if that's all you want from it."

As they talked the twilight had come. Within a few minutes it would be dark, Arnie was thinking, and then he could show the others what he had noticed on the previous night. Perhaps it was a natural phenomenon. In that case Bill should know about it.

"Where did you learn about Sputniks, Bill?" John asked.

"I was in on a series of experiments during the International Geophysical Year. Our particular section was mainly concerned with the exact shape of the earth, and for that we relied on information sent back from instruments we'd put into orbit. As a matter of fact, we learned quite a lot."

"But not enough," Arnie said bitterly. "None of us learned enough to prevent a war."

John shrugged. "Eighteen million dead in the first World War, mostly combatants. Over twenty million in the second—no one will ever know just how many—but that time there were as many non-combatant as combatant casualties, maybe more. They didn't keep accurate records at places like Auschwitz and Belsen and all those other little pieces of hell the Nazis and Japs successfully created here on earth. They wouldn't have had enough clerical staff to do it. And don't forget we weren't entirely guiltless ourselves. Hamburg, Dresden, Hiroshima, Nagasaki. Oh, I know there might have been some military justification in all those, where there was no justification for the genocide the Nazis deliberately and ruthlessly carried through, but we killed innocent people just the same. But we forget, you see. We not only forget our own atrocities, we even forget the hideous things *they* did." He paused and looked at Arnie. "What was the Sputnik message again?"

Arnie repeated the message. By now it was dark, and he directed John's and Bill's attention to the iridescence he had noticed the previous evening. He asked Bill if this was a natural phenomenon.

No, I don't think so," Bill turned round and looked south. "You can see it to the south too. Not as bright, but it's there all right. No, I don't think it's natural; I wouldn't like to guess what it could be."

Arnie said, "If it's not natural, I think I can. This has happened before, on a strictly limited scale, after they detonated a couple of devices at very high levels. Now, if Geraghty was right about the start of the war, if it happened when he said, that radioactivity—which is what it is—has persisted for seven months. I expected that in the Northern Hemisphere if a major war had been fought, but not in the Southern."

"Why not?" John asked.

"Well," Arnie said, "it's tied into this question of global fallout. I've been trying to remember everything I've ever read, and I was almost sure until now that I was near an answer." He hesitated for a moment, but went on more confidently. "Maybe it doesn't affect my idea too much anyway, if we assume there've been large-scale explosions in the Southern Hemisphere as well as in the Northern. Understand, I'm not stating that as a fact, I'm just trying to draw a conclusion from what I've observed. You see, predictions of global fallout were based on a weather theory developed by two scientists who had made an intensive study of the stratospheric circulation of air. I think they were British scientists, weren't they, Bill?"

"That's right. Brewer and Dobson. Their theory was that there was a north-south circulation of air in the Northern Hemisphere. They suggested that the air that was moist and warm rose slowly toward the stratosphere in the low latitudes near the equator. When it reached the tropopause it was dried by condensation in the cold boundary layer, then passed into the stratosphere and moved slowly toward the Pole of whichever hemisphere it originated in. Later it would descend again in the higher latitudes. So there would be two separate circulations for the two hemispheres."

John shook his head. "But what does it mean in terms of fallout? how does it affect us?"

"Well," Arnie said slowly, "I'm going to skip the short-term effects. We were under the ice when those occurred, which is probably why we're still alive. But basing it on the Brewer-Dobson model of air circulation, and actual soil tests made for, I think, Strontium 90, they drew up a graph that showed stratospheric fallout would be at its peak between about sixty-five and twenty degrees North, and at its lowest about ten degrees South, with a smaller peak between thirty-five and fifty-five degrees South. The reason for the peak being much smaller in the Southern Hemisphere was that at the time the surveys were made the only thermonuclear explosions had been in the Northern Hemisphere; and because there's only a limited mixing of air at the equator most of the fallout stayed in the Northern. Reasonable, Bill?"

"Based on the circulation theory, yes. I didn't know about the soil tests."

"They confirmed the theory. Now, as I said, the model of fallout was based on explosions in the Northern Hemisphere only. If there've been numerous explosions in the Southern as well, it would alter the pattern. But it doesn't really affect my main point, which is that the minimum fallout would still be between about ten degrees North and ten South. Unfortunately, only about five per cent of the world's population lives in that belt. And that goes a long way to explain why we can't receive anything on the radio. But," he added hastily, "it's just a guess. It could simply be atmospheric interference due to abnormal radioactivity."

"It would seem from what you've said that we should be fairly safe where we are," John said. "I mean, we missed the short-term fallout, and Bill here figures we're about ten degrees South. Shouldn't that make us safe?"

Arnie shook his head. "It depends how much megatonnage was employed." His voice was bitter again. "They made a lovely new language, my colleagues, didn't they? Megatons for a million-ton equivalent of T. N. T. Easier to say, isn't it? Better still, megadeath. So much nicer and cleaner than just saying a million people killed. Let's apply the terms to the two wars you talked about, John. World War One was an eighteen-megadeath situation. World War Two was a twenty-plus megadeath situation—" He broke off and turned away from them, staring out at the lagoon and the sea beyond it.

"Arnie." John's voice was soft. "It was hardly your fault."

Arnie swung around to face them. "Sure it was." He was speaking rapidly. "Sure it was my fault, and your fault, and everyone's fault who was idiot enough to think piling up more and more bombs on both sides would ensure the peace. Yes, we had a test-ban treaty, but only when both sides knew they had enough weapons to destroy the other completely. And of course they had to allow for overkill— another great word, *overkill*. It meant some targets would literally be overkilled, killed twice, maybe three times over, because there was always the chance the first weapon might miss, and that was militarily unacceptable. So overkill it was, but it didn't matter because there was a hot line, and a system to prevent accidents, and so everyone was safe. Only it didn't work out that way. I don't know how much explosive the Russians and ourselves had piled up, but I'll bet they threw it at each other until there was nothing left to throw, or maybe nothing to throw it with."

"I think you're right," Bill said. "And I do have an idea how much explosive the two sides had piled up."

"How could you?" John asked. His voice was calm, while Bill and Arnie were speaking nervously and fast. "That kind of information was never released. Unless you were working on some project for the government?"

"No," Bill said, "I wasn't. But I had a friend at M.I.T. who had been. We used to go to New York occasionally over the weekend and tie one on together. I remember once we got talking to an Air Force officer in a bar. We weren't exactly sober, but he was drunker than we were. It was just after the Cuba crisis, and I remember feeling sorry for him because when we finished up in my room with a quart of Scotch he was telling me about the number of hours he'd put in on airborne alert while the situation was hot. By that time Ben, my friend from M. I. T., had passed out, and I was bloody hazy myself, but I remember him saying if they'd got the word they'd have gone in with everything they had. They'd have thrown it all, just as Arnie said.

"That's the first point. Here's the second. Next day I asked Ben how much stuff we had, how much the Russians had. He was pretty cagey about it; but it interested me, and I did some checking of my own. About a year later I found a magazine item that just about gave me the answer. All Ben had told me was that we had too much. He also said the Russians had about half what we had, and that was still too much.

"Then I found this article. It gave exact details of the offensive forces available to the United States during the crisis. For example, six hundred and forty B-52's, each carrying about fifty megatons; seven hundred B-47's. I allowed twenty megatons each for those. That already added up to forty-six thousand megatons. I can't remember the exact figures for the B-58's, the Atlases, the Titans, the Minutemen, and the Polaris subs, but I added all those in. Then there was the carrier-strike strength, and all the tactical nuclear weapons NATO had and a few hundred megatons for the R.A.F. and the French.

"Anyway, the total figure was round sixty thousand megatons. Then I added half that, to represent the Russian capacity, and I had about ninety thousand megatons. Of course, that represented only what was available for immediate use. It didn't include reserves and stockpiles. I have to admit I didn't realize the significance of the figures in terms of actual physical destruction and casualties."

"I can tell you the significance," Arnie said. "I heard two of my colleagues discussing it one day. They were talking about a report that had just been issued. This was back in sixty-one. It was an unofficial report, I believe, but it postulated roughly one million people dead or fatally injured for every seven megatons. The ratio would be higher in the urban areas, lower in country areas, but the average was one megadeath for seven megatons. Now let's take another look at Bill's figures. Divide ninety thousand megatons by seven. That gives you a figure of twelve and one half thousand megatons. And the population of the earth is, or maybe I should say *was,* three thousand million, so that on Bill's figures alone there was enough explosive available to kill every man, woman, and child in the world four times over." He paused. "And that, my friends, is what they meant by *overkill.*"

"But wait a minute," Bill said. "It doesn't necessarily follow. There might have been an overkill factor of, say, ten in America and Russia, none at all in Brazil."

"No," John said. "I've been thinking about the message Arnie picked up from the Sputnik. Those are the words of a dying man, a man who is determined even in his death throes to involve as many people as possible in his own destruction. Look, I know nothing about technicalities or nuclear weapons, but I do know something about people. It was my job. Let me quote you just one case that I know about personally. The police had surrounded a murderer in Chicago. He knew there was no chance. But he had a high-powered rifle. Before they got him he'd killed one policeman, wounded another, then fired at random into a crowd of people that had been allowed to get too close. He killed three of them before he died himself, and none of them had anything to do with him or the police. I suppose you can say he was a psychiatric case, but it doesn't alter the fact he did it."

"You mean the Russians might have gone mad when they realized they were beaten, and started throwing weapons at anyone and everyone?"

"It's quite possible," Arnie said. "I see what John means. But there could have been a military reason too. There were quite a few bases on or near the equator. A lot of airfields in South America and South Africa and Australia that they might have thought would be used by SAC for refueling. Anyway"—he waved his hand at the southern sky—"there it is. I don't suppose we'll ever know what really happened."

"That's the worst part," Bill said, "the not knowing. But at least when the submarine reaches the coast they'll be able to tell us what's happened."

"Yes," Arnie said, "but in a way that's what I'm afraid of most. Look at it this way. Let's assume it's heading for San Diego. How far would that be, Bill?"

"I'd say around four thousand miles."

"And Australia? Japan? China?"

"Australia about two thousand, Japan three and a half, China a little more. But I'm guessing."

"That doesn't matter. All those places are nearer than San Diego. All right, let's assume we can receive when the sub reaches the American coast. I figure that will be in seven, eight days from now. But if we can receive when it does, don't you see *we should be receiving from all those other places now?*"

"South America, too," Bill said quietly. "That wouldn't be much farther away. I'm afraid I get your point, Arnie. The sub will be able to give us local information. But if it does, and we receive the message, it means it isn't just interference that's preventing us hearing all those places. It means . . . well, let's face it, it means there's no one there to transmit."

"Exactly." Arnie thought for a moment, and added, "Well, maybe not quite that, but certainly no technical capacity left, no organized system, no civilization as we knew it."

John said, "I think we ought to get back. I'm hungry enough to eat even that slop they gave us."

They walked slowly back along the beach. For a while none of them said anything. Then John said, "I think there are two things we have to consider. The first is your speciality, Arnie. The second concerns us all."

"Okay," Arnie said, "shoot."

"We can guess from everything we've discussed that there's been very heavy fallout. But what about our chances here? You said we were in about the safest latitude geographically. But how safe? Are we getting fallout right now? Is there any way we can tell?"

"John, I just can't answer that question. So much depends on the kind of bombs used, whether they were fused for ground or air burst, where they actually landed. I'd say we'll certainly get fallout, maybe we're getting it now. I'll also say it will be less than anywhere else in the world except the two Polar regions. But that's about all I can tell you, except that it will probably continue for several years."

"Can't we measure it, tell exactly what we're getting?"

"Listen," Arnie said. "Pistols we have, also carbines, whatever the hell good they think those will be to us. Axes, binoculars, all the way through the alphabet you name it, we got it. And spades. Though why we'd want spades except maybe to dig our own— Sorry, I open my mouth too much. Anyway, we have everything we need except the things we need most. Radiation meters. Without them we just don't know what fallout rate we're getting. There's nothing we can do about it. But I don't think it's too high at the moment."

"Why not?" John asked.

"Well, the short-term fallout, if there was any in this area, we've definitely missed. We were under the ice. And if there was any, the rains in March or April would pretty well have cleaned the island. That's why I asked you about them this morning, Bill."

"Yes, I wondered."

"Now the long-term fallout, that's something else. From what I remember, the radioactive dust can hang around in the stratosphere a long time. Months, maybe years. But we'll have no way of telling if and when it starts coming down. Maybe it's coming down right now. That's about all I can tell you. What was the other thing, John?"

They were close to the huts now and paused for John to speak.

"I don't think we ought to tell the girls too much," John said. "Agreed?"

"Agreed," Bill said quickly. "I don't think Jane could take it. But she's much better today."

After they had eaten, they all went outside and sat on the sand. They did not talk much, though Arnie tried several times to introduce some topic for general conversation. He got little response. So they sat quietly under the brilliance of the stars, a brilliance seen only in equatorial latitudes but which was partially masked by the iridescent glow in the sky that had caused Arnie so much concern.

After about five minutes of near silence, Helen said, "There's something that concerns us all." Her voice was crisp and authoritative, the voice of someone accustomed to giving instructions to junior nurses.

"We all know we've more or less paired off. It would be the most natural thing in the world if those of us who wished"—she glanced quickly at John, then looked away again—"were to live together, especially since we may very well be the last people alive, as Jane said. But it's impossible. It mustn't happen, and I'll tell you why. Arnie checked the stores they left us, didn't he?"

"Yes," Arnie said.

"But there was one thing you didn't find."

"You tell me."

"Contraceptives. We have to accept danger from radiation, but it is imperative for us not to pass on that danger, at least until we know more. I don't blame the people who decided what the supplies should be. They couldn't foresee this situation. But if we have no contraceptives, and if we are receiving even moderate doses of radiation, we can't live together naturally without appalling risks. We can't, because of the genetic danger."

"But surely," Bill said, "there are other ways, other—"

"Other methods? No. Because in our position we have to be one hundred per cent sure. Don't forget, I know about these things. I know all about the so-called natural methods, and I can tell you they most certainly aren't infallible. So we have the choice of living together or living apart, both of them potentially disastrous. If we live apart there's no genetic problem, but psychologically it might injure us and our relations with each other."

"I agree," Jane said quietly.

"But if we live together and radiation is sufficiently high, we risk one of two possibilities. The first is sterility, and that would be disastrous psychologically. The second is we might produce monsters, terrible mutations who would bear no resemblance to human beings. Of course, if radiation isn't high, we might have perfectly normal children. We might in time create an oasis of life in the middle of a desert of death. But we wouldn't know until perhaps it's too late."

John said, "I'm impressed by your knowledge of mutation."

"There's nothing strange about that. I've actually seen it in my own hospital. A woman accidentally exposed to a massive overdose of X-rays. I won't describe to you exactly what the poor baby looked like, and fortunately it was born dead. I'll only say that both the doctors and myself were physically sick when we left the delivery room."

"It's something we can't decide until we know," John muttered, "and we have no way of knowing. God damn those bastards and their bombs. God damn them all."

"Yes," Helen said. "It was a world where people starved in the millions, where there were no funds for cancer research but the sky was the limit for armaments. It was our world, ours and the Russians, and a few other highly developed countries, and all of us carry part of the responsibility, part of the guilt."

Bill said, "I agree with what you've just said, but I don't agree with your assessment of the genetic danger. We may be getting a certain amount of fallout, but it's going to be less here than anywhere else in the world."

"How much is less?" Helen said.

"Well, that's difficult to say. But I'd be willing to take a chance."

"Then you're a fool. Let me ask you this. Is there the slightest chance the level of fallout is high enough to be dangerous—to the embryo, I mean?"

"I don't think anyone could say that, but personally I'd guess not."

"And you'd be prepared to take a chance on a guess?"

"Yes, I would," Bill said stubbornly.

"All right," Helen said, "you'd take a chance on a guess, but I'm not guessing about the baby I saw. You didn't see it, I did. And I can tell you this, anyone who'd take a chance without definitely knowing is both idiotic and a danger to the girl he takes a chance with."

John Anderson broke in quickly, "Now, why don't you two cool down?"

Helen stood up. "I've said what I have to say. That's all." She turned and walked quickly to her hut.

The rest sat in uneasy silence for a few minutes, then as if by mutual consent they separated and went off to bed.

In the days that followed, John Anderson sensed that they were falling apart as a group. The hostility between Bill and Helen was obvious. Jane naturally sided with Bill. Arnie did his best to ease the situation by joking and wisecracking, but his efforts all turned sour.

For three days they did little except listen for a message from the submarine. Finally John suggested they should explore the island thoroughly. To his surprise the other five instantly agreed. They also agreed that each day while four of them were learning about the island, two would remain behind to monitor the radio in case something came through. None of them really believed anything would.

The next day John and Helen arrived at the top of the West hill. They had taken the path leading from what Bill believed to be a gun position and followed it to the top. They found here a square of concrete at least six times the area of the gun position they had left behind. John looked round carefully. He noted that again the concrete seemed to be fairly new. He left Helen and walked slowly across the white surface.

Almost immediately he saw a dull patch in the center of the square. He went toward it quickly and knelt down to make a close examination. It was a circular piece of metal, about twelve inches in diameter, and with a small projecting handle. He grasped the handle and pulled. The metal lid came away from the concrete easily. Inside was a heavy cable, of a type he had seen frequently during his service in the Navy. It was a power lead, heavily insulated, carrying eight similar but smaller insulated cables inside the main one.

Helen called, "John, come quickly, there's something strange."

John carefully replaced the lid over the cable aperture, then hurried across to where Helen stood on the edge of the concrete. She pointed down to the level ground between the hills. Looking down, John saw a ribbon of concrete stretching across the island. It ran slantwise in relation to the shape of the island, so that its ends pointed a little to the north and south of the two hills.

"What is it?" Helen asked.

John focused his binoculars on the concrete. It was about a mile long, he thought, and though at a distance it looked narrow, he guessed it was at least a hundred feet wide. He lowered the binoculars and said, "What would you think it was?"

"Well, I know it's impossible, but it looks the way a runway looks from an airplane."

"I think," John said, "that's exactly what it is. See how the approach at each end is clear of the two hills? That's how they'd build a runway, to give the pilot a clear approach over low ground. Let's go down and look at it closer, but first come over here and look at this."

He led her to the center of the concrete and showed her the power cable under the metal lid.

Helen looked up at him. "What is it?"

"Well, obviously it's a power lead. I'd guess it's for some kind of radar installation. This is the highest point of the island; it's the obvious place to site it. Given the right type of radar, you could detect a ship a hundred miles away, maybe farther."

"But why? Who'd be interested? This is supposed to be an uninhabited island."

"Perhaps it isn't supposed to be. Why the runway, if it *is* a runway? Why power cables to a radar site, if it *is* a radar site? Why the gun positions, if they *are* gun positions?"

"Yes, why?"

John looked around. "There's a path over there in the corner. Let's follow it down. I think it'll take us down to the runway."

As they walked down the gently sloping path, Helen felt the tension between them that had been growing each day. She wondered how long it would be before it became intolerable, before the breaking point came.

The path did, in fact, lead to the concrete strip. When they reached it, Helen sat and rested while John paced out the distance across the concrete. When he came back to her he said, "It's a runway all right. Fifty yards across, as near as I can judge, and a clear approach at each end."

"But why a runway?"

John shook his head. "I don't suppose we'll ever know. Anyway, we must get back. Let's walk along the runway; there may be a path to the huts." He turned and began to walk.

Helen followed him wearily. She was conscious of a tiredness that was not entirely physical. She caught up with him and took his hand.

They did not speak much on the way back, even when they found a path. They could walk the path to the huts, but they could see no path to the future.

A few days later John sighted a ship from the top of the West hill. On the first day of sighting, it was only a smudge on the horizon. By the third day it was close enough to the island for them to see its exact shape, and to know it was not under power but was drifting with the current. On the fourth day they thought it would probably pile up on the reef of their island. They looked forward to this, for it was possible that by boarding the ship they could discover something about what had really happened. There would be a ship's log, and perhaps something recorded there would give them a clue. There might even be people. . . . But on the fifth day the ship drifted past the west side of the island. At its nearest point it was only about five hundred yards away. All six of them climbed to the top of the West hill and watched it pass. With binoculars they could see three sprawled heaps inside the wheelhouse. There were more sprawled heaps on the deck. The high-power binoculars left no doubt what those heaps had once been. So the ship of the dead passed away from them, and three days later it vanished forever over the southern horizon.

The next day Mary was walking along the road leading up to the West hill. Suddenly she became aware of a rustling in the foliage above her. She looked up, and started back in surprise as a brown form swung down to the road in front of her. It was a monkey about two and a half feet in height, with extremely long arms that reached well below its knees. It did not seem to be at all afraid of her. Mary thought it was a chimpanzee—she had seen chimpanzees in zoos. The animal stood there watching her, chattering to itself.

Mary spoke gently and the chimpanzee moved a little closer, unafraid but seeming rather timid. She wondered if she could entice it back to the huts. It would be a discovery of her own, she thought, and perhaps the others might be able to learn something from it.

She began to walk back toward the huts. She heard sounds behind her, glanced back, and saw that the monkey was following.

It followed her right back to the huts, and when she came out onto the beach and joined John and Arnie, it peeped at them through the green foliage, then squatted on the sand only ten yards away from them.

John said, "Why, it's a chimp. Kind of tame, too."

"I thought it was a chimpanzee," Mary said, "but I wasn't sure. I don't know much about monkeys."

"Not monkey," John said. "Ape. An anthropoid ape of very high intelligence. We used them a lot in behavior-pattern experiments. They can be very smart, and very friendly too if they're tame. I'd say this one is definitely tame. Maybe escaped from a ship, or something."

The chimpanzee was now very close to Mary. She lifted it onto her lap and it immediately put its arms round her neck and clung to her, obviously delighted.

Helen came out of the hut and joined them. "Well," she said, "I see we have company. Where did you find him, Mary?"

"I didn't. He found me." Mary paused. "And I don't think you should say he. You should say she."

Bill and Jane came out of the foliage onto the beach. After they had heard about the chimpanzee, Jane explained that they had been to their favorite pool. They had not seen anything new, but they had heard something peculiar.

Bill said, "What she means is *she* heard it. Damned if I could."

"I'm quite sure I heard it," Jane insisted. "It was a very high-pitched, throbbing kind of sound. I heard it very faintly at first, when I was lying on the grass—"

"On the grass?" Arnie broke in.

John Anderson smiled and said, "Be quiet, Arnie. Go on, Jane."

"Well, when I pressed my ear to the ground, I could hear it quite clearly."

"I couldn't hear it," Bill said. "Not a bloody thing."

"But that isn't all. I listened for about five minutes, then suddenly it stopped. One second I could hear it as plain as anything, then it just wasn't there any more. I know Bill doesn't believe me, but I'm sure."

"Wait a minute," Arnie said quickly. "You say high-pitched?"

"Yes, very."

"Then that could explain why you heard it, and Bill didn't. The human ear varies in its capacity to pick up high sounds. I forget the figures, but I think the top limit is about sixteen thousand vibrations per second. Dogs can hear still higher. So it could be your hearing is more sensitive to high-pitched sounds than Bill's."

"But even if he's right," John said, "that still doesn't explain what was causing it."

"Could be lots of things," Arnie said. "Sympathetic vibrations from our generators, even. They're cutting in and out all the time."

Mary stood up and handed the chimpanzee to Helen. "I think I'd better get started on the food."

Arnie said quickly, "I'll come with you." Together they walked away.

Helen put the chimpanzee down on the sand. The animal approached each of them in turn, allowed itself to be patted, then quite suddenly turned and went off into the vegetation.

John said, "She seems to have accepted us. She'll be back. And she's tame, and also healthy, as far as I can tell. Bill, what do you say the four of us take a walk now while Mary's preparing the food? We can all listen for this strange sound."

When they arrived at the side of the pool, Helen and John were both enchanted by the beauty of the surroundings. Jane showed them the exact spot where she had heard the sounds, and they all listened for quite a while. At first there was nothing, then both Jane and John heard the sound. Bill did not hear it, and neither did Helen. But John definitely confirmed he had heard the same sound as Jane. And he revealed that he had taken tests for high-tone deafness during his physicals in the Navy. He had passed them, but about half the sailors had not. They decided that Arnie's theory was correct. Later they sat for a while beside the pool.

"I wondered why you two were always talking about this pool," John said. "How did you find it? It certainly is lovely."

"Well," Bill said, "we stumbled on it. Literally. We were pushing our way through the undergrowth when I tripped and fell. As I got up I suddenly saw this clearing and the pool."

The pool was about thirty feet wide and almost circular in shape. Jane looked around her, first to the right, where a hill stream coursed into the pool itself, then to the left, where the overspill of water continued on its way to the sea. "It *is* lovely," she said. We come back here often because it's so peaceful. I suppose the gentle movement of the water, the quiet sound of its flowing helps relax me. Anyway, we like it here."

"And so do I," Helen said, "but I think we ought to be getting back."

They got up, but before they moved off toward the well-defined path through the undergrowth that Bill and Jane had trodden in the past few days, Bill said, "I find it relaxing too, but that's not the only reason I come back. I have a feeling there's something near here that could give us the information we've been looking for. Information that could make Helen's ideas about genetics as out of date as they are—well, frustrating for all of us."

"Now, what in hell does that mean?" Helen said.

"Never mind for the moment." In the last few seconds the veneer of New England had dropped from his voice, and now his Welsh accent was clearly distinguishable. "I'm a scientist, if you can call geography a science, and I won't present my argument until all the facts are in. Let's leave it at that, shall we?"

Without giving Helen a chance to reply, he began to walk across the clearing toward the path. The other three followed him: Jane, puzzled; Helen, still angry; John Anderson, with an uneasy feeling that the group was very close to its own deadly explosion.

SAFE BASE ONE: JULY, 1966

Geraghty was sitting at the desk in his cabin. Although he had arrived at the Safe Base fourteen days before, he and his crew had been instructed to remain on the ship. In front of him on the desk were piles of reports and over a hundred aerial reconnaissance photographs of various areas.

On the day of their arrival a ship-to-shore telephone link had been set up, and through this they had been ordered to remain aboard until they were declared free from infection and, more important, free from contamination. This had puzzled Geraghty until he had personally received an explanation. He then organized the inoculation of all his crew members, and also of the three observers who had been on the cruise. He had been warned that it was quite possible a few of the men who were inoculated might become severely ill, and might even die.

One of those who had become seriously ill was his Lieutenant-Commander Executive. Geraghty's own Medical Officer thought that his chances of survival were very poor. Geraghty had called in Doctor Jones, and he had agreed with that of the ship's M.O. Under these circumstances Geraghty had promoted Lieutenant Perkins to the post of his personal executive.

Geraghty sighed as he looked at the piles of reports and photographs. Barnard had been right, he thought. It was certainly no land of milk and honey they had returned to. On the other hand, he had been amazed and delighted to find that he was junior to only one officer at the Safe Base, a major general of the Air Force. Geraghty had spoken with him twice on the ship-shore line, but General Richards had sounded extremely weak and feeble. Much of what he said to Geraghty did not make sense; but tomorrow, Geraghty thought, he would be able to go ashore himself and determine the exact position there. Tomorrow was the end of the quarantine period.

He felt the need to talk to someone, and picked up the phone. Perkins answered immediately. Geraghty said, "Perky, how about organizing two cups of coffee and coming here?"

"Right away, Commander."

Geraghty replaced the phone. It was good, he thought, to have someone like Perkins to rely on. He had been thoroughly efficient in his duties since he took over as exec. Geraghty decided that once they got ashore he would recommend to the General that Perkins should be promoted to Lieutenant Commander. This, he felt, was the least he could do to reward Perkins for his valuable services in the past. He reached forward and picked up the pile of photographs again, riffled through them quickly. So far, he was the only person on the ship who had seen the photographs or read the reports.

Perkins arrived with the coffee and took a seat opposite Geraghty. They sipped their coffee and exchanged a few unimportant remarks.

Then Geraghty said, "Perky, I don't like the set-up here. I wanted to talk about it with someone I could trust."

"You can sure trust me, Commander."

"I know that. It's why I'm going to do a thing I don't often do, and break orders." He waved a hand at the reports and photographs. "This tells me exactly what went on, but it would take you a week to go through it all. So I've prepared a summary myself. It's in my writing, but I guess you can follow it."

"Well," Perkins said, "I certainly should be able to, Commander. We've been together a long time."

"Yes, a long time," Geraghty said. He flipped a three-page hand-written report onto Perkins' side of the desk. "You just read that while you drink your coffee. To me, there are three really significant points in it. Let's see if you can pick them out."

Perkins read the report quickly. Then he read it again more carefully. He finished his coffee and put the summary back on the desk. "I'd say that the three most important points are: first, the intercepting of a radio message from Peking the night it all started; second, the use of weapons other than thermonuclear; and third, the fact that we can't survive here, but we can on one of the islands in the minimal-fallout zone."

Geraghty lit a cigarette. "Absolutely right. But there's a fourth thing, which I haven't mentioned in my summary. Have you been up top yet?"

"Well, no, Commander. I have looked through the periscope, of course, but I haven't been up top. If you remember, your orders specifically forbade that to anyone except yourself."

"Yes, I remember," Geraghty said. "But I've been on top and it's a pretty amazing sight. Did you have any idea places like this existed?"

"No, I didn't."

"I knew," Geraghty said, "but I didn't know their exact location. I understand now why they ordered us to return submerged and without breaking radio silence. It's very simple, Perky. I've learned a lot in the past fourteen days. Both from the reports and from talking with Major Ryan. By the way, he is, or should I say was, the second in command to General Richards until we arrived. Originally there were three of these Safe Bases. They think the enemy got the other two. There's been no radio contact with them, and although they sent out helicopter reconnaissances they got no positive result. To put it more simply, the helicopters just did not return. So that leaves us."

Perkins said, "What about the freighter berthed beside us? It looked to me like the U.S.S. 'Savannah'."

"Yes," Geraghty said, "very much like the 'Savannah'. But this one doesn't have a name yet. She was built in secrecy and brought here in secrecy. There's no doubt they knew what they were doing, the boys who planned all this. Now when we go up top and you can see more clearly, you'll understand— But that can wait. For the moment, let me assure you I haven't been sitting on my butt for fourteen days without working out a plan."

Perkins said nothing, waiting for Geraghty to continue.

"Yes, I've worked out a plan, but to implement it I'm going to need several things, and I just don't see how I'm going to get them if I'm not allowed a free hand."

Perkins said quietly, "May I ask exactly what is your plan, Commander?"

"You may, Perky, you may. It's very simple, really. We have the submarine, we have a nuclear-powered freighter that can carry two or three thousand people if necessary. We have a devastated homeland — Maybe I shouldn't do this, but I want you to look at some of the photographs." He picked up a pile of photographs, selected a few, and placed them one by one before Perkins.

"Here's Los Angeles. As far as we can tell, the epicenter was about five miles north of Santa Monica."

Perkins looked at the photograph and said quickly, "But there's nothing showing."

"No," Geraghty said, "nothing showing, but if you look more closely you'll see grid reference numbers that give the exact geographical location. That one explosion took out everything from Long Beach to Lancaster, from Oxnard to Upland. Outside the area of total destruction you could go a hundred miles farther all around and say that although everything there wasn't totally destroyed the damage would be substantial enough so that no human life would be possible."

"Except for those lucky people on the islands off the coast," Perkins said.

Geraghty shook his head, "No, even places as far away as Catalina Island got it, either from the blast or the heat. Nothing left alive there."

He flipped another photograph across. "New York City. Anything left of the boroughs? And it wasn't just New York City. Do you see anything of Newark? Of White Plains? Everything within a hundred miles was blasted or burned."

He put another photograph on the desk. "Chicago. Can you see Joliet? Or Evanston? Or Custer Park? Do you see how the shore line of Lake Michigan has changed?"

"I don't know Chicago too well," Perkins said. His face was pale.

Geraghty went on. "Do you know Washington?" He pushed another photograph across to Perkins. "Look for the Potomac River. Or rather, don't look for it: it isn't there. It flows into the sea about a hundred miles south of where Washington used to be. And here's London. You know London."

"Well," Perkins said, "I've flown in and out of London Airport a few times."

"You won't find London Airport in the photograph. There's a little smudge that might be what was left of Staines Reservoir. Over there on the east could be what's left of Southend. Can you make sense of the photograph? I can't." He pushed four more photographs across the desk. "There's Omaha, or what *was* Omaha. There's Dallas, and Detroit. But look at the fourth one carefully."

Perkins looked at the last photograph. "I don't recognize anything —not that I recognized much in what you'd already shown me."

"No," Geraghty said, "but this one is Moscow. Look at the big difference in the grid numbers."

"What scale are these photographs?"

"The one of Moscow covers approximately nine hundred square miles."

"But there's absolutely nothing left."

"No," Geraghty said, "there wouldn't be." He swept aside the remaining photographs. For a moment he looked like an old man. It seemed to take an enormous effort before he was able to speak again.

"These are all the photographs we have. God only knows what the rest of the world looks like. I haven't any photographs of South America, or India, or Australia, but these are sufficient to tell me we underestimated them. In my opinion this continent isn't going to be fit to live in for maybe fifteen or twenty years, perhaps more. As you said, we must live on the islands while we get things organized. And that brings us to the fourth point I referred to earlier. It seems there's trouble here. There are two factions, the military and the civilian. I don't know yet the exact facts and figures about who is here and who isn't, but Major Ryan tells me there's an ex-Senator from one of the northern states who is trying to get in on the act. He maintains the only solution for survival as a nation is for everyone here to wait it out until it's safe to go outside and start reclaiming ground. Obviously he's wrong, but General Richards is apparently too weak, physically or mentally, to argue with him. Oh, the hell with it! Let's go up top and you can see exactly what this place looks like."

Geraghty stood up, put on his cap, and walked toward the door of the cabin. Perkins fell in behind him, but just as Perkins was going to close the door the ship-shore telephone rang.

Perkins said quickly, "I'll get it, Commander." He picked up the telephone, listened for a few moments, then said quietly, "I see.

Commander Geraghty will be in touch with you in the next few minutes."

Geraghty had already gone through the door and a few steps along the passage. Now he turned back and pushed open the door of the cabin. "Perky, what the hell was that?"

"I have to inform you, Commander, that was a message from Major Ryan."

"And?"

Perkins stood stiffly to attention. "General Richards has died. You are the senior surviving officer, Commander."

"Well, now," Geraghty said, "that's bad news about Richards. Maybe we'll defer that trip up top for a while, Perky. This does change things."

He sat down behind the desk and reached for a telephone.

THE ISLAND: JULY, 1966

The days passed slowly. They had explored the island thoroughly, with few new discoveries.

Their diet of dehydrated foods did nothing to help the increasing tension between them. They could not vary their diet by adding the abundant fruits of the island because one of the things Arnie was certain about was that Strontium 90 was very easily absorbed into plants of all kinds, and from their products—for example, bananas—could equally easily be transmitted to the human body.

John Anderson had found that though the fish were plentiful they were not so easy to catch as he had imagined. He had fashioned himself several spears from lengths of bamboo, sharpening one end to a point, and he spent hours each day attempting to spear fish to supplement their diet. He was rarely successful. Once he had managed to get a turtle, though they seemed even more difficult to catch than fish. That night they ate the turtle after Mary had prepared it. She removed certain parts and from them prepared a soup. The rest of the meat she baked. They all agreed the meal was excellent, and temporarily their spirits rose. Temporarily.

Arnie, with Bill Evans, managed to pick up only one message. The transmission was faint and distorted, and it followed the same general pattern as the transmission from the Russian Sputnik. First there was a very weak, indecipherable transmission. Then two minutes later another, slightly more distinct, from which they picked up a few words and phrases. This was followed by another, much too weak to be decipherable. They waited by the radio for two hours, hoping to hear the message again, but it did not come through. They never heard it again, just as they never heard the Russian Sputnik again after the first time. They had no doubt it came from an orbital vehicle, but this time the language was English. This was an American transmission that said much the same as the Russian message, but with a reversal of roles. The Americans declared they had not started the war, the Russians had. They called on the world to witness this, and declared that just retribution would follow.

Later, when John joined them, they agreed that the two messages represented the dying spasms of two giants, or two children, who were seeking to justify themselves. The message added nothing to their knowledge of who had actually started the war, but it confirmed their belief that at one stage of the war both countries knew they were dying.

During these days the chimpanzee was a frequent visitor. She became extremely friendly with them, though they had little to offer her in the way of titbits. She was quite content to sit with any of them, but of the six she preferred Mary. One night, though, when Mary and Arnie were preparing food, she sat on Helen's lap.

In the last few days Helen had spoken little to Bill Evans. But now she said, "Bill, you've wandered about the island more than the rest of us. Have you seen another chimpanzee?"

"Well, no," Bill said. "No, I haven't. Why?"

"Because unless I'm wrong, and I don't think I am, this one is going to be a mother chimp before long." Helen paused, then added, "She could hardly have managed it on her own. In any case, she's swelling in the appropriate place."

"Well, I suppose you know about things like that."

"Yes," Helen said coldly, "I do."

John Anderson broke in to interrupt what he thought might become a quarrel that would aggravate the tension between Helen and Bill. "Another mystery, but not too important," he said. "She probably has a mate somewhere. We noticed the female chimps were always more inquisitive, more ready to make friends than the male. But in the end the males came around too."

Bill Evans stood up. "I have to be going now. Jane, will you ask Mary to keep some food for me?"

"Sure I will. How long will you be?"

"About twenty-four hours, I think." He grinned. "I don't mean I'll be gone that long. I should be back in two hours at most. But in twenty-four hours I think I'm going to have the evidence I want." He looked directly at Helen and continued, "Not only the evidence I want, but the evidence all of us need. See you later."

He turned away and went into the undergrowth. Only Jane knew exactly what he was looking for, and she had promised Bill not to reveal it.

The next day the male chimp appeared. At first he watched them suspiciously from about forty yards, and though they tried to entice him to come nearer he remained aloof. When John walked toward him he disappeared hastily.

That evening the five of them were stitting outside the huts. Bill had been away all day and had not yet returned, though they had already eaten their evening meal. They were drinking coffee—instant coffee, but precious because it was the one luxury that had been permitted. In the early days they had drunk quite a lot of it, but now, with the realization that relief might not come for a long time, perhaps for years, perhaps never, they had agreed to ration themselves to two cups a day, one with the morning meal and one with the evening.

As they drank the coffee they did not talk at all. The silence was broken by the sound of vegetation being trampled and by a strange, high-pitched squeal, and then came Bill Evans' voice, cursing fluently but cheerfully.

"Hold still, you little bugger, or I'll slit your bloody throat for you."

Bill emerged from the high growth, carrying something that wriggled and squealed, trying to escape from him. In the twilight that had come rapidly, they could not see clearly what it was.

"Over here, Bill," Arnie shouted.

Bill walked toward them, and he was laughing. As he approached they saw that the animal he was carrying was a pig, a very small pig.

When he was still twenty yards from them he shouted, "Get a piece of rope, somebody. I can't hold this little bugger much longer."

"I'll get it," John said, and he disappeared.

Bill joined them. They crowded round him. "You caught one, Bill!" Jane said. Her voice was animated, bright. There had to be some reason for Bill's laughter, and she thought she knew what it was.

"You're bloody right I caught one. A whole bunch of them, about twenty, came down to drink at the stream. This little one wandered away from the rest, so I grabbed him and ran—mother pigs can be very nasty if you interfere with their family. And let me tell you I had one hell of a job getting him back here. He wriggled worse than a bucket of eels."

John came back with a piece of strong cord. Bill took it and, while Arnie held the squirming animal, expertly slipped a knot round the little creature's left hind leg. Then he said, "All right, Arnie, let's carry him into the hut. I want us all to see him properly in the light."

They took the pig inside, and Bill tied the end of the cord to the leg of a chair. The pig immediately made a dash for freedom, then squealed in outrage as the cord pulled it up short.

Bill said excitedly, "He's food, he and the others, and there were at least three families of them. But he's even more. He's your measuring instrument, Arnie, he's your living Geiger counter. Hold him still a moment, John."

"Now," Bill went on, when John had secured the struggling animal, "I want you all to look at him closely. You see any imperfections? You see anything other than a perfectly healthy young pig about six weeks old?"

"How do you know his age?" Mary asked.

"I used to help my uncle on his farm, made a bit of extra cash during vacations. Take it from me, this one's about six weeks, no more. Now look him over. He's strong, lively, fit as a flea. Look him over closely."

John said, "There's nothing wrong with his muscles, I'll say that."

"Or his voice," Helen added, as the squeals rose in a shrill crescendo.

"All satisfied?" Bill asked. "All right, I'll take him out and let him go." He bent and untied the cord that was knotted to the chair, then slipped the cord from the pig's leg. He picked up the animal and took it outside the hut. As soon as it was released it disappeared at high speed into the vegetation. They listened to the sounds as it went away from them, and then they went back inside.

"We should have a name for the piglet," Bill said. "He's important.

"I don't see why," Mary said. "Maybe I'm just dumb."

Arnie patted her arm. "Sure you are, but beautiful too. Bill was right, that little pig's a living Geiger counter. So how about Geiger for his name?"

They all agreed. Then Arnie said, "Bill, would your knowledge of pigs stretch to how long the gestation period is?"

"It would," Bill answered promptly. "The average is one hundred and thirteen days."

"Well," Arnie said, "you all know I hate talking, but I'm just going to have to force myself. One hundred and thirteen days, I want you to remember that. A perfectly healthy, normal pig. Remember that too. What would his mother have been eating, Bill?"

"Anything that grows. Anything at all. Breadfruit, fallen figs, bananas, probably yams—I've seen a few of those."

"So there's our answer to the problem Helen brought up," Arnie said. "I'm no biologist, but I figure pigs would be affected by radiation as much as human beings, maybe more. Would you agree with that, Bill?"

"Definitely."

"There's our answer. We're safe. Those pigs have lived and bred while we were under the ice. If the island were receiving heavy radiation they'd certainly have ingested some of the products from their food, in addition to suffering the direct effect of fallout. Young Geiger, God bless him, is a perfectly normal, healthy pig. Which he certainly wouldn't be if his parents, particularly his mother, had suffered any sizable dose of radiation. Bill, did you see any abnormalities in the other pigs, particularly in the young ones?"

"No," Bill said, "absolutely none. There were some older than Geiger, some younger. I couldn't get close enough to tell how much, but they were all absolutely normal. We're safe, Arnie."

Arnie was silent for a few moments. Then he said, more quietly,

"Yes, thank God, we're safe. We can live normal lives. And in time we can round up the pigs, domesticate them."

"So far as any pig can be domesticated," Bill said. "They go wild very quickly. But if we round up the young ones it should work out all right. I'm not sure of the breed, but I'd say they were Middle Whites. At least that's what we'd call them back home."

"The breed doesn't matter too much. But as you said, Bill, they're food. They've survived, and so can we. They've produced normal, healthy offspring, and so can we. Let me tell you right now, *we're going to survive.*"

"I don't agree, I don't agree at all," Helen said. "Certainly that young pig appeared to be healthy, but that's no proof. There could be a dozen reasons for it. And remember that it has a less complicated nervous system than human beings. I don't think the argument is conclusive."

"No," Bill said, "you probably wouldn't agree that two and two make four either."

Once again John intervened. "I think we must consider the fact that we are in the area of lowest fallout. I think that must explain a lot of things that have been puzzling us. The roads, for example, the gun positions, and the runway. Those things weren't installed for us. Then who were they for? It's my guess this was a getaway island, a place the top people could fly to if a big war made the North American continent uninhabitable. Somewhere they could hide out in safety. And that means a place where there would be an acceptable level of fallout. They deliberately picked a place where they knew it would be low; and this is it, as Bill and Arnie have demonstrated. I think they evacuated the population, probably only a small number of people, and made this island a reservation where they could live safely if the worst ever happened. We were just lucky someone decided to dump us here for the experiment."

"But they never came," Arnie said.

"No, they never came. It's my guess things moved too fast for them. From what Geraghty told us, the war started at Christmas. Who'd expect a war to start at Christmas? There was no crisis, everything was peaceful. They had a system to prevent accidents, and a hot line as the ultimate insurance, but somehow everything failed. And then there just wasn't time for the big boys to escape. They were clobbered before they could make the move."

"I'll go along with that," Bill said, "except for one thing. If you're right, John, why wasn't the island stocked with stuff ready for them? All the food supplies that are here were landed from the sub."

"I can't answer that one. Probably they had some cargo planes preloaded to fly in what they'd need. But things moved too fast."

Arnie said, "I think you're probably right, John. There's no such thing as a foolproof system. And the more complex you make it, the more intricate, then the quicker things can happen if it ever breaks down. If a system is geared to prevent instant war, and the system breaks down, instant war is what you get. We know there was war, we know they didn't arrive, and it must have happened just as John said. And I agree they probably had supplies prepacked, stored so they wouldn't deteriorate."

"All this doesn't affect the main issue," Helen said. "I know I'm not a qualified doctor, just a nurse with a hell of a lot of obstetrics experience, but the evidence Evans has produced is not enough for me. I refuse to accept it as conclusive." Her face was very white, and a small vein stood out in her right temple.

Bill Evans walked over until he was only a yard or so away from her. "Just what do you want in the way of evidence?" he asked. "Maybe we can find a colony of bloody aborigines on the island. Maybe that would satisfy you?"

Arnie said quickly, "Now look, let's not—"

"I'm telling you the evidence is not conclusive," Helen interrupted, "and I'm not prepared to accept anything less. And you, Mary?"

"That's not fair," Arnie said. "It isn't just a question of Mary, it's a question of me too. Why don't you ask both of us?"

"Because," Helen said calmly, "it affects Mary far more than it does you. The greatest fear of a mother is that her child will be abnormal in some way. It's something that men just don't understand. I repeat my question. Mary, how about you?"

"Well," Mary said hesitantly, "I think you're right. I'm sorry, Arnie, but I do think we ought to have more evidence."

Arnie shrugged. "If you feel that way."

"I'm afraid I do. I think we'll just have to wait. I know I just couldn't face the risk of producing an abnormal child. Do you remember those terrible pictures of the Thalidomide babies? Please try to understand, Arnie; I just couldn't take a risk like that."

Arnie put his arm around her slim shoulders. "Listen, I understand. I'll wait."

"And you're right," Helen said. "Jane, how do you feel?"

Jane's face was flushed. She moved closer to Bill Evans and slipped her hand into his. She said, "I'm not denying you're the medical expert, Helen, but I'm going along with Bill. I agree with him, and I disagree with you. I think the evidence *is* conclusive, and if Bill and I want to live together, which we do, then we will. I don't think we're running any undue risk."

"I'm sure we're not," Bill said. "We've already discussed this, and we agreed that if I could get positive evidence we'd live together. And I did. I produced the pig."

"Hardly surprising," Helen said acidly.

"Very funny, especially for an interfering bitch. We're going to do exactly what we want." He spoke quickly, his Welsh accent thicker and more noticeable than it normally was, which happened when he was extremely angry.

John Anderson said, "Now, wait a minute. We're all individuals, and therefore we have the individual's right to decide his or her course of action. But remember we are also a group, and each of us owes a certain loyalty to that group. Otherwise we'll destroy ourselves."

Bill replied quickly, "I'm sorry, John, but we've made our decision." He looked directly at Helen. "I apologize for calling you an interfering bitch, but you must admit I was provoked. Let's all try to remain friends, even if Jane and I go our own way on this one thing."

"As far as I'm concerned, you can go to hell."

"Well, we're not going to hell, but we're leaving you for the night."

Mary said, "Please, Jane, just wait a little longer. Then perhaps we'll know for sure."

"How long is a little longer?" Jane asked. "Twenty years? Thirty years? Forever? I'm sorry, Mary, but we've made our decision. Let's go, Bill."

Helen turned away as Bill and Jane left the room. Bill went to his room and picked up a blanket. The nights were warm, but sometimes it became a little chilly just before dawn.

They were sleeping when dawn came, lying in each other's arms beside their favorite pool.

INTERLUDE: Nanyang, Honan Province, August 15, 1965

When Chuang arrived exactly—and deliberately—five minutes late for his meeting with Li, he saw that Chen was not present.

Li murmured a conventional greeting as Chuang sat down, then followed it by saying, "Comrade Professor Chen isn't with us."

"I had already observed that," Chuang said. "Probably held up by bad roads. Some of them are getting into a really bad state. We'll have to attend to them after the operation. I need good internal communications for my armies." He poured beer from the bottle that stood ready in front of him on the table.

"No," Li said, "he's not late. He's not coming. His part in the operation is over except for one very important detail. Otherwise he has fulfilled his purpose, now that you have the devices." He paused. "You do have them, I suppose?"

"Yes, I have them."

"Then from now on there's no further need for his presence here. All future meetings will be between the two of us."

Chuang said, "I see. Have you the date for me?"

Li shook his head. "Regretfully, no. But one thing I can assure you, it will be two months at least."

"I already knew that."

"Yes, but I can also tell you it will not be more than six months." He held up a hand as Chuang was about to speak. "Don't ask me how I know, because the Chairman has instructed me not to tell anyone. I'm afraid, my dear Marshal, that includes even you."

"I don't care how you got the information, or where you got it from. All I want is the date. And as far as I'm concerned, the nearer six months the better."

"Why?"

"Darkness," Chuang said. "November, December, January—

those would be the best months for my trawlers. The sub-marines—well, they don't matter too much, except that they will have to carry out the important part of the operation at night."

"Oh, yes," Li said, "I see your point. One further question, then we can perhaps close this meeting."

Chuang said angrily, "You mean you brought me five hundred miles just to ask one question?"

"But an important question, Marshal. I could hardly come to you, because the Chairman expects me to remain here so that I am instantly available to him. Besides . . ." He let his voice drift delicately away.

Chuang instantly grasped the implication behind Li's words. "All right," he said, "let's get on with it. What's the question?"

Li spoke quietly. "Are you completely satisfied with the front organization we have set up in the United States?"

"Yes," Chuang said, "I am."

"Could you explain to me exactly why?"

"They are an entirely respectable San Francisco trucking company. San Francisco, as you know, has a very large Chinese population, and there are many of our people among them. It has been comparatively easy to infiltrate some of my personally trained men over the past two or three months. Only six were required, and we got them in without any trouble. The company, of course, is entirely controlled by our people. Every employee is a member of the Party, though they have been warned from the start that they were not under any circumstances to disclose this. In fact, they have been prominent in helping to organize the Double Tenth festivities each year. For example, last year each of the company's six trucks carried both the American and the Kuo Min Tang flags. My six men have now taken over the identity and the documents, such as social security cards, of six of the most trusted employees."

"And the six who have been replaced?"

"They are being kept safely in hiding."

"Excellent," Li said. "Then everything is arranged."

"Except the date," Chuang said stubbornly.

"I have already told you, my dear Marshal, that I myself do not yet know the exact date. But"—he paused reflectively—"I should know it soon. I would guess, since you press me, that it would be about four months from now."

Chuang said, "Now *I* have a question. About the trade fair—you understand that this is absolutely vital to my plan?"

"Of course," Li said. "I realize that it is a vital part of *our* plan. Agreement has already been reached in principle. As you are aware, relations between us are not exactly cordial. We have, so to speak, broken through the thick ice from Khrushchev's reign, but the water beneath is still cold. However, the idea of our wanting to send our exhibits to Moscow has flattered the Russians. You are aware that they sent six experts to examine some of the goods we propose to display?"

"No," Chuang said. "I'm too busy with military matters, and especially this operation, to bother with such things. I have my aide prepare a summary of the more important items from the *People's Daily* each day, but I don't remember seeing anything about that."

"There wasn't much publicity. But the visit served its purpose."

"Which was?"

Li smiled benevolently. "To convince them of our inferiority. We didn't show them any of the new items we are developing, merely the older types. Our textiles, of course, we showed in full, and they were impressed, as indeed they should be. But it was different with the various types of mahinery and manufactured goods. Openly, they said very little, but we were able to record one or two private conversations between them in which they seemed to be highly amused by our backwardness. They will welcome the textiles, the beautifully embroidered silks, and other things of that nature. They would, I think, even be prepared to buy them. But at the same time they have suddenly seen the chance to make us lose face before the whole world. They will be able to demonstrate without having to say a word that we are a primitive people. This, they hope, will put them in a much stronger position in the Communist bloc. Naturally they accepted our proposals very warmly.

"But, of course," Li continued, "they don't have the subtlety and wisdom that we have possessed since they were running about in bearskins. They regard us as peasants, ignorant peasants. No, the trap was admirably baited and they gobbled up the bait. Everything is prepared, but the date of the fair is not yet definitely fixed. It will be, when I have received from the Chair-

man the date for S-Day. I think you will find that the fair will be
scheduled to open a few days after that date, which would of
course mean transporting the exhibits there two or three weeks
previously. Would that be satisfactory?"

"Perfectly satisfactory," Chuang said. "One further point . . ."

Li inclined his head politely to indicate he was listening.

"Technicians," Chuang said. "I have already used the four
Chen sent me. They are allocated. Naturally they don't know
anything about the nature of the operation."

"Naturally," Li said. "We are not, after all, Japanese bar-
barians."

"Well, then, I shall need another for Moscow."

"But who better than Comrade Professor Chen?" Li spoke
softly, his voice almost a purr. "It will be a great honor for
him." He smiled gently at Chuang.

For the first time since they had met, Chuang laughed out
loud. But at the same time he made a mental note to increase
his own personal bodyguard to at least a company of highly
trained troops; and all of them would be veterans of the Long
March; all of them personally known to him; and all of them to
receive special privileges and payment as double insurance of
their loyalty. He finished his beer and stood up to leave.

Li said, "Just one further thing, Marshal. Aside from emergencies, and I don't anticipate emergencies, the next time we
meet will be when I give you the date of S-Day. Immediately
after that I shall report personally to our beloved Chairman. I
shall require you to have in your mind the fullest details of the
operation. You are not to put anything in writing. I myself
shall write down the relevant information and present it to the
Chairman." His voice suddenly became hard and incisive. "Do I
make myself clear?"

"Perfectly clear," Chuang said. He turned and left the room
without bothering to say the customary words of leave-taking.

When the door had closed behind him, Li gently caressed
the hairs on his face. He placed the tips of his fingers together
and commenced to think. The Chairman was in excellent
health, but he could not live forever. And he was fifteen years
older than Li. The future held many interesting possibilities.
He began to contemplate them.

SAFE BASE ONE: JULY/AUGUST, 1966

Geraghty and Perkins went ashore at exactly 09.00 hours the morning after General Richards had died. Geraghty paused halfway down the companionway and noted with pleasure that Major Ryan had turned out a guard of honor for him. He acknowledged the salute of the officer in charge of the guard and followed him as he led the way to Safe Base Headquarters.

Ryan was waiting at the entrance of the hut, which was the Headquarters building. He saluted, and Geraghty acknowledged the salute. Then he extended his hand and Ryan took it.

"Welcome, Commander," Ryan said. "It's great to have you with us, sir."

"Thank you, Major. Now let's go inside and we can all be a little less formal." He smiled at Ryan. "When you get to know me better, Major, you'll know that I reserve formality for formal occasions. Those officers I *trust* can be as informal with me as they like." He turned to Perkins, who was standing a little behind him and to his right. "Isn't that right, Perky?"

Somehow in the short interval between their hearing of General Richards' death and their coming ashore, Perkins had arranged to have his best uniform adorned with the extra thin stripe that Geraghty had awarded him when he learned that he was now the senior officer at the Safe Base. So it was Lieutenant Commander Perkins who now stepped forward to shake Major Ryan's hand. "That's absolutely right, Major. The Commander has a great rapport with his officers and men, and I'm sure you'll get along just fine."

"Well, then, if you'll follow me, gentlemen."

He led Geraghty and Perkins through the entrance of the building to a large office at the end of the main corridor, opened the door for them, and waited as Geraghty stepped into the room. He had noticed that although paint had been brushed over the name that should have been on the door, the title Commander in Chief had been left. He looked round the room.

It was large, not luxuriously furnished but with an adequacy of chairs and other appointments. Facing the door was a large desk, and behind it a comfortable swivel chair. Geraghty walked behind the desk and sat down in the chair. Once he was comfortably seated, he said, "I shall require a shingle on my desk, Major. I take it you have removed the——"

Ryan said quickly, "Yes, Commander. We removed the General's shingle when he died. Also, we deleted his name from the door. You may have noticed it."

"Yes," Geraghty said, "I did. And the General himself?"

"He has already been cremated, sir. Standing Orders call for immediate cremation of anyone who has died. I understand there's a risk of infection."

Geraghty nodded. "Very good, Major Ryan. I always approve of immediate attention to Standing Orders. Now, let's see. Apart from me, you're the senior officer here?"

"Yes, I am," Ryan said. "I've been a major for seven years. I was expecting promotion any time, but then everything blew."

"All right," Geraghty said, "from here on, you're second in command. I'm going to make your special responsibility the day-to-day running of the base. Perkins here will assist me as my personal Executive. And in due course I would like a report and assessment of all officers who managed to make it here."

"I don't know many of them," Ryan said. "Mostly they're young; the older ones simply didn't survive the trip. General Richards was an exception." He glanced at his watch. "If you'll excuse me, Commander, I'll have to leave you for about half an hour."

"Now," Geraghty said, smiling, "you don't have to bother with that Commander stuff. You can call me J.G. when those of us of senior rank are together."

Ryan said, "Well, thank you, J.G."

Geraghty smiled again. "And now, just what do you have to do that calls you away at this moment?"

Ryan said quickly, "I have to check the defenses. You may not have seen them as you came ashore, Commander."

"J.G.," Geraghty said gently.

"Sorry. You may not have seen them as you came ashore, J.G., but we've had to establish barricades between ourselves and the civilians. I inspect them four times a day." He glanced at his watch once more. "I'm a little late now, so if you'll pardon me."

"Of course," Geraghty said. "You carry out your inspection, Ryan, and then I'll want a detailed report from you."

"I'll be back in about thirty minutes, but I'll tell you this now, the situation isn't good. The arrival of your boat has helped, but it still isn't good."

"Not boat," Geraghty said quietly. "Ship."

Ryan colored. He had a fair skin and red hair. "I'm sorry, J.G., I didn't know."

Geraghty looked at him with approval. "Now, don't let's worry about that, Ryan. I suspect there'd be quite a few things in Air Force terminology I wouldn't get right. You go ahead and inspect the defenses while I get settled in here. Oh, yes, one other thing, Ryan. I think we'd better have the designation on the office door altered. I want the whole thing painted over. Just my name, and below it, Commander."

"I understand," Ryan said. "I'll be back in about thirty minutes with a report."

Ryan saluted and went out of the room. Geraghty turned to Perkins. "Sit down, Perky. I want to talk to you about Ryan. A good man, don't you think?"

"I'd say so, J.G. He seems to have been very efficient. I mean, the guard of honor, the way he carried out Standing Orders regarding the disposal of the late General Richards. Yes, I'd say a pretty good man."

Geraghty passed a hand across his forehead. "I feel kind of rough," he said. "Nothing bad, maybe migraine, or maybe a hangover from those shots we had. I think perhaps I'd better see Doctor Jones. Have him brought ashore and escorted here."

Perkins went out quickly. Geraghty sat back in his chair and thought about the barricade, which worried him. There had to be some strong reasons for Richards putting them up.

Jones arrived, and Perkins ushered him into the room. Jones immediately went behind the desk and looked closely at Geraghty. "You're running a temperature, Commander."

"I know," Geraghty said, "I've got a hell of a headache too. Can you do anything about it?"

Jones pushed a thermometer into Geraghty's mouth, held his wrist while he took a pulse count. He looked at the thermometer after he had taken it from Geraghty's mouth. "About three degrees above normal. Your pulse rate is a little higher than normal, nothing to worry about. I'd guess it's probably the after effects of the injections. What do we have in the way of drugs?"

"One of the files against the wall there should tell you."

Jones found a file marked "Medical Supplies," sat down and began searching through it. Meanwhile, Geraghty and Perkins reviewed the list of people who had made it to the Safe Base.

"It's fantastic when you think about it, Perky. We're twenty miles inland, yet we and that freighter are floating on natural sea water. You know how they did it?"

"No, I don't."

"Well, it's all in the reports. I don't pretend to understand technical details myself, but it seems they concentrated on protection against radioactivity, for here we've got the advantage of a mountain above us, and they constructed a canal ditch leading into here. They increased the protection by coating the inside of it with lead. The reports aren't specific, but I'd guess that when the time came they exploded something that let the sea water in and transformed an empty deep ditch into a canal. What they didn't foresee was the conflict that has apparently arisen between ourselves and the civilians, who stubbornly refuse to be shipped to the islands, where we know they can be safe. A hell of a problem."

Doctor Jones looked up from his file. "Commander, we're very well provisioned with drugs. I think I have the answer to at least your personal problem."

"Well, that's great," Geraghty said.

Jones closed the file. "I think I may have the answer to another problem too. I couldn't help hearing your discussion just now."

"That's all right, Doctor," Geraghty said. "I trust you, after our talks on the ship. But what I want to know is what you mean about an answer to the other problem. Never mind me—I'm pretty fit, and even if I run a temperature for a couple of days it won't hurt me too much."

Jones said, "I'm a physician, and I must make sure before I tell you positively. First, I will need to inspect the drugs that are stored here. Where are they?"

"Hell, I don't know," Geraghty said. "You'd better wait for Ryan to come back. Oh, you wouldn't know him. A Major Ryan, Air Force, but he seems to me extremely efficient."

"Do we need to wait for Major Ryan, Commander?" Perkins said. "I'm sure one of the staff here will be able to take Doctor Jones to the stored drugs." He moved over, put his hand on one of the telephones, and said, "With your permission, Commander."

"Go ahead."

Perkins picked up the telephone and said, "Operator, connect me with whoever was orderly to General Richards."

"And while you're about it, Perky, I could use a cup of coffee."

Perkins spoke rapidly into the telephone, put it down with a satisfied smile, and said, "General Richards' orderly will be with us very soon. He'll bring two cups of coffee, Commander."

The coffee was brought by a jovial, red-faced able seaman, who immediately identified himself as the orderly of the late General. Geraghty said, "You know where the medical supplies are stored?"

"Sure, Commander. Nobody's supposed to know it, but I heard the doctors and the General talk about it."

"All right," Geraghty said. "I want you to take Doctor Jones here and let him look through the supplies."

"That's very easy, sir. Only half a block from here. If you'll follow me, Doctor."

"Wait a minute," Geraghty said, as the sailor and Doctor Jones were going out the door. "What's your name, sailor?" He felt it important at this early stage to make sure *his* importance was known among the military personnel in the Safe Base. And the Commander's orderly, he reminded himself, was always a useful source of rumor, trial balloons, and the like.

"Phillips, sir."

"Okay, Phillips, how would you like being my personal orderly?"

Phillips' face broke into a large smile. "I'd like it fine, sir."

"All right," Geraghty said, "consider yourself engaged. But on probation, you understand."

Perkins suddenly broke in. "Commander."

"Yes, Perky?"

"Do you think it might be a good idea if I went along with Phillips and Doctor Jones? To sort of get the feel of the place, you know?"

"Why, yes, Perky, I think that would be a very good idea."

When the three had gone, Geraghty sat back in his chair and considered the situation. He wondered first just what Jones had meant. Of course he could not blame him for being noncommittal at this stage. He was certain of Jones's reliability. Next, he thought again about the islands. It was the only solution, he decided. There the really big stocks of supplies had been stored. There he could start a new world. But of course there remained the problem of how to deal with the civilians in the Safe Base, and particularly how to deal with Brecht, the ex-Senator from the North.

He was still absorbed with this problem when Major Ryan returned, a moment later joined by Perkins and Jones. All three took chairs facing the Commander's desk, and Geraghty said, "Gentlemen, I heard only the first few words of Major Ryan's report before you came back. Maybe you'd better repeat it, Ryan, and I can assure you that anything these gentlemen hear will remain confidential."

"All right, Commander. The thing I'd better tell you is that I met Senator Brecht personally."

"Ex-Senator," Geraghty said quietly.

"All right, ex-Senator, but I met Brecht personally. He seems a very determined man."

"Determined about what?" Perkins asked.

"Determined that the people he claims to represent will tell *us* what to do. I should explain, they appear to blame us for the war. What is more important, they're armed; they probably wouldn't have made it to the Safe Base otherwise. Mostly they're armed with shotguns and pistols, but they're armed."

"Shotguns and pistols," Geraghty said, "don't constitute an effective deterrent to a determined force. I believe that we can trust the soldiers, sailors, and airmen?"

"All but a few of them," Ryan said. "A few have gone over to the other camp. But of course the arrival of your submarine makes a big difference."

"Yes, it does. All right, so they have pistols and shotguns. What do we have?"

"Nothing very much. A few automatic rifles, and that's all."

"But I have more," Geraghty said. "I have at least one hundred fifty automatic rifles, four machine guns, and at least twenty submachine guns, with adequate ammunition. If it comes to a fight, Ryan, we're well equipped. Shotguns and pistols aren't going to be much use against weapons that can pick you off at six hundred yards range. You agree?"

"Well, yes, Commander," Ryan said, "but it isn't the kind of agreement I find pleasant."

"In war nothing is pleasant."

"But we're not at war," Ryan said.

"Then why do you have the barricade? Why are you concerned about them having weapons? Let's get one thing straight right now. We're still at war, because we're fighting for the future. We're fighting not for ourselves, but for the human race. Now forget your hypothetical worries, Major, and join the team. How do I contact ex-Senator Brecht?"

Ryan said, "That's easy. You only have to go to the barbed wire and the sentries will get in touch with him. Of course, you'll need an escort."

"I don't need any escort, and I'm going unarmed."

"It could be dangerous, J.G." Ryan's tone was disturbed. He went on, "The General once went in there to talk to Brecht, but he never went again. After that they met at the barbed wire."

"Does Brecht know the General is dead?"

"No," Ryan said. "I thought it more discreet to carry out the cremation arrangements in secrecy, pending your arrival to take command."

"Excellent," Geraghty said. He pointed at a plan on the far wall. "Is that a plan of the Safe Base?"

"Yes, J.G."

Geraghty came from behind his desk and went up to the plan,

indicating with a motion of his hand that Ryan and Perkins should join him. "Perhaps you'll read it for me, Ryan. It's a big plan, pretty detailed too."

"It represents a big area, J.G. I'll take the bottom half first. You'll see in blue the dock where the two ships are berthed. Here on the left are the administrative offices where we are now, and a hundred huts, originally designed to house the Headquarters staff." He pointed with his finger. "Here are food supplies for the Headquarters staff. I should have mentioned one other thing about the huts—they each accommodate forty men. So over seventy of them are empty." Again his finger pointed, and he began to speak rapidly, pinpointing each of the important buildings for Geraghty. "Drug storage; armory; mess halls; hospital. Naturally I'll show you around these when you have some time to spare."

"All right," Geraghty said. "Now the rest of it."

"The red line you see here is the barricade we have established. It's eight hundred yards long, and we have sentries every fifty yards. They're equipped with automatic weapons, but we've very few left. Now, here beyond the barricade in the top half of the plan is the main living area. That's where all Brecht's people are. They have ample accommodations and living space, because there are sufficient huts there to accommodate comfortably about a hundred thousand people. And there are only just over nine thousand of them. They have enough food to live on indefinitely, plenty of water, and electricity."

"Accommodate nearly a hundred thousand?" Geraghty queried. "In an area that small?"

"Well, J.G., it isn't so small. That area you're looking at is about half a mile wide and a mile long. You can get a large number of people into that space."

"It's fantastic," Geraghty said. "On what basis were these people selected?"

Ryan shrugged. "I don't really know. Technical skills, I suppose."

"You have documentation for them?"

"Yes," Ryan said, "we have. Every one of them had been issued a special identity card prior to the war, and when those of them who made it arrived here at the Safe Base—incidentally there's another entrance here, you see it at the very top of the plan—those cards were collected by the men on duty here and filed in Headquarters. Even the children have identity cards.

Geraghty swung around sharply. "There are children?"

"Not many. About two hundred. The people selected were mostly single, but I presume they had to include a few married men who happened to have a particular skill they felt would be necessary, and of course in that case they had to issue entrance permits for wives and families too."

"I understand," Geraghty said. "Now I'm going to see Brecht."

Perkins said tentatively, "J.G., I don't think you should go alone."

"Thanks, Perky, but no. I go alone, and also I go unarmed."

"You'll have a long walk," Ryan said. "Nearly a mile after I drop you at the barricade."

"You have transport?"

"Sure," Ryan said. "I can take you up to the wire in a jeep, but then you'll be on your own."

"Right," Geraghty said. "Let's go."

Geraghty, Perkins, and Ryan went out of the room. Outside the hut a jeep was waiting for them. They rode in silence over the half-mile that separated them from the barrier. When they arrived there, Ryan climbed out of the jeep and said a few words to the sentry at the wire.

The sentry blew a whistle, and immediately men emerged from a building tucked away to the left. Geraghty noted that they were in different uniforms and came from all Services. In a moment the barrier was opened for him, and he went into Brecht's territory.

As he walked, his footsteps loud on the concrete, he thought how a few hours previously Barnard and Goldfinch, together with the dissident members of the crew who had refused to grow beards, had preceded him. By his orders they had gone ashore and had been escorted into the civilian portion of the Safe Base about three hours before he and Perkins had gone to see Major Ryan.

He walked forward stiffly, as though he were taking part in a formal parade at Annapolis. When he had gone about five hundred yards from the barricade, he saw ahead of him a group of men carrying arms. As he approached them, he noted that they were armed mostly with shotguns and pistols. A few of them had hunting rifles. They made no move toward him, but when he reached them, they formed into a silent, untidy group around him. He realized that they were an escort to take him to Brecht, and continued at the same pace. They showed no open hostility, but they were hardly friendly. Ten minutes later, he was in Brecht's office.

Brecht greeted him politely, but without rising from his chair behind the desk. Geraghty sat down and removed his cap, while at the same time looking closely at Brecht. He saw a tall man, thin almost to the point of emaciation, with close-cropped white hair and clear blue eyes. The appointments of the office were scanty—just the one telephone on the desk, two chairs, some kind of plastic floor covering. He nodded and waited for Brecht to continue.

"General Richards doesn't seem to speak to me anymore," Brecht said. His voice was quiet, light and yet strong. "Apparently he and I don't agree about the future of the people here. I suppose you have some message from him?"

"General Richards won't be seeing you again. Not ever."

"I don't understand."

"General Richards is dead."

"I didn't know. I'm sorry."

"Why should you be sorry? I've read copies of the correspondence between you and Richards. You didn't seem to like each other much, you didn't agree about the future of the community here, you don't have any particular reason to be sorry."

"And yet I am. A man is dead, so I am sorry. I wouldn't expect you to understand that, Commander Geraghty. Oh yes, I know your name, and why you're here. Does that surprise you?"

"Not particularly." Geraghty's voice was as level and calm as Brecht's. "I presume you've been speaking with Barnard and Goldfinch."

"That's right. Mostly with Barnard. But you tell me Richards is dead. I presume you are in charge of the military subsection?"

No, Geraghty thought, you're not going to rile me, you bastard. Maybe it was a mistake letting those two get here before I did, but it doesn't alter the facts. They couldn't have known about the fire power we have available on the sub. But play along a while, see what this man thinks.

"I am the senior officer, yes," he said. "As such I am in charge of the base, just as General Richards was, although you didn't seem to agree about that, either."

"No, and I don't agree now. There can only be one person in charge, Commander, and that person must be a civilian, duly elected by the people he represents. There are approximately nine thousand of us here, you know, and if I weren't a man of peace we would have torn down that stupid barrier months ago and taken complete control."

"Why didn't you?"

Brecht sighed. "I told you, I'm a man of peace. I hate killing, I've seen enough of it. You missed it, Geraghty, you were under the ice when the people who managed to reach this base got here. Ask any one of them, ask them what they saw on the way. Death and destruction, Americans killing Americans like animals, for survival. Death in all its most grotesque and horrible forms. You didn't see it, but we did. We saw where military power had taken us. And we don't want any more of it. Have I answered your question?"

"The administration before the war was not controlled by the military."

"Not controlled, perhaps, but certainly under its influence. Why else did a war start?"

"Didn't Richards tell you?"

"He said something vague about us not starting it. But that's unimportant. What is important is that the war started. The great system you people had created failed. That's what is important. You put your faith in armaments, more and more armaments each year, but it didn't work. Now tell me what you want, Geraghty, but before you tell me, let me tell *you* something. We don't trust you, or your kind. We never will. Now please make it brief."

My God, Geraghty thought, this is going to be impossible. But be fair. This man has probably seen terrible things. Accept that. But convince him somehow that we weren't responsible for them. Convince him that the only future for the people is on the islands.

He began to talk rapidly. First, he outlined exactly how the war had started. Then he described the islands, the huge stocks of equipment and food, supplies of all kinds, that had been stored there, enough, he pointed out, to ensure the start of a new civilization. Finally he appealed to Brecht to realize that only on the islands could a new civilization be created. He talked for more than ten minutes, but even before he finished talking he knew he had failed.

As soon as Geraghty stopped, Brecht said, "Now let me get this absolutely straight. You propose that the people here be divided among the six islands?"

"Correct."

"And your people—the military—where do they fit in?"

"Well, they'll be split up also. After all, the islands have to be defended."

"Against whom? Are you really serious, Commander?" Brecht gave a laugh, but there was no amusement in it. "What you mean is you will appoint a military governor of each island, with enough troops to control the population. Richards made this clear, though I don't think he intended to. You've made it equally clear, but I don't think you intended to either. In any event, the answer is no. We are here, we remain here, and we will go out from here and create our own civilization. We will reclaim the land—it will be possible about twenty years from now—and we will form a community where every man is free, every man has a vote, and every man can take his part in government if he wishes, and that's the way it's going to be. We don't want any part of your islands. We have enough food to keep us going here, and we're determined to wait and to emerge into open, clean air as free people."

"You think you'll be alive to see it?" Geraghty's voice was bitter now. He knew that he had lost, that he could never talk this man around. But at least he could demand that Brecht prove he really represented the wishes of the people. "Who do you mean by 'we'? How do I know you're really talking for all the people here?"

Brecht said nothing for a moment. Then he reached for the phone. He held his hand over the mouthpiece and said quietly, "No, I won't see it. But an elected representative of the people will. As for your other question, in a few minutes you will be able to hear how the people feel." He spoke a few words into the phone, listened, then spoke again. He replaced the phone and said, "They'll be here soon."

"Here?" Geraghty glanced round the room. "Are you serious?"

"Twenty people will be here. They represent the others. You can take my word for it they have been properly elected. Also, if you want an independent opinion, I've asked that Doctor Barnard come along."

"I don't want to see him."

"I'm afraid you'll have to. Now, if you'll excuse me, I have to welcome the delegates."

Brecht rose from his chair and walked out of the room. Geraghty sat still. He did not really need to see the delegation. Brecht would not have called them unless he was sure they would support him. And Barnard! But what could he, Geraghty, do in this situation? He could see no answer to the question, but he waited quietly until he heard voices outside; then the door opened and Brecht said, "They're here, Commander."

Geraghty stood as the delegation entered.

"A tight fit, Commander, but you see they're all here."

Geraghty looked at the delegation. About twenty people—he did not bother to count them. And Barnard well to the rear. Suddenly he felt almost powerless, with a sense of physical pressure upon him from the presence in this comparatively small office of so many men. He wanted to say something, but he could not. Instead, he backed against the wall while Brecht moved behind his desk and sat down.

"Are you satisfied, Commander?" Brecht asked quietly. "Are you satisfied that this delegation represents the people? I have already assured you that you have my word on that."

"All right, I accept it." Geraghty's voice was thick; it sounded almost strangled.

"Very well, then, we shall proceed. Gentlemen, the Commander has suggested to me that we should all be shipped to the six Pacific islands I have told you of. I have replied we have no such intention. I have told him we intend to stay here and in due course to emerge and build a new civilization right here in America. Do you agree?"

The response, from twenty voices, was almost deafening to Geraghty. But he understood quite clearly what they had said. The answer was YES.

As the delegates went from the room, Geraghty forced himself to looked at Barnard. Then he looked away, and presently only Brecht and he were left in the room.

Brecht said, "So you see, Commander, it is as I told you. Now, if you have nothing further to tell me?"

"I have nothing further to tell you."

"Then perhaps you will leave."

Geraghty nodded. He turned away, hating Brecht, but somehow not able to put his hatred into words. Outside the office he found the same group that had escorted him. They walked with him again until they were about five hundred yards from the barrier. Then they left him.

For nearly two hours Ryan and Perkins had waited by the wire. At last they saw Geraghty returning.

He was walking slowly, tiredly, almost like an old man. Ryan snapped an order, the sentry blew his whistle, and the barrier was opened. Geraghty stepped through.

"How did it go, Commander?" Perkins asked.

"Back to Headquarters," Geraghty said, and climbed into the jeep. Ryan tapped the driver, who immediately gunned the jeep into loud action, swung around, and drove back to the Headquarters building.

When they were in his office, Geraghty sat down and lit a cigarette.

Ryan and Perkins stood in front of the desk. Doctor Jones had apparently not moved from his seat while Geraghty had been gone. The file marked "Medical Supplies" was open on his lap, and Jones was making calculations on the back of sheets in the file.

Geraghty said suddenly, "It's no use. It's absolutely no use at all. The man's a lunatic. He's completely unreasonable; he just doesn't see that the only way for us to survive is to get out to the islands. I told him what we had there—unlimited food, weapons, and fuel, plus the nuclear reactors we have on three of the islands."

"And didn't that convince him?" Ryan asked.

"No," Geraghty said, "it didn't. He just doesn't understand. But I'll tell you one thing right now: we're going to go in there and take those arms away from them. What the hell we'll do after that I don't know."

Jones looked up from his file. He said, "I've been making some calculations, Commander, and I think I have the answer for you."

Geraghty looked at him. "You're sure?"

"I'd say I'm over ninety per cent sure. Looking through the list of drugs we have available, I found a very peculiar one. I won't bother you with its chemical name, but I recognized it immediately, because I've used it a lot."

"What are its effects?"

Jones smiled briefly. "You could call it a hypnotic drug. Administered in the right dosage according to the height and weight of each subject, it renders the subject extremely suggestible under its hypnotic influence."

Geraghty said, "You mean we could drug these people, then tell them they're wrong."

"Oh, more than that. Once the drug has its full effect—and that takes about seven days—the subject can be induced to believe everything he's told. We found in experiments that we were successful in approximately ninety-five per cent of the cases. You must understand it was still in its experimental stage when I worked with it, but I can guarantee the results are spectacular."

"Then that's the answer. We disarm those people—Ryan, I want you to get out a plan immediately, and bear in mind that we want as little loss of life as possible. Once we've disarmed them, we can administer the drug, and then convince them the only future for mankind is on the islands. But remember, Ryan, I don't want any unnecessary casualties. Bear in mind that you have the fire power of four modern machine guns. You may have to use them if there's determined resistance, but you won't have to use them more than once or twice. They'll soon surrender." He rubbed his hands together. "Jones, you're sure this is the drug?"

"Absolutely sure, Commander. But there's a snag."

"What?"

"The quantity of the drug. That's why I've been calculating. We've enough for three thousand people, maybe three thousand five hundred. Not more."

Perkins said softly, "But that would be enough. It would give us a numerical equality, and it would maintain what we've already got, an absolute superiority in automatic weapons. We could force the rest of them to accompany us and do what they're told."

"No," Geraghty said. He was thinking quickly. "We classify them by age, sex, and skill. We decide who will be most helpful to us in our new life, and we select those. Doctor!"

"Yes, Commander?"

"Once they're disarmed we'll have no trouble bringing them along here in groups. How many do you think you can deal with each day?"

Jones said, "About two hundred, if I have at least four other doctors to help me."

"You shall have them, Doctor. Better begin preparations right away. We're going in tomorrow."

THE ISLAND: OCTOBER, 1966

"Look," Bill said, "you just have to ask her. I know you're hardly on speaking terms, but after all she's the expert."

"I don't like to," Jane said. "When she does speak to me it's as if she were speaking to a whore."

"But be fair. She has a sense of professional ethics. This is a professional matter, and though she may not like you personally, I'm pretty damn sure she'll do everything she can. You've been sick every morning for the past three weeks, and there are the other signs too. You just have to consult her."

"Well, all right," Jane said, "but I'm not going to like it."

"No, but if what we suspect is true you're going to need her badly when the time comes." He held out his hand and lifted her to her feet. They walked slowly from the pool to the huts.

When they arrived there Bill was relieved to see that only Helen and John were sitting on the beach outside the buildings. He took John to one side while Jane spoke to Helen. A few minutes later the girls disappeared into the center hut where Helen had her small dispensary. They were gone about half an hour while Bill and John made small talk. Bill did not mention why the girls had gone inside, but John Anderson thought he probably knew the reason and he said nothing about it.

When the two girls emerged from the hut Bill sprang to his feet and went quickly toward them. He looked anxiously at Helen.

Helen spoke briskly. "Well, it certainly looks as if Jane is pregnant. But of course I can't be one hundred per cent sure without making tests, and I don't have the facilities I need to make them."

"Thank you, Helen," Bill said. It was the first time he had spoken to her since the night he and Jane decided to go their own way.

Helen shrugged, and said, "It's my job. Don't think I approve. But I promise you that when the time comes she will be properly looked after."

John Anderson had joined them and he asked, "What's new?"

Jane spoke for the first time. Her voice was firm and had a proud note. "Helen thinks I'm going to have a baby, John."

John said, "Well, congratulations." He turned to Helen, "Are you sure?"

Again Helen shrugged. "So far as I can tell."

Jane said, "I'm absolutely sure, and I'm very glad. Thank you, Helen, for your kindness."

"It wasn't kindness, it was my duty. There are some things even a nuclear war can't wipe out."

During the past few weeks there had been little communication between Bill and Jane and the other four. Now, in an atmosphere that John was delighted to see was more relaxed than it had been, they talked freely. By this time Arnie and Mary had joined them. Arnie had heard absolutely nothing, he told Bill, since the very weak transmission from the American space vehicle. But each day at noon he continued to tune to the frequency that he had been given by Geraghty. He spoke as if he did not think there was much hope that anything would ever come through.

Another item of news for Bill and Jane was that the chimpanzee had not been seen for several days. This was unusual, because she had made a habit of visiting them each day.

Later that evening they ate their food together for the first time since Bill and Jane had detached themselves from the group. The atmosphere was still a little awkward but, John thought, a great deal less tense than he could have ever hoped. Perhaps the prospect of new life on the island had caused this, especially new life in a world that perhaps was dead.

On the next day the missing chimpanzee came to them again. They heard her before they saw her. She was making quite different sounds from those they associated with her. There was an almost human quality in the high, moaning cries. They saw her twenty yards away from them in the fading light. They called to her, but she would not come to them. They walked toward her, and she did not attempt to move away. She was crouching on the sand, and as they got nearer they saw that she was holding something in her arms.

Helen and Bill knelt beside her, and Helen very gently eased her clutching arms away from her chest, then looked up in sudden alarm as she saw what the chimp was holding. She tried to put herself between the pathetic little monstrosity and Jane, but it was too late. Jane had seen the dead, horribly deformed baby chimpanzee quite clearly. The pupils of her eyes dilated in shock, her face became pallid as the blood drained from it. She slumped to the sand.

"Carry her into the hut, Bill," Helen said quickly.

Bill picked her up and carried her into a room in the women's hut. He laid her gently on the bed, and looked helplessly at Helen.

She said crisply, "Leave us, Bill. Tell Mary to bring— No, never mind, just send Mary in, I'll get it myself while Mary watches her."

Bill tried to say something, but Helen cut him short. She said, more loudly than before, "Leave us, Bill!" She caught sight of John, who was standing anxiously at the door. "John, you send Mary, then stay with Bill."

John took Bill to the leisure room and pushed him into a chair. Then he went swiftly from the room and told Mary to go to Jane. She went at once, and Arnie went back with John to stay with Bill.

They waited for nearly an hour. They did not talk. Once John slipped quietly from the room. He was gone only a few minutes, and when he returned his face was grave. Bill did not notice either his going or his return.

When Helen came into the room she went straight to Bill and put her hand lightly on his shoulder. He tried to speak, but no words came.

Helen said slowly and distinctly, as one might speak to a child, "The first thing you must realize, Bill, is that she's going to be all right."

"Thank God for that." His voice was thick. "And—"

"No, Bill," Helen said gently, "I'm afraid not. There was nothing anyone could do to prevent it. It's always possible at an early stage, especially when there's shock." She paused a moment. "She's lost a lot of blood and she's very weak, but she's going to be all right, I promise you."

"All right. She's going to be all right." He spoke with a controlled anger, which was all the more savage because he spoke so quietly. "Those lousy, power-crazed bastards." He rose to his feet.

John went forward, but Helen moved her hand slightly to stop him. Bill walked across the room to the far wall. He smashed the side of his hand against the wall, and said slowly and distinctly, "Fuck them! May they rot in flaming hell."

When he turned around he shook his head like a fighter who has taken a heavy punch. "Sorry, Helen," he said. His voice sounded almost normal again.

Helen moved forward. "Let me fix your hand, Bill."

He looked down at his hand as though it were not a part of himself. A thin trickle of blood was coming from where he had smashed it against the wall. "Doesn't matter," he said.

"Come along and I'll bandage it for you."

"Can I see her?"

"After I've put a bandage on for you," Helen said. "But she's asleep, Bill. It would be bad for her if you woke her. But you can see her just for a moment after I've bandaged you."

"All right," he said.

She took his arm, and he went docilely with her from the room.

John said, "I think we ought to find the chimp and bury that poor little thing."

"Yes." There was sadness in Arnie's brown eyes.

They went along the beach, but the chimp had gone. It was hopless to look for her in the darkness. They returned to the hut, moving slowly, as though carrying an impossibly heavy load.

Helen was waiting for them. John, who knew her so well, could detect the lines of strain at the sides of her eyes and at the corners of her mouth. She said, "Mary's sitting with Jane. I've put Bill in another room. I gave him a sedative, and he's asleep."

"I wouldn't have thought he'd have taken it," John said.

"He didn't know. I told him I had to give him an anti-tetanus shot. Arnie, if you'd like to sit there with Mary she'd probably like it. John and I will spell you later."

"Sure," Arnie said. "Helen?"

"Yes, Arnie?"

"Does this mean you were right all along?"

Helen shook her head. "I just don't know. But it certainly looks like it."

Arnie said nothing. He went slowly from the room.

When he had gone, Helen turned to John. He held her close, comforting her, while the tears ran down her cheeks. It was the first time in many years she had cried, but now she could not stop.

Helen kept Jane under heavy sedation through the night, the next day, and the next night. During her brief waking moments they fed her nourishing soups. She said nothing to them, not even to Bill.

On the third day Helen cut down on the sedation, and Jane was awake for six hours. Still she said nothing to them.

On the fourth day Bill insisted that Helen and Mary should relax. Jane looked much better now, and she had spoken a few words to him, though they were only monosyllabic, listless replies to his questions.

About eleven in the morning, while Bill stayed with her, the other four went for a walk. Almost immediately after they had left, Jane asked for a sleeping tablet. Bill gave her the tablet, and went to get some fresh water to help her swallow it. She drank the water, and for the first time she smiled at him. Then she turned on her side, and soon she was breathing deeply. He bent over her and saw that her eyes were closed.

He sighed and sat down in the comfortable chair on the other side of the room. As he relaxed his weary body he closed his eyes for just a moment, hoping it would rid them of the gritty feeling, the heaviness he had experienced in the past few hours. It seemed to help. . . .

Then he opened his eyes. The bed was emtpy.

He looked at his watch. It was a little after three. He had slept for almost four hours.

He called, "Jane," and rushed from the room and through the three huts, opening every door, shouting her name. She was not there, and neither was any of the others.

He thought quickly. She had not taken the tablet. She had pretended to be asleep. She was not in any of the huts. He hurried back to the center hut, to the room where Helen kept the medical supplies. The door of the small cupboard that contained the drugs was open. He fought against accepting the idea that immediately came to his mind. He must find her, he knew, and fast. He thought he could guess where she had gone. He ran out of the hut, but suddenly checked himself as he realized that when he found her he would need help immediately. He went into the room he had been using while Jane was sick, and buckled on his gun belt. Then he ran along the beach and into the vegetation, and with all his speed and strength kept on to the place where he knew she must be.

It took him only ten minutes to cover the distance between the huts and their pool. He burst through the last clump of thick ferns into the clearing, and saw her lying beside the pool. She was wearing the white nightdress she had used in bed, and he saw that it had been torn as she pushed through the undergrowth. Her feet were bare, and low down on the nightdress was a crimson stain.

He lifted her, cradling her in his arms, and then he saw the bottle, the same bottle from which he had seen Helen take sleeping tablets to give her.

The bottle was empty.

He lowered her very gently to the grass, pulled out the Colt automatic, and fired two shots in the air. Then he eased the nightdress from her shoulders, pushed it down below her breasts, and bent his head to listen, his ear pressed against her smooth flesh. He thought he detected a faint heartbeat but he couldn't be sure.

He remembered something he had been taught in the Army. He drew the watch from his wrist, polished the stainless-steel back, and held it close to her lips. He held it there for ten seconds, then looked at it. There was a faint mist on the steel. She was alive!

He fired another shot, hoping that Helen was close by, that she would get there in time.

He polished his watch with his handkerchief again and held it close to her lips. Again there was a slight mist on the polished surface.

Suddenly she breathed deeply and convulsively, the breath coming from her in a long gasp.

He fired another shot, and once more bent to listen. He could hear nothing. He tried the watch again, holding it for the full ten seconds. There was no mist on the bright steel. He tried again, and again, but the result was—nothing.

Slowly he pulled the nightdress up until her shoulders were covered. Then he sat down on the grass beside her and held one of her dead hands tightly between both of his.

From where he sat he could see, through gaps in the vegetation, the blue of the sea. Beside him the water made gentle, tranquil sounds as it flowed into and out of the pool. But he did not see the blue of the sea, did not hear the gentle water sounds. He saw instead the valley where he had been born, a green valley once. He heard the deep gurgle of the mountain stream where he had passed many happy hours tickling the small, fat, brown trout that hid beside stones in the stream, flicking them out onto the bank with the sure, scooping movement that looked so easy and took so long to learn.

As he looked at the green valley he saw it for what it was. A green loveliness made ugly by the black, bubonic excrescences of the slag heaps, the hillsides defaced by the black, endless terraces of mean, soot-encrusted dwellings, the air polluted by the coal dust that blew from the loading yards of the deep mines. He remembered his father, who had been killed in an accident three thousand feet below the surface of the ground, and all the other men who had been maimed and killed during times of prosperity, and those who had quietly, patiently starved during times of depression so that other men could live in luxury. He remembered his oldest brother, who had rejected the mines, and had died in a blazing oil tanker during the second World War, died so that there should never be war again.

In the distance he heard John shouting. He did not reply. He looked down at the body of the girl who had been destroyed by a war that important men, men of power, had said was "unthinkable." He heard John again, and Arnie, closer now. John and Helen, he thought; Arnie and Mary. Himself . . . He could not pray for Jane or for himself, because he no longer believed in God. Instead he leaned over her and kissed her dead lips. He heard John and Arnie moving through the undergrowth, There was very little time left.

He picked up the automatic.

John heard the crash of the shot very close to him. He ran, with Arnie a few yards behind him. In seconds he reached the clearing. When he saw them from the edge of the clearing, John knew he had been right. . . . Bill had fallen across Jane. Even from twenty yards he knew they were dead. He waited for Arnie, and together they walked slowly to the bodies.

When they saw what was left of Bill's head they turned away. After they had recovered a little, Arnie said, "How did he do it?" They still could not look at the bodies.

"Through the mouth," John said. "Oh my sweet Christ, through the mouth!"

They waited another minute, then they drank a little water to help clear away the sour bile taste in their mouths. Because it had to be done, and because these two people had been friends whom they loved, they lifted Bill's body off Jane and laid him close beside her. John stripped off his shirt and covered Bill's head with it. Arnie was holding the empty bottle. They heard the two girls approaching.

"Stop them," John said quickly. He pointed to places on the grass where the evidence of Bill's death was visible. "They've suffered enough without seeing this."

Arnie nodded, and he stopped the girls at the edge of the clearing. Helen looked at him. It was a question.

"Yes, both of them," he said. He paused, then went on, speaking deliberately, "We don't want you to go too close. Bill shot himself."

"And Jane?" Helen asked.

Arnie held out the empty bottle. Helen looked at it. She said tonelessly, "It's my fault. I should have anticipated this. I should have hidden those tablets and all the other drugs she could have used. It's my fault."

Arnie said harshly, "It's nobody's fault. Nobody who's here. It's the fault of men who were just exactly what Bill said they were that night." John called to him. "Wait here," Arnie said to the girls. "Please wait here."

Helen and Mary watched him as he and John talked briefly together. When he came back to them he said, "We three will go back to the huts. I'll bring back the spades and two sheets." He shrugged his shoulders hopelessly. "It's all we can do for them." He began to walk. The two girls looked once more toward the two bodies, and followed him.

When Arnie returned with two spades and two sheets they began first to clear up the visible evidence of Bill's death. They dug a small hole ten yards away, dropped the bloody pieces of bone and flesh and brain into it, and hastily filled the hole again. Then they picked a place to dig the grave. They had no doubt where it should be. Here in this clearing Bill and Jane had passed many hours of happiness and love. Here, then, they should rest together. John, using the side of his spade, marked out a rectangle about six feet long and four feet wide in the grass. They began to dig. Although the earth was soft and easy to shift, they found that after about twenty minutes they had to rest.

Arnie suddenly spoke. "I just remembered something. You know what I said that night we were talking about our supplies?"

"Well, you said a good many things," John said.

"Yes," Arnie said bitterly, "but one particular thing. I said I couldn't figure out why they had supplied us with spades, unless it was to dig our own—"

"Forget it," John said. "Let's dig."

Another twenty minutes, and the hole was about two feet deep. They decided it should be at least three feet. They continued digging. It was John who hit the hard, impenetrable surface. "Must be rock," he said.

Arnie pushed his spade down into the earth. It grated on something hard. They looked at each other, and then quickly cleared away the remaining earth. Soon they saw that it was not rock they had hit, but metal. Arnie hacked at it with the side of his spade. The hard steel of the spade scored lines across the metal.

Arnie bent down and looked closely at the shallow penetration his spade had made. He looked up at John and said unbelievingly, "It's lead."

"You're sure?"

"One hundred per cent sure."

John said, "Let's not worry too much about it now. We can discuss it later." He took his automatic from his gun belt and fired a shot in the air. It would take perhaps twenty minutes for the girls to get there. They used the time wrapping the bodies in the sheets Arnie had brought, and moving them to the side of the grave.

When Helen and Mary arrived, Arnie climbed down into the grave and took the two sheeted bodies as John handed them down to him. He placed them carefully side by side. Then he climbed out of the grave. They all looked down for a few moments and then, still without speaking, John and Arnie shoveled the earth back into the grave. When they had finished, there was a little mound that rose about six inches higher than the surrounding earth.

Helen and Mary had each brought some wild flowers, and now they placed them on the mound.

Again they stood in silence for two or three minutes, then as the light quickly faded they turned and walked back to the huts.

SAFE BASE ONE: SEPTEMBER, 1966

Geraghty was right. When the force of about two hundred had gone into the attack, each armed with an automatic rifle and backed by the covering fire of four machine guns, there were only one or two patches of isolated resistance. Within an hour everything was over. Geraghty accepted Brecht's grudging surrender, and disarming began immediately. The arms were piled in untidy heaps, each heap guarded by a squad of riflemen, and elements of Geraghty's remaining forces then moved in from the wire to begin the process of escorting back the people whom Geraghty had selected from a list prepared for him by the Headquarters staff.

The wire would not be removed before the ships sailed.

Ryan had suggested this, and Geraghty had agreed at once. Ryan had proved himself very reliable, and Geraghty agreed with him that even now there could be a sneak attack or some form of reprisal.

He sat behind his desk looking at the reports he had received from Jones and his team of doctors, then flipped them across the table to Perkins. "You've read these, of course?"

"I have," Perkins said. "Last night. They all seem to be very satisfactory."

"I quite agree. Now let's get down to considering the Table of Organization you've drawn up for our new society. I like it. I like the flavor of it." He looked at the large sheet of paper on which a pyramidal shape showed a breakdown of the new organization.

"Why, thank you, J.G.," Perkins said.

"Just two small points. I don't quite think I like the designation, 'Workers.' It sounds undemocratic, somehow. After all, we'll all be workers in a sense. Why not call them 'Citizens'?"

"I think that's a very good idea, J.G."

"All right, then. And here at the top." He pointed at his own name and the names in the two rows underneath. "I'm not too sure I like the expressions, Supreme World Leader, Deputy Supreme World Leaders, and Assistant Deputy Supreme World Leaders. Maybe I'm sentimental, but I prefer to see myself designated as Commander One. And the ranks below me as Commanders Two and Three respectively. Aside from that, I think it's fine."

He looked up as Jones came in. "Yes, Doctor?"

"Well, Commander, it's all finished. We're running the last batch through today. That means we should have them ready for their indoctrination talks seven days from now."

"And how soon after that can we sail?"

Jones shrugged. "Three or four days."

"All right," Geraghty said, "make a note of this, Perky. Set the provisional sailing date for the freighter—we still have to think of a name for her, by the way—two weeks from now. Now we have to work out a plan of disembarkation on the islands we're going to use. With our reduced numbers I think we should use first the islands already equipped with nuclear power plants. Later, as the population expands, we'll be able to occupy the other islands. But for now I think three will be enough. You and I, of course, will be following a few days later in the submarine. You've been very unselfish about this, Perky, and I won't forget it. You could easily have been a Commander Three."

"I'd rather hold a rank lower and remain with you as your personal exec."

"Very unselfish," Geraghty said.

He turned to Jones. "And you, Doctor Jones, have also, I feel, given absolutely invaluable service. I want you to come with me in the submarine and land with me on the main island. You remember it. It's the one where we dropped the people from the experiment, and it's the biggest and best equipped, and I'm sure the best base for our operations."

Perkins said quietly, "I think I have a name for the freighter, or at least a suggestion."

"And what is it?"

"Nova Terra," Perkins said slowly.

"Nova Terra." Geraghty pondered the words. "New World. Now,

that's very appropriate, Perky. Yes, I think I like it. Get it painted on right away."

"Right away, J.G." Perkins stood to leave, then suddenly said, "What about the six guinea pigs?"

"What about them?" Geraghty asked sharply.

"I mean, shouldn't they receive protective inoculations, as we did when we came back to this base?"

Geraghty looked inquiringly at Jones.

"Yes," Jones said, "I think they should. None of us are infected, but we may be carriers. I think it's a precaution well worth taking."

"All right," Geraghty said. "Now, the 'Nova Terra' carries two float planes, doesn't she?"

"That's right," Perkins said.

"All right. Make plans for one of the planes to fly the drugs in to them. Oh, and while we're about it, they might also do a quick radiological survey of the island. I'm pretty sure it's clean, but we might just as well be certain."

"I'll arrange it all, J.G." Perkins saluted and left the office.

Geraghty said, "One further point, Doctor Jones. We'll have to have a doctor examine them just before we arrive to make sure the protective drugs have taken effect. Have you anyone you can spare?"

Jones thought for a moment, then he said, "Yes—Dietrich. He's too old for settlement on the islands anyway. He's going on the freighter, so he can return with her when she comes back to pick up the garrison you're leaving behind, and the extra food supplies." He looked at Geraghty curiously. "I understood you to say, by the way, that we'd have plenty of food on the islands."

"Plenty, yes, but you can never have too much. That's why I'm leaving a small garrison behind, as a sort of police force to ensure those people up there don't wantonly destroy huge stocks of food, or damage the docking facilities. Don't worry, Doctor, this place was stocked for a hundred thousand people. They're down to about six thousand. We'll leave them enough for twenty-five years on that basis, and take the rest back to the islands. The garrison will withdraw at the same time, because we won't need this place any more. Everything's been thought of. Incidentally, how is our supply of hypnotic drugs?"

Jones said, "We've enough for about ten people."

"Okay, leave them here. I'll be sending the six guinea pigs back, and Dietrich can give them the shots. Then they'll sail back in the 'Nova Terra.' By the time they arrive the shots will have taken effect, and you can indoctrinate them personally."

"I understand," Jones said. "And now, Commander, I've a lot to do." He turned and left the office.

Geraghty walked to the window. Nova Terra, he thought, a New World. His world, and the world of his successors. He remembered that he had not checked with Perkins on whether the standard uniforms had been issued to everyone. He picked up a telephone. Perkins was not in his office. Well, he thought, it did not matter; he was quite sure Perkins would not have overlooked this. He began to go over in his mind the details of the planned embarkation and disembarkation. Again he was satisfied that nothing had been overlooked.

He sank back in his chair and closed his eyes for a moment. Under his leadership there could be a great future. And he was confident that when the time came, there would be an able successor to follow him in his huge task. He was a very proud and satisfied man.

THE ISLAND: NOVEMBER, 1966

In the days that followed Bill Evans' and Jane Nichols' deaths, the four survivors suffered from the knowledge that now there would be nobody to follow them, that they might be the last four people alive in the world. Yet strangely, it brought them closer together as a group; they seemed to find mutual strength in each other.

John and Arnie used some of the time to test diggings on the West hill. The lead they had discovered when they had buried Jane and Bill had puzzled them. After they had made about thirty test diggings they felt certain that underneath the hill there was a man-made construction at least a mile across.

"Look," Arnie said, "we plotted out the rough shape of this artificial cavern, or whatever you want to call it. We have to ask ourselves why it's there. And I think I know the answer. Remember your idea about prepacked cargo planes?"

"Yes," John said. "Yes, I see. You mean that it's a huge storage depot?"

"It's the only thing that fits. Look at it this way. The runway was to land them here. It would take too many cargo planes to ensure they had enough stores. The stores had to be here already, and it's my guess they're under this hill."

"But why lead?"

"Well," Arnie said, "lead is the most effective material for stopping radioactive penetration."

"And why haven't they come?"

Arnie said slowly, "I think, John, we guessed it right the first time. We didn't know about this artificial cavern then, but I don't think they had time. As we guessed, they were probably clobbered before they could get off the ground. I don't suppose we'll ever know, but one thing is explained: the sound we heard—or at least some of us did, after Jane said she heard it."

John said, "Well, I don't exactly see how what we're thinking explains that."

"An air-conditioning plant," Arnie said. "If they have stores in there, they'd need to be kept at a regular temperature—a lower temperature than we have out here in the open. And that would mean an air-conditioning plant, and something else too."

"What else?"

"It would mean a power unit to keep the plant going. And in its turn that would mean a source of power that could be relied on not to dry up in three years, or in thirty years."

"But what in hell could guarantee that?"

"A nuclear power unit. It's my belief, John, that beneath this hill there's a nuclear power unit that may be capable of supplying power for the next hundred years or more. Don't ask me to go further than that because, as I told you, I'm no nuclear physicist."

"Well, they haven't come," John said, "and it's my guess they never will come."

"I agree."

"But if there are stores under there, then we've got to find them. You know how short we are running on food."

"Sure I know. But how do we get through a lead roof, probably reinforced by concrete underneath?"

"We don't," John said. "We find the entrance. It shouldn't be too far from one of the roads. Listen, in the next few days you and I have got to look for that entrance, because if we find it we also find security, and perhaps ultimately safety and survival."

So for the next seven days they searched for the entrance to what they were convinced was a storage depot. They did not find it.

Arnie had instructed both Mary and Helen on how to operate the radio. Each day at noon one of the girls listened on the frequency to which Arnie now kept the set constantly tuned. And though Arnie and John did not find the entrance to the depot, on the eighth day of their search, when they returned shortly after noon, they learned that the radio had at last given them the message they had been waiting for.

Mary and Helen were by the radio, and both of them looked

excited. Helen said quickly, "They just came through. They told us to stand by for a vital message in the next fifteen minutes."

"Vital?" Arnie asked. "You're sure they said vital?"

"Yes, we both heard it," Mary said.

They sat in tense silence for about ten minutes. And then came the message: *A float plane will land on the lagoon an hour from now. Do not attempt to go near the men in the plane. They will leave a package of medical supplies on the beach. You will follow the instructions contained in the package for protective inoculations. The men from the plane will conduct a preliminary survey of the island. Under no circumstances are you to approach nearer to them than fifty yards. They will contact you on this frequency after their survey is completed.*

The message was repeated three times; then the carrier wave died out.

The minutes went by with agonizing slowness. They filled the time by speculating about why they should not approach the men, what the inoculations were for, where the plane would be coming from. They covered these and other questions over and over, but not even Arnie could suggest an answer.

They heard the plane before they saw it, and jumped to their feet. Then they saw it. It was a two-engined machine of a type immediately recognized by John as a Grumman SA-16 Albatross. Usually these were used for air-sea rescue operations, but John knew they had a good range. The plane flew over the island, circled, and then let down on a long approach into the lagoon. It touched the water about three hundred yards out from the beach, throwing up a high wave of spray that momentarily obscured it. Then it settled lower in the water, losing speed rapidly, and they heard the roar of its motors as it finished its landing run, changed direction, and taxied swiftly across the water to the beach.

Several minutes went by, then four men came one by one from the plane. The men were dressed in grey suits of a shiny plastic material. The suits covered them completely from their necks to the soles of their feet. Their heads were covered by inverted bowls of transparent material. Each of them had tanks of some kind—later the four learned that they were oxygen tanks—strapped to their backs, and each carried some sort of implement that seemed to consist mainly of a long nozzle that looked like silver.

The men walked slowly along the beach, then split up and moved purposefully toward the vegetation. As they moved they held their nozzles in front of them a few inches from the ground, almost as if they were using vacuum cleaners. Three of them completely ignored the group standing outside the huts, but the fourth man carefully placed a small bag on the sand and waved to them. He pointed to the bag and beckoned to them, indicating they were to pick it up. Then he too turned and disappeared into the interior.

"Just like spacemen," Arnie said. It was the first time any of them had spoken since the plane had landed.

John said, "I'll go pick it up."

The others watched him pick up the bag and return with it. He handed it to Helen. It was made of plain rubber, and was quite small and light. There was no sign of movement from the plane.

Helen said, "I'll take it inside and open it."

The others followed her into the hut. The bag was held closed by four snap fasteners. Helen opened it, carefully removed a transparent polythene container that held a dozen ampoules, two hypodermic syringes, and several needles, and placed the container on the table. Then she opened the envelope that was also in the bag.

The message was brief; it was mainly medical instructions about protective shots. It told them merely that there would be a message from the plane when the preliminary survey had been made. In the meantime nurse Dimarco was to give each of them, and herself, protective shots as detailed. Of the twelve ampoules in the polythene container, six labeled "A" were to be administered immediately; six labeled "B" seventy-two hours later. The message also repeated the warning that they were not on any account to approach the men, and stated that they were not to leave the vicinity of the huts.

Helen handled the shots with the efficiency they had come to expect from her. The shots were quite painless after the first small pain as the sharp needles penetrated the skin. She gave the last shot to herself, and John noticed she did it as detachedly and cleanly as she had the others. He could never do that, he thought. Yet if he were a diabetic he would have had to learn to do it to stay alive. He wondered briefly about diabetics and others who had depended on drugs to keep them alive. They would not have lasted long, he was sure, even if they had escaped the initial holocaust.

After Helen had finished, and had carefully, sadly, put into the drug cupboard the ampoules that should have been for Bill and Jane, they all went outside again to await the return of the men who had gone into the interior.

They weren't sure of the reason for the shots, but Arnie remembered reading somewhere that it was possible to give a degree of protection to the human body against radiation by injecting certain chemicals. He did not recall any of the details.

During the time they waited, there was no message from the plane. It was possible, they thought, that the plane had carried only the four men. But they could not understand why they had not been told immediately at least a little of what had happened. It seemed to them both perverse and cruel that, after waiting so long for the knowledge, they should now have to wait even a minute longer. They talked about these things while they waited, and Arnie explained that almost certainly the silver nozzles were connected to Geiger counters, and the men they had seen were dressed in suits that gave protection against heavy doses of radiation. They waited without hope, because they already knew what the report of the survey team would be. They had seen proof of it for themselves.

The waiting went on for about forty minutes before the four men came out of the vegetation onto the beach. They did not emerge individually but as a group, which suggested they had been in communication by walkie-talkie during the survey. They were still wearing the plastic suits, but all of them had pushed back the transparent headpieces so that now they hung like goldfish bowls upon their backs. They were talking together animatedly and, in contrast to the way they had ignored the four survivors when they first landed, they now turned and waved to them before walking toward the plane.

Arnie said quietly, "It's impossible, but it has to be true. We're not hot. The island isn't hot." He shook his head. "Why would they expose themselves if it weren't true?"

A few minutes after the men got into the plane they heard first the hum of a carrier wave, then a voice: *By order of the Commander, I send my congratulations to you. The level of residual radiation on the island is below danger level. You will probably feel slightly ill as a result of the injections you have been given. This is nothing to worry about, and it will disappear within a few days. Fourteen days from now you will recieve a further visit. Good-bye.*

Almost immediately after the radio became silent they saw the propellers of the plane begin to turn. The motors caught, and the plane backed away from the beach to the middle of the lagoon. Its take-off run was about one thousand yards, then it climbed steadily into the sky. They watched it diminish in the distance until it was no longer even a tiny speck.

They sat silently, each of them thinking that Jane's death had been unnecessary, and therefore Bill's too.

Helen broke the silence. "Of course, we have to realize that Jane miscarried because of shock. But it still doesn't explain why the chimp had that monstrosity."

"I've been thinking about this too," John said. "Look, we agreed that the ape and her mate had come on this island before we did. We know they certainly didn't land from the sub. But suppose they landed from a ship that arrived on the island before us, to bring some of the stores Arnie and I think are here. Suppose that ship was only a day or so out from port when the attack occurred. It's quite possible the ship would have been heavily contaminated and the chimp could have received a dose of radiation sufficient to produce a monstrosity."

Arnie said, "I think I'll go along with you, John. But there's something else puzzling me. You saw how they exposed themselves when they completed the survey?"

The others nodded.

"So why the shots? I know I said earlier they had been working on some kind of protective inoculations against radiation. But if the island's clear, why did we need the injections? Why were we kept away from the people who came? And just what were those shots?"

"I think I know," Mary said. "My father is—" Her voice faltered for a moment. "I suppose I should say *was*—an agency correspondent. So was my brother. Well, he was a free-lance correspondent. His specialty was defense, and he had a lot of knowledge about the weapons we were making.

"He was in England when one of their leading scientists was killed in an accident at Porton, near Salisbury. My brother told me the scientist was killed by some bacterological poison he was working with. My brother was very interested in bacteriological warfare, and for years he had been trying to research all he could about it. He told me that in addition to the research at Porton, he was sure experimental research was going on at Suffield in Canada, and at Fort Detrick in the United States. He was also sure there was a big story in one of those places; and when this scientist died he happened to be in England. Of course, he said, the security people slipped up somewhere, otherwise the man's death would never have been reported. My brother was one of the correspondents who tried to find out exactly how it had happened.

"He was unsuccessful, because the authorities moved very quickly, but he did find out that they were working on something they were very anxious to conceal, and he had no doubt that although all the places in England and Canada and the United States were supposed to be research centers developing antidotes for bacteriological and toxological agents, they were really working on bacteriological warfare. He told me this one night in California, and I know him well enough to believe what he said was true.

"He had been approached by a certain government agency. I don't know just what they said to him, because he wouldn't tell me, but I know he was afraid to publish anything about what he had uncovered. He also said that governments quite willing to boast about the huge number of bombs they had were strangely shamefaced when it came to admitting that they were developing even more terrible weapons. And he also said he was sure if it ever came to a big war, both sides would use weapons of that type. For a long time I didn't really understand what he was talking about: but if the shots Helen gave us aren't to protect us against radiation, then I think we have to assume they're to protect us against even more terrible things."

Helen said slowly, "That could be why we were told not to approach the men from the plane. Is radiation contaminating, Arnie? I mean, can one person pass it on to another, like measles?"

Arnie said, "No, definitely not."

"Well, then Mary could be right. I don't see any reason for the shots or for keeping us away from the survey team unless there was a danger they might pass on some terrible disease to us."

"But," John said, "they all looked perfectly healthy."

"That's immaterial," Helen said. "You don't have to be suffering from a disease to be a carrier. I think Mary is right, and I also think the reason we have to wait for two weeks before someone else comes is that it takes that long for the vaccine, whatever it was, to give a full protective effect."

Arnie said thoughtfully, "I wonder who they mean by the Commander. I don't know that I particularly like the word."

John said, "Well, we have to remember Geraghty told us some form of government existed. Obviously it would have a leader. Maybe he calls himself Commander."

"I still don't like the sound of it."

"Well, the important thing is we know we're safe," John said. He looked at Helen questioningly.

Helen said slowly, "No, John, we must wait at least until they've been again, until we can be sure. Anything can happen before they return. I think we have to be absolutely sure."

"All right," Arnie said, "I understand. We'll wait."

And so they waited. A great fear had been lifted from them but the shadow of Bill's and Jane's death was still over them. . . . They waited.

INTERLUDE: Nanyang, Honan Province, October 15, 1965

When Li and Chuang next met, for the last time before the S-Day operation, the Chinese had startled Western experts by another atomic explosion. But that was not all. Analysis of the dust that had been collected in the upper atmosphere by high-flying American planes had shown clearly that the Chinese had employed enriched Uranium 235. This meant that they were far more advanced technically than the West had thought. But of course they had no delivery system. Therefore there could not yet be any real danger from them. It was on this assumption by the West that Chuang had based his plan.

When Chuang had settled himself at the table he said immediately, "You have the date?"

"Yes, I have the date." Li's voice was very polite. This was not a day he felt he should annoy Chuang, who would be extremely busy from now on.

"And?"

Li smiled. "A most appropriate day," he said. "In the West they call it Christmas Day. December 25. I think that gives you slightly more than your required two months, Marshal."

"Yes, it's enough. But why that particular day?"

"For two reasons. There is, first, the psychological reason. The Americans would expect the Russians, whom they regard as anti-Christian heathens, to pick that day. The Russians, on the other hand, will reason that this is the one day when the Americans would assume the Russians would be least likely to expect an American attack. And so the Russians will reason that this is precisely the day the Americans will pick to attack." He paused and smiled briefly. "You see the delightful subtlety of it?"

Chuang said grudgingly, "It doesn't hurt my plan, that's true. Maybe it even helps. What is the second reason?"

"This, of course, comes more into your province. We have absolutely reliable information from a highly placed official inside Russia that they plan a series of multiple-rocket test launchings timed to coincide exactly with the start of the American Christmas. That is, during the night of December twenty-fourth, twenty-fifth. The Americans will think these launchings to be an attack upon them. And if you then destroy one of their radar stations, as you have already suggested, they will also assume that it has been done deliberately to prevent them from tracking the missiles."

Chuang was silent for a moment. "And this informant—you can trust him?"

"Absolutely. He is an old friend of mine. I won't reveal his name, but I can tell you that he is one of a group still faithful to the Stalinist ideals, which come closest to what we know to be true Communism. Further, he is in a position where he has access to matters of this kind. You may be sure that unless there are technical delays this will be the date. In fact, he has assured me the launchings will be timed for exactly midnight American Eastern Standard Time. How does your plan fit with this?"

Chuang looked at Li with something like respect. Certainly it would help, he thought. One of the American satellites would definitely pick up the launchings, and if after that— He broke off this thought and said, "Comrade Li, I have, as you know, committed nothing to paper. I shall require ten minutes to consider the implications of what you have told me."

"Naturally, Marshal. I shall leave you to your considerations." He rose from his chair and moved quietly out of the room.

Midnight, Chuang thought . . . He began to plan his schedule. When Li returned ten minutes later, Chuang was ready. Li sat down and waited politely.

Chuang said, "I have the details."

"Excellent. But one moment, Marshal." He pressed a bell on the table. When a servant appeared Li spoke rapidly to him in the national language. Chuang understood perfectly well what Li was saying, but gave no indication that he did.

The servant left the room and returned quickly with a roll of fine paper and a pen. An American-made one Chuang noticed.

He had one himself, taken from an American colonel in a prison camp in North Korea. He watched as Li uncapped the pen, held it poised over the paper.

"Now," Chuang said, speaking more slowly than usual so that Li would not miss any of his words. "First we have to consider intention: to cause an all-out war between the Americans and Russians. It is possible that some accident or crisis might precipitate this, but there is also the possibility that before that accident or crisis would occur they might form an alliance against us. My conclusion, therefore, is that the war must be provoked as soon as possible.

"Date: We have already agreed on December twenty-fifth. Forces available: Four ocean-going submarines, fully equipped with simple launchers. Crews are fully trained. They are also equipped with sufficient modified ground-to-air missiles to simulate an attack by Russian nuclear submarines."

Li looked up from his writing. "You will excuse me for interrupting you, Marshal, but did I not recently read that the Americans are installing a chain of underwater listening devices off the Atlantic and Pacific coasts of the United States to give automatic warning of enemy submarines?"

"Yes, they are, but we're told that it won't come into use, except experimentally, for at least another three or four months."

"Ah," Li said. "Please continue, Marshal."

"Also, two trawlers, one carrying one device, the other two. These devices will be armed before they are transhipped from the trawlers to land and, in one case, to ice. I have the necessary technicians to do this. Finally, one device to be placed at the most appropriate geographical point where it will disrupt the workings of the so-called hot line between the Pentagon and the Kremlin. All these items of equipment are assembled and in perfect order. Crews have been fully briefed, though they are of course ignorant as to the exact nature of their mission.

"Method: Here I will have to detail the function of each separate unit. The first is simple. Components of the device can be shipped in to Moscow with machinery for our trade fair. I take it this fair is now scheduled for early January?"

"Oh, yes," Li said. "Yes, they've been very co-operative. I'm sure they're very much looking forward to seeing us make fools of ourselves in front of the world." He smiled gently. "It's a pity the fair will never be held."

"Very well, then. Comrade Chen will accompany the device, which will be taken directly to the Chinese Embassy, and not to the site of the fair. It will be better if a few agricultural items are taken along with it to be placed on display before the fair opens. This should allay all suspicions."

Li murmured, "I agree," and made a note on the paper.

Chuang went on, "One of the trawlers will head for the California coast, where it will remain outside territorial waters. From it, two devices will be landed by landing craft. They will be loaded onto trucks from the trucking company I have already told you about, taken to San Francisco, and stored in the company's garage there until the appropriate time. One will leave for New York ten days before S-Day. It will proceed slowly and cautiously, and should be in position in New York three days before S-Day. We have, I may add, acquired a warehouse in New York where it can be safely stored until the time comes. The other truck will leave a day later, since it has less distance to go, and will head for a filling station we have acquired a few miles south of Scott's Hill, near Wrightsville Sound. It will be concealed there until the appropriate time. These trucks will, of course, be in radio communication with us. They will report by prearranged code word when they are in position, and similarly we will order them by code word to start their mission. You're sure the President will be at his holiday residence?"

"Yes, I'm sure. The Americans make a practice of announcing these things well in advance. He always goes there."

"Very well," Chuang went on. "The first and second trucks will be instructed to leave their hiding places in time to reach New York and Scott's Hill, respectively, by midnight. In the case of New York, the truck will cruise around central Manhattan. It doesn't matter where it is when our signal is received, except that it be somewhere central. The other truck is a rather more awkward matter. But it will be only ten minutes from the point on the road closest to the President's home, which stands only a few hundred yards back from the road. If it arrives at the correct moment, well and good; but if it's a few minutes before, then the driver will have with him an expert who can simulate a breakdown. The device, I need hardly add, will be concealed by assorted items of machinery, all of them quite harmless. Even if the driver is questioned, an examination of the contents of the truck will show very little, and in any case in the few minutes available they will not be able to make a thorough search.

"The other device landed from the trawlers presents a more difficult logistic problem, but one we think can be effectively overcome. We have a suitably tracked snow-vehicle, and that will proceed across the ice and snow to the vicinity of Clear. I do not anticipate any trouble with this, as it will be completely dark and it is hardly likely there will be far-flung patrols in that temperature." He paused.

Li said, "It sounds admirable, Marshal. How will the devices be detonated? You understand I am not a man of science."

"By radio signal from Peking," Chuang said. "It's a very simple technical matter."

"Simultaneously?"

"No. It will be better if a state of confusion is permitted to continue for at least a few minutes. My suggestion would be this. First, as soon as the report of the Russian launchings is received we should detonate the device at Clear. Then after, say, two minutes, we'll add to the confusion by causing the explosion in New York. By this time the Pentagon will certainly be in contact with the President. They would not respond to just one explosion, or even two; so third, the device near the President's home is exploded, and simultaneously with that, or a few seconds after, the one in Moscow. And that, I think, will do it. Consider: they will have no knowledge of any missiles approaching over the segment that Clear covers. There has been an explosion in New York, and probably they will have no communication with New York. And after the third, they will have no communication with the President."

Li interrupted him. "But does that matter? Surely they have some system to cover such an eventuality. I recall that when a former President was assassinated it was over an hour and a half before his replacement was sworn in. Surely they won't do anything until a similar process has been repeated?"

Chuang said sharply, "They're not fools. Nor am I. They will certainly have set up a system whereby a deputy has been allocated—and I'd guess be permanently on duty in the Pentagon —for just such an emergency. In fact, I have reason to believe this is the case. He will now be faced not only with three proven explosions, but also with the threat of missiles heading in from the sea. He will have tried to use the hot line to Moscow and will find that the Russians are not replying. What can he deduce from this? Simply that the Russians have launched an attack and are not interested in anything Americans have to say to them. Undoubtedly he will give orders for a response. In his position I certainly would. It is true it will probably only be a limited response, but the Russians will detect it. What are they to do? They will respond, again possibly in a limited fashion. This response will in turn be detected by the American satellites, and whoever is the deputy for the President at the Pentagon will decide the Russians are launching a full-scale war. He can't afford to have his bombers caught on the ground, so he will order them off. I think he will also order Polaris submarine strikes against Russian offensive bases. The Russians will, in turn, detect this, and from then on they will be kept very busy. But"—his voice became suddenly deeper than usual—"there is one other possibility."

Li said affably, "Surely not, Marshal. It seems to me your plan is completely logical and foolproof."

"There is no such thing," Chuang said harshly, "as a foolproof plan. I lost two of my best divisions in Korea in one day because some idiot misinterpreted an order. A *simple* order. No, there is nothing that can be completely foolproof."

"And?" Li asked quietly.

Chuang shrugged. "It's difficult to say. They may guess it was us. Or, of course, they may assume that their system has somewhere gone wrong. But if they guess it was us, they may well turn on us."

"But surely our air defenses are excellent?"

Chuang laughed. "Excellent? Oh, yes, I know we publish that sort of garbage in the newspapers every day. They'd last about ten minutes. What have we got? Obsolescent Russian fighters for which we don't have spares. A few squadrons of obsolete bombers that couldn't even reach the coast of America, let alone return. No, if things do go wrong, we must be prepared for very heavy attacks."

Li said, "But one thing you've forgotten, perhaps the most important thing of all. We have men." His voice became almost dreamy. "More men than they can possibly imagine."

"Yes," Chuang said, "we have men, we have rifles, we have artillery." He looked at his watch. "And, incidentally, I have a hundred men waiting for me outside. I must leave now. I think the plan will succeed. But I cannot guarantee it. Perhaps you will annotate your report to that effect."

"Naturally, if you wish it. But I think your fears are groundless."

"I must leave immediately to join my men. Otherwise they will be"—he looked directly at Li—"shall we say anxious?"

The implication was not lost on Li. But he merely said, "You will not forget to inform me if there is any disruption in your arrangements before the operation takes place. You have fulfilled your part admirably. Now all the Chairman and I require from you is to ensure the devices are in position when we need them."

"They will be," Chuang said, and he turned and went out.

Li returned to the report. He considered it with care. One or two of the characters perhaps were not as perfect as they might be, one or two of the phrases not clear enough. He ordered another roll of paper and began carefully transcribing the report, which he personally would hand to the Chairman the next day.

When he had finished writing the report he read it through several times before deciding it was perfect. Chuang was an insolent, drunken lout, but he had certainly utilized the very limited resources at his disposal to put together what Li considered to be a foolproof plan. It was nonsense for Chuang to say no plan could be foolproof. Given sufficient care and thought, any plan could be made so. He could recall many examples of this in Chinese history.

The inference, the threat almost, of Chuang's remark about the hundred men outside had penetrated deeply into his consciousness. The fool, he thought. He did not know that one of his drunken, unguarded remarks made at a party of high military officers had been reported to the Chairman by an informant planted among Chuang's personal staff. The informant was no longer available. He had apparently died of a mysterious disease, but the important thing was that his report had reached the Chairman. And the Chairman, while realizing Chuang's inestimable value at that particular time, had been appropriately displeased when he learned that the Marshal regarded him as "one of those ninnies in Peking."

Li closed his eyes and began to contemplate the glorious past, and the even more glorious future. China had already established herself in Africa. When the time came she would easily be able to dominate the African states. Puppet governments would be set up under Chinese control. The only remaining major problem, once America and Russia and the rest of Europe had wiped themselves out, would be India and Pakistan. But by then more bombs would be ready, and in any case the huge armies that China could put into the field would soon overrun these countries.

Li permitted himself a small smile as he contemplated the golden future.

SAFE BASE ONE:
EARLY DECEMBER, 1966

Before they boarded the submarine Geraghty and Perkins looked at the Safe Base for the last time. The "Nova Terra" had left some weeks previously, and the submarine, big though it was, seemed somehow small and lonely in the huge dock. On board, they went immediately to Geraghty's cabin.

Behind them they had left a garrison of about one hundred officers and men, mostly infantry, who would maintain order and discipline while they were away. The barbed wire was still in place, but it had been reinforced by four machine-gun emplacements and by arc lights that clearly lit up the zone six hundred yards from the wire that Geraghty had decreed none of ex-Senator Brecht's men should cross. It reminded Geraghty, in a way, of the Berlin Wall. But of course this was different; this was an action in defense of liberty, not against it. Major Ryan had designated a former infantry captain to command the garrison, and he was quite sure that with the uninterrupted field of fire available to the machine-gun posts, no attempt would be made to storm the wire. A white line had been painted across the width of the Safe Base six hundred yards from the wire. Brecht had been warned that anyone crossing that line would be shot without warning.

Geraghty said, "They're a disorganized rabble."

"They sure are," Perkins agreed. In the past few weeks he had assimilated much of Geraghty's growing confidence and authority. He went on, "You remember that song about 'They're either too young or too old'?"

"Hell, yes," Geraghty said. "I remember all right."

"That sure was a smart thing you did, pulling out their potential fighting men, as well as the women of child-bearing age." Perkins' tone was warm.

"Well, I wouldn't exactly say that. In a way I'm sorry I had to do it, because it wasn't altogether humanitarian, and you know how I believe in humanitarian principles." He did not wait for Perkins to reply, but continued, "In the long run, however, I think it was the *right* thing to do. They'll be better off with us than here. Maybe in a few hundred years people will be able to say: 'My people came across in the "Nova Terra".' You know, the way people used to boast about their folks coming across in the 'Mayflower'. Well, now, let's forget about all that. What's our crew state?"

"We're undermanned, of course. But we can get by on a short cruise. We gave quite a few of our sailors to the 'Nova Terra', but we have enough to maintain adequate watches. I'm afraid it's going to be twelve hours on, twelve hours off, but under the circumstances we can't help that."

"Hell, no," Geraghty said, "it's a short cruise." He glanced at his watch. "Ten minutes before we sail. All checks complete?"

Perkins reached for a telephone. He spoke into it briefly, waited for a reply, and said, "All checks complete, J.G."

"Fine. Go ahead, Perky, you take her out."

Perkins flushed. Taking the submarine out meant backing down a narrow canal. It was a difficult feat of seamanship, and he was very proud that Commander One should have placed such trust in him. Geraghty seemed to sense what Perkins was thinking. He smiled. "You can do it with your eyes shut. Better keep them open just the same. You can buzz immediately if you need me. Let me know when we're in clear water, and I'll come up top before we submerge."

Perkins saluted smartly and went out, closing the door quietly behind him.

Geraghty looked around his cabin. It was like coming home, he thought. For a moment he wished he had a cigarette, because this was the sort of moment in which he enjoyed a cigarette, when he could relax, confident in the knowledge that his ship was in good hands. And he was certain it was, because he had assessed Perkins as a man who was capable of dealing with any situation. Any within his experience, naturally. But the experience would come with time, and Perkins still had lots of time.

He ran over in his mind once again the supplies that would be available to him when he reached the main island. He thought of the sixteen Polaris missiles that were safely stored there. And the jeeps, the guns, the fuel, and the food. And not least of all, the huge sperm banks that he knew from the reports had been carefully stored in great containers, constantly monitored for correct temperature and humidity. He thought what a blessing nuclear reactors had proved to be. He knew there was one already functioning on the main island, and he also knew there was one in reserve there, waiting to be activated if the primary reactor should give any trouble. So he had available an unlimited source of power. In fact, he had power, period. He made a mental note to record this thought some time in the future. It would look well in his journal.

He felt a slight vibration as the propellers began to turn. He waited contentedly, his mind full of the infinite possibilities that the future held, until a call from Perkins informed him they were in the open sea.

He went up to the bridge. "I'll take her from here, Perky. Well done." Perkins smiled and stepped back.

Fifteen minutes later the submarine was cruising comfortably at a depth of twenty fathoms.

THE ISLAND: NOVEMBER, 1966

Three days after the first inoculation, Helen gave them the second shots from the "B" ampoules. The first shots had not affected any of them; the second gave Mary and John slight temperatures, and Mary complained of pains in her legs and arms. But the symptoms disappeared quickly.

John and Helen, during one of their walks, found the chimp's body at the side of the road leading to the West hill. They could not tell the cause of death, and there seemed to be no outward sign of radiological damage. John returned to the huts for a spade, and they buried the dead animal where they had found her. They did not find her mate, and assumed that he was dead also, his body hidden somewhere in the thick vegetation of the interior. In any case, they did not see him again.

Fourteen days after the first visit, the plane returned. When it had taxied to the beach two men emerged from it. John focused on them with the binoculars.

"They're wearing some kind of uniform with collar badges, but I can't quite make out what they are," he said.

One of the men walked briskly toward them, carrying a medium-sized black bag. This time they had not been given any instructions to stay away from the visitors, but none of them went forward to meet him. It was almost as though they were afraid of this personal human contact, as opposed to the impersonal instructions of the radio, after so long a period of isolation.

The man came up close to them. He was about six feet tall, very thin and wiry, with sparse grey hair and a face so pale in contrast to their faces that it was obvious he had seen little sunlight in the recent past. He wore rimless bifocals, and behind them were penetrating eyes of a cold, pale blue.

He shifted his bag from his right hand to his left, and said, "It's good to see you. But where are the other two?" His voice was clipped, with a hint of an accent that was not American. He added, before any of them could reply, "I am Doctor Dietrich."

John Anderson said, "Welcome to the island, Doctor. The other two, well . . ." His voice faded away.

Helen glanced at John, and said quickly, "They're dead, Doctor." She explained how Jane and Bill had taken their own lives. She sketched in briefly the fears they had all felt; the lack of knowledge they had suffered from; the way in which they had made a discovery that appeared to Bill and Jane to guarantee their safety; and finally the incident which had led to tragedy.

Dietrich merely nodded.

Arnie had been watching him closely as Helen spoke. He did not know why, but he felt distinctly uneasy.

Dietrich said, "In less than two hours we must leave. First I have to give you all a physical check, then there'll be time for questions before Leader Four Smith joins us." He turned to Helen. "You are Nurse Dimarco?"

Helen nodded.

"Very well, then, I shall examine you first. Please take me to a suitable room."

After the physical examinations, he told them they were all in good shape. They had not, so far as he could see, suffered any bad effects from their time on the island, and he was not surprised by this, because the radiation level on the island was very low, according to the survey team's readings. He began to explain why it should be so low, and was surprised when John told him they had worked it out for themselves.

"We're not sure about the injections, though," John said. "And why the instructions to stay by our huts?"

Dietrich shook his head sadly. "I can tell you about the injections."

Arnie looked hard at him. He thought he had detected a coldness in the doctor, but the way Dietrich had conducted the examinations had gone quite a way to change his mind. And now Dietrich seemed sympathetic toward them.

"The injections were to protect you against disease."

"What disease?" Helen asked sharply.

"Nurse Dimarco, it was not just one disease. There were many."

"From fallout?" John asked.

Dietrich looked at his watch without answering her question. "I told Leader Four Smith I would not be through with the examinations for an hour. We have perhaps fifteen minutes before he comes. I will try to tell you all I know, but I know nothing about how it all started, only about the effects."

"How many people are left alive?" Arnie asked.

"No one can do more than guess," Dietrich said. "In the United States, perhaps one hundred thousand. Most of those will die in the next few years from the long-term effects of fallout. Or they will starve, or kill each other fighting for food. That is already happening in many areas. In the rest of the world, perhaps a million, and practically all of those will also die in a few years."

They sat in silence, their attention riveted on him. They had known, or at least suspected, this would be the case. But that did not lessen the horror they felt.

Dietrich went on, "In the countries directly involved in the fighting, most people died in the first or second day. They died from blast, or from the immediate short-term fallout, or from the thermal effects of high-altitude explosions. I have heard it said that after the first few hours the defenses on both sides had ceased to function. Both sides had kept their big load-carrying weapons, their bombers, in reserve for that time. As soon as the defense broke down they sent the bombers in. They were able to pick off their targets at leisure. Some of the Russian bombers carried as many as twenty bombs in the megaton range. They systematically destroyed every worthwhile target. About eighty per cent of the people died in the first two days.

"But then came the real horror. It is why you were given protective inoculations. Each side realized they could not completely destroy the other with radiological weapons only. So they started using the ultimate weapons. You know, people talked a lot about the bombs, but there were even worse weapons than the bombs."

"You mean germ warfare?" Helen asked quietly.

"It is a loose way of describing it," Dietrich said, "but you could call it that. Two general types of weapons had been developed. First, there were toxicological weapons, what you might call poisons. There were nerve gases, of course, and such things as botulinus toxin. But as weapons these had disadvantages. Botulinus, for example, becomes harmless in twelve hours. The gases require favorable winds. So mostly the second type of weapons were used.

"These were bacteriological. They included highly developed forms of—among other bacteria—cholera, psittacosis, syphilis, and plague. These had the advantage that they could be passed on from human being to human being. They were specially developed to be almost impossible to counter without the suitable serums, and their effects were much more virulent than those of the bacteria from which they had been developed. Some people, a few only, were naturally resistant. In some remote areas—deep jungle, for example—the diseases never penetrated. And they were not very effective in the polar regions. But in thickly populated areas they swept through whole countries, destroying virtually all life. As I said, the population of the world is now estimated at about a million. Twenty years from now it will be down to about one hundred thousand, as the long-term effects of Strontium 90, Carbon 14, and other isotypes with a long half-life are felt."

"But surely," John said, "there were some countries that were not affected by all this—countries with huge populations like China and India and Pakistan? Like some of the South American republics?"

"The Russians saturated China," Dietrich said. "I believe we did too. There were SAC bases in Pakistan and Japan. We suspected the Russians might be using Indonesian bases. Panama was attacked, of course, and many other places. Once the attacks were made, once the diseases began to spread! . . . Plague, you see, does not recognize international frontiers. And neither does fallout."

John said, "I can't imagine anyone developing such filthy weapons, let alone using them. There's no defense against them."

Dietrich said quietly, "They were filthy weapons, yes, but logically no more filthy than other weapons of mass destruction specifically designed to slaughter millions of people. And there *was* a defense against them. Of course, it applied only to a limited number of people, but the research establishments had already produced enough serum to inoculate about sixty thousand carefully selected people before the war ever started. They were instructed to report to certain safe bases if war broke out. I believe about ten thousand of them actually made it."

Mary said, "Then there were research centers against disease, places like Fort Detrick and Suffield and Porton, weren't there?"

"They were concerned with the finding of antidotes, yes. But that was only a part of their work. It was known that the enemy had these weapons, and the government was able to convince most people that these establishments—there were others in addition to those you mentioned—were only developing antidotes. But of course they did more than that. If you could study the lessons of history you would see that if your enemy has a weapon of great potency, it inevitably happens that you yourself will produce a weapon of similar potency to use against him. They call it deterrence."

He looked at his watch. In the distance they heard a man's voice calling. Dietrich stood up. "I must go. You will please not tell Leader Four Smith I have given you this information." He shook hands with each of them. "We shall not meet again."

Arnie said, "Please tell us this, Doctor. How come you are safe? How come you know so much about what went on in these germ-warfare establishments?"

Dietrich paused at the door. He did not turn to look at them. "I know because I worked in one of them."

Smith was tall and well built, about the same size as John Anderson. His hair was cropped close and he had a clean, well-scrubbed appearance. His summer khakis were immaculate, whereas Dietrich's had been dirty. Also, while Dietrich had worn simply a plain khaki shirt and slacks, Smith had insignia of rank on his collar—two silver bars. He said to them, "My congratulations. Dietrich tells me you're all very fit."

John Anderson came forward and held out his hand. "Let's introduce ourselves. I am John Anderson, and this is Helen Dimarco." Smith shook hands with both of them, and then Arnie Levin stepped forward and introduced himself and Mary.

Smith said, "Well, I guess Dietrich told you who I am. I am Leader Four Smith." He touched the badge on his collar momentarily. "We had to use what was available for insignia. Later we'll probably work something else out. Now, I'm quite sure there's a lot you want to ask me. Or perhaps," he added casually, "Dietrich has already told you most of it?"

John said carefully, "He told us we were healthy, and that there had been a huge loss of life, but not much else except that he wouldn't be seeing us again."

"No," Smith said, "that is true. He won't be seeing you again. He's too old for settlement on one of the islands. But I'm quite sure the first thing you want to ask me is who won the war." He looked at them expectantly.

"All right," Arnie said, "so who won the war?"

"We won it. They're finished, and they'll never trouble us again. Even more important, we have a stable government, and thanks to the foresight of some of our military thinkers we're well equipped for the future. It will probably surprise you to know there are huge supplies of equipment and food right here on this island. We're well fixed, except numerically of course, but future generations will take care of that."

"Then we'll survive as a nation?" John asked.

Smith laughed. "Not just as a nation. As the world. Within twenty years there won't be anyone else left anywhere except a few primitive and isolated communities. They won't have efficient weapons or transportation. Most important, they won't have communication with each other. They will exist without knowledge of similar communities, and therefore, for all practical purposes, each single community will be the only one left in the world. Perhaps it's true to say today we're still a nation, though as I've pointed out, for practical purposes we're more than that. Tomorrow we'll really be the world. We already have a world leader."

"How come he survived?"

Smith smiled. "The same reason I did. When everything blew up we were both in safe places. I was in the reserve War Room a thousand miles from Washington. We saw most of what went on, even after the Pentagon War Room was blotted out. So we just sat it out for three weeks until the air had cooled enough for us to make a fast break to S.B. One. A few of us got through."

John said, "S.B. One?"

"Sorry, of course you wouldn't know. Safe Base One. There were

three Safe Bases, but S.B. One was—is—the biggest. The other two
don't exist any more. But you'll want to know what happened in the
fighting."

Arnie said quietly, "It would be interesting."

"Yes," Smith said, "well, I can't tell you a great deal, because after
a while things got kind of chaotic. The defenses on both sides didn't
function much after the first few hours. Carefully placed air and
ground bursts knocked out their communications early, and of course
modern defense systems just can't operate without efficient control
and communications systems. There was termendous jamming by
both sides, too, and all kinds of electronic interference. We didn't
know much except that if we kept hitting longer than the enemy we'd
win. And we did, by God, in spite of what he pulled on us the second
day.

"His attacks were getting weaker, and we still had plenty left. But
then he started with bacteriological weapons. Fortunately we had
plenty of those weapons ourselves, more efficient than his, I'm glad to
say. So we gave it back to him. And to China, and a lot of other
countries we suspected were helping him. And that did it. Yes, the
fact we had an adequate stock of those weapons was a marvelous
thing. Thank God!"

Arnie looked at John incredulously. John stared straight ahead, his
face expressionless.

Smith continued, "There isn't much more to tell. After about a
week there were no more attacks. Once or twice our aerial reconnaissance revealed attempts at a build-up inside Russia, and one of the
subs patrolling the coast lobbed in a few missiles. That ended the
build-up. Nine months ago was the last time, there haven't been any
incidents since."

John said, "Just what is this Leader system? I mean Leader Four,
and whatever else there is."

"You have to understand we've created a new democratic order
of things. We had to; after all, we're the world now. So a structure
was created where we have a World Leader—though he prefers the
designation Commander One. Then we have a Commander Two, who
is in fact the Deputy World Leader; three Commanders Three, nine
Leaders One, twenty-seven Leaders Two, eighty-one Leaders Three,

and two hundred-plus Leaders Four. It's a thoroughly democratic system and it works like this. When the present Commander One dies, the Commander Two automatically moves up. Then he appoints one of the three Commanders Three to succeed him. The two remaining Commanders Three choose a Leader One to join them. The Leaders One elect a Leader Two to join them, and so on down the line. It's simple, practical and—"

"And very democratic," Arnie said. "Who do these leaders lead? Do you have *people* in your democracy?"

John flashed him a warning glance.

But Smith didn't notice Arnie's anger. "The remaining survivors are classed as Citizens," he said. "They rank from Citizen One down through Citizen Three. And all of them have a chance of moving up through the grades if they are suitably recommended. Of course, later there may be modifications in the system, but for the present it seems to be working well. Incidentally, you're very honored. The Commander One is going to establish his headquarters right here on this island in person. You'll like him. A fine, democratic man. Why, do you know, if he likes you he doesn't mind at all if you don't call him Commander One, but simple address him as J.G."

John said quickly, before Arnie could speak, "Another question. Did the Russians start the war, or did we? And why?"

Smith stood up. "I can't answer that question here." He looked at Mary and Helen, then continued. "But I am authorized to pass it on to you, Anderson, and you Levin, because I don't mind telling you both you've been selected as provisional Leaders Four. I suggest you walk with me back to the plane."

He nodded to the two girls and went abruptly from the room.

John said quickly, "Come on, Arnie. What the hell, we can tell the girls later. Right now we should find out all we can."

Arnie said, "Right now I'm not sure I want to find out any more." But he followed John out of the room.

Outside the huts Smith was waiting for them. He said pleasantly, "Let's walk along and sit down."

They walked about fifty yards from the huts and sat down on the sand. Smith said, "Sorry I couldn't answer your question in there, but you see the answer's classified for anyone below Leader grade."

"How are the girls graded?" Arnie asked sharply.

"They're not," Smith said. "But now I can tell you we didn't start it and the Russians didn't. Who does that leave?"

"Well," John said, "the British or the French, I guess. But that wouldn't make sense. They'd know they'd be wiped out, so why should they do it?"

"Precisely," Smith said. "And they *were* wiped out. We think the British lasted about six minutes, once it started. The French a little longer perhaps—they were bigger geographically. We have reason to believe two or three R.A.F. bombers—not more—got off the ground before they were all destroyed. They had no influence on the war, of course. Now, what country had repeatedly said they weren't afraid of nuclear war? What country had objected strongly to the Russians' peace line?"

Arnie said slowly, "You mean China?"

"Yes. I mean China."

"It's impossible," John muttered. "They may have had a few bombs, but I remember reading some expert who said that even if they had bombs they wouldn't have the means to deliver them for at least ten years."

"They had the bombs. And they delivered them." He paused, then went on. "Only four or five bombs, but they placed them just where they'd hurt most."

"But how could they?" Arnie's voice was puzzled. "Without effective delivery systems, how could they?"

"They did," Smith said. He glanced at his watch. "I guess I have about fifteen minutes more. You'll get all the details later when you're indoctrinated, but for now all I can do is give you an outline. You have a rough idea what our defense system was? Against surprise attack?"

They nodded.

"All right," Smith said. Then he began to talk rapidly. First he sketched in the organization of the defense system, the B.M.E.W.S. stations, the MIDAS satellites, the Teepee system and other bending radars, the converted KC-135 that SAC always kept flying in case of emergencies, the missiles from the hardened and non-hardened bases, the Polaris subs, and the SAC bombers on airborne alert or ground stand-by. They constituted the deterrent.

But, he pointed out, there was no way of detecting missiles the Russians might send the long way round by the South Pole instead of across the top. He cited the example of Korea where, in spite of Allied air supremacy, hundreds of thousands of human ants every night humped a hundred pounds of ammunition each from the supply dumps to the guns. He outlined the events of the previous Christmas, the three nuclear explosions, the detection of missiles heading in from the sea. He repeated that it was believed that when the Chinese decided to start a war, they had only four or five bombs available.

Then he came to what had been deduced, by logically fitting pieces of information together, to be the Chinese plan. They had picked on Christmas partly for psychological reasons. The Americans would assume that was the day the Russians were most likely to hit them because the Russians would assume their guard would be lowered that day. And the Russians would assume the Americans would pick that day because they had decided the Russians would never expect a first strike from a Christian nation at Christmas, and might therefore reasonably be caught off guard.

But there was another reason for deciding on Christmas. There had been something of a rapprochement between the Russians and the Chinese after their bitter quarrels. Either because the Russians had told them or because their agents had found it out, the Chinese knew the Russians intended to use Christmas to display once again before the world the superiority of Communism over the West by launching the first orbital space platform. That decided them. They had blown three bombs, at Clear, at New York, and near the President's vacation home. In the case of Clear the bomb had been transported over ice—and Smith pointed out that at that time of year there was perpetual night around Clear; the other two bombs were transported overland, one to a point near the President's home and the other to New York City.

Arnie tried to interrupt, but Smith waved a hand to silence him. "At the time the Chinese learned of the successful orbital platform launch, their bombs were already in position. They knew the American MIDAS satellites would detect the Russian launching. They then detonated the first of the bombs, at Clear, by radio signal from Peking. They allowed time for this to register on the Americans, then detonated the bomb which wiped out the President, followed shortly afterward by the bomb they had placed in the center of New York City. After a carefully calculated interval, they fired what were apparently ballistic missiles from submarines about forty miles off the coast. These were immediately picked up by coastal radar, and their numbers reported back to the Pentagon. The coastal radar was very effective.

"Of course we saw all this happen in the duplicate War Room, or Command Post, and we also saw the response. Whoever was on duty at the Pentagon—I don't know his name—was very careful to avoid a spasm response. He ordered off in reprisal only about forty missiles from the non-hardened bases. Those were the bases that couldn't have survived a Russian first strike.

"The Russians assumed an American first strike was under way. They had no contact with the Kremlin from Strike Headquarters, so the commanders there initiated their own graduated response to the apparent American threat. In their initial launch they sent off, we believe, between fifty and sixty intercontinental missiles.

"These launchings were in turn picked up by another American satellite, and the Pentagon C.P. decided on all-out war. It's difficult to blame them, because with one of their main detection stations out, and the possibility that some of the Russian missiles would be coming around the South Pole, they assumed some would have multiple warheads—a lot of ours did. Under those circumstances there was only one order they could give, and they gave it." He paused, then said, "The whole process was known as escalation. Nobody on either side realized exactly what was happening. But from then on in, both sides reacted with everything they had."

"As I told you, things became pretty chaotic after that, but I probably saw as much of what happened as anyone." He looked at his watch again. "I have a few minutes to answer questions if you have any."

Arnie said quickly, "I certainly do—in fact, several. First, you say the Chinese had four or five bombs. How big were they?"

"About a hundred kilotons each. You can say roughly they were five times the size of the bomb we dropped on Hiroshima. That meant they destroyed everything up to a distance of about a mile from ground zero."

"All right," Arnie said, "but let me ask you this. How did they deliver them? We know they didn't have long-range missiles. At least," he added, "I assume they didn't."

"No," Smith said, "they didn't."

"Then how?"

"You remember I mentioned Korea? How the Chinese used coolie labor to bring supplies up at night? Well, we think they planted these bombs the same way. Don't forget at the time of the year it happened places like Clear are in darkness all day long. We think that a team of Chinese trained in arctic warfare—and some of the remoter provinces of northern China have a pretty arctic climate—transported a bomb over ice to about half a mile from Clear. That would have been close enough. Hell, you could knock out most radar antennae with a couple of well-placed conventional mortar bombs. But it was important for the Chinese that it should be a nuclear explosion."

"So, as I say, we think a Chinese combat team moved a bomb over the ice to Clear. On the American coast it was easier. We think they landed two bombs on a lonely stretch of coastline, loaded them in trucks, and moved the trucks in position on the night they intended to start things. Again these devices were fired by radio signals from Peking."

Arnie said, "They couldn't have done it. Those things are huge. How could they have got them there?"

Smith smiled. "Huge? Let me tell you something. You could pack a fission bomb that could destroy a city into a space no bigger than a couple of good-sized golf bags. They would have weighed about six hundred pounds each, but that wouldn't present any problems."

"All right," Arnie said. "But what I can't understand is the missiles coming in from the submarines. We know they didn't have any submarines equipped with missiles. Or did they?"

"No, they didn't have missile-equipped subs. They didn't need them. All they needed was to fire off objects that looked like missiles when they were picked up on the radar screens. This is how they did it, and we don't have to speculate too much about this because a survey team found one of the projectiles. A few years ago the Russians supplied the Chinese—this was before the big row between them—with over a hundred ground-to-air missiles. Now, these obviously had a limited range. But the reason they had a limited range was they had to deliver a warhead to the target. The Chinese simply removed the warhead, boosted up the power of the rockets, and they had a missile capable of traveling two or three hundred miles. They launched them so that the coastal radar would think the objects on their screens were genuine missiles coming in from submarines. And don't tell me it isn't possible, because it worked. Coupled with the three nuclear explosions on the continental United States, that triggered an initial response from us, and then as I've told you the whole thing escalated into an all-out war."

John said, "I didn't think the Chinese knew anything about rockets."

"They invented rockets," Smith said quietly. "People tend to forget it, but the Chinese were the first to use rockets in war. We don't know all they did to the Russian ground-to-air missiles to boost their performance, but we know they could boost it considerably just by taking off the warheads. Whatever they did, the blips showed up on coastal radar as short-range ballistic missiles. A radar screen could detect things coming in, but it couldn't detect the fact that these objects were completely harmless."

Arnie said, "I still don't understand why it had to lead to all-out war. What in hell happened to the hot line?"

"It didn't exist."

"What the hell do you mean it didn't exist? You mean all the stuff we were given in the papers was—"

"Don't jump to conclusions. Sure it existed, but only until just after the Chinese blew their third bomb. After that the hot line wasn't there any more. After that there was no communication."

"But," John said, "the third bomb was in New York. How did that affect the hot line?"

"It didn't. You have to remember, though, that a teleprinter link requires two ends and a cable connecting them. Or to be more accurate, cables. Our end was all right, and the cables too, but the Russian end was not. It terminated in the Kremlin, and just after the New

York bomb was detonated the Kremlin apparently ceased to exist."

Both John and Arnie looked at him blankly. He continued, "We don't know exactly how or why, probably we never will. But we can guess. There was a big Chinese delegation in Moscow at the time. A trade fair was due to open there in a few days. We think they smuggled one of the devices into the Chinese Embassy and, incidentally, we know the cables of the hot line passed very close to it. We think that at the appropriate moment they blew it, and that was the end of the hot line. Radio Moscow went out, of course. In fact, when the Russian stations started broadcasting civilian alerts, Moscow was the one station that was off the air. So there was no hot line left. Does that answer your question?"

"Yes," Arnie said quietly, "I suppose it does. It's like something I once told John and Bill—you heard about Bill?"

Smith nodded.

"Well, as I said to them, if a system is geared to prevent instant war and the system breaks down, instant war is what you get. We had a beautiful system designed to prevent our main enemy getting away with any sneak attack. It was also designed to prevent any act of madness or malice or just plain damn stupidity on our side. It was a beautiful, elaborate, delicately poised system. It was like the mechanism of a fine watch, infinitely perfect and precise. But that was its strength and its weakness. It was complex and delicate. Both sides knew that. So did the Chinese. They simply disrupted the delicate mechanism and that was it. The mechanism didn't function any more."

Smith shrugged. "Well, I don't think we ought to blame the system too much. It was as perfect as we could make it. And perfect enough so that we survived. Also perfect enough so that the people who upset the delicate mechanism were destroyed anyway."

Arnie said, "Yes, they were. So were about three thousand million people in the world. You balance it out for me." He looked directly at Smith and went on, "We were talking about the megadeath situations created in World Wars One and Two. Now we can assess the megadeath situation for World War Three. Three thousand megadeaths—has a nice ring, doesn't it?"

"I have about five minutes," Smith said. "Why don't you walk me to the plane? You know about the storage dump under the East hill?"

"No," John said, "but we found something that could have been a man-made construction."

"And the fuel tanks under the West hill?"

"No, we didn't find them."

"They're well concealed. One tank of diesel, one of avtag—that's aviation fuel. Enough for a long, long time."

As they talked they were moving down the beach toward the plane.

Smith said, "These are the last few hours you will have the island to yourselves. In about four hours they'll start arriving. First, about five hundred Citizens to complete the roads, erect the huts, and get everything ready for the World Leader. That will take about two weeks. The day after they've finished I expect the World Leader himself will arrive. Also the S.F.L.B.'s."

John asked Smith just what *that* meant.

"S.F.L.B.? That's simply the initials for Selected Future Leader Breeders. About two hundred of them. It's all been very hygienically and democratically arranged."

"I'm sure," Arnie said. "And what about this indoctrination you said John and I would have? What does that mean?"

"You'll find it very easy," Smith said. "And a great experience too, once you've had your shots. They give you those in the first week. I don't remember too much about the first week except that I slept a lot, but after that it was great. I found, we all found, we could think more clearly about things. We could see our part in the new order, see exactly *what* we should do, and *why* we should do it. You come to realize the great concept of it all. Even the Citizens realize it. They realize they have to give up certain things, but it's absolutely necessary for the future. But they're proud to give up those things because they've begun to understand the role they have to play. I assure you both, you'll find it a marvelous experience. Mystic, was the way I heard one of the Leaders Two describe it, and I think that's about the best description. It's kind of a mystic experience that prepares you for everything to come, even the inevitable sacrifices."

John asked quietly, "And the inevitable sacrifices? What are they?"

"Oh, mostly small things," Smith said quickly. "No alcohol or tobacco, of course; we can't waste resources on petty luxuries. Anyway, they're injurious to health. No settled family relationships, for the first generation anyway. Later we'll have to see. We were hoping the numbers of men and women reaching the Safe Bases would be roughly equal, or perhaps we'd even have more women than men. It didn't work out that way. We have roughly five men to every three women. It will mean a certain amount of sharing, but of course that's inevitable, and the Citizens realize it. After they're indoctrinated they understand the family doesn't really matter any more, because they're all part of one big family. The essential criterion for the women of the first generation is that they should be strong, sturdy, active breeders."

"And do the Selected Future Leader Breeders breed with the Leaders of the new order?" Arnie asked. He asked the question very slowly.

Smith smiled. "Of course not. They've all been selected for their intelligence and physique. And to ensure the quality of the children they'll produce, the children who will be the Leaders of future generations, they've all been inseminated with sperm taken from men of proven leadership and physical qualities. We estimate they will produce four children each during their breeding life, and then in the next generation those children will breed together, their numbers increasing with each generation and providing always an increasing and self-generating body of Leaders to supervise and direct the increasing number of Citizens. As I told you, it's all very simple and logical, but you'll understand better when you've been indoctrinated."

"There seems to have been a great deal of foresight in all this," John said.

"There certainly was. That's where our system was so good. And secure too. No one knew that sperm banks had been set up in absolutely secure conditions on the islands where no radiation could possibly harm them. But the men who governed us were making provision for the future, and because of their foresight there's going to be a future." He smiled at them again, and there was something almost boyish in his smile. "Listen, men, I'm going to have to leave pretty soon."

They had arrived at the plane now. Arnie said, "I have just one more question."

"I guess I can spare the time," Smith said. "But make it fast."

Arnie said, "All right: why can't we tell the girls about this?"

"I think I already told you that women don't have any classification. They are neither Leaders not Citizens. Instead, they have been restored to the status of being simply women, and as such the breeders of future generations. After all, that's really their function, isn't it? They will even be permitted to keep their children with them until the age of four, when the State will take over. They'll feel quite happy about this, because by that time they'll probably have one or two more children anyway. Do I make myself clear?"

"Yes," Arnie said. "Crystal clear."

Smith turned to John. "And you?"

"My question is the same as Arnie's."

"Look," Smith said patiently, "I've already told you the information about who started the war is classified for everyone who isn't a Leader. Women aren't classified, so they can't be told. You'll see the necessity, once you've been indoctrinated. But I'll put it as simply as I can for you. You can't have a Garden of Eden without a serpent, can you?"

"I suppose not."

"Well, there's the parallel. The Citizens must have something to hate. It's no use telling them the Chinese started the war. It would make our Leaders look ridiculous. After all, many of them helped create our defense system. It would undermine discipline. They have to be taught that a great and powerful enemy attacked us, but because we had the greater strength—and the strength of God also; that's very important—we defeated him. So, now we are the elect of God, and in that spirit and that knowledge we can go forward into the future with confidence. We have defeated an evil and powerful aggressor. Surely you can see the necessity for that?"

"I understand perfectly," Arnie said. "I understood before you ever told me. Since I reached an age when I could think for myself I've always understood that the first casualty in war is truth."

Smith did not reply to Arnie's remark, but said, "Don't worry too much. I'll probably be seeing you again. Leaders rate air transportation. I repeat, you are not to tell the women. That is an order."

He turned abruptly and went to the plane. He did not offer to shake hands with them.

Arnie and John walked slowly back toward the huts, and John said, "Will you tell the girls or shall I?" They knew each other so well, their thoughts were so close, that there was unspoken agreement between them that the girls should be told.

Arnie said, "Let's do it together. You know, John, I have a rotten feeling I've heard all this before."

"Yes, I know what you mean."

They did not speak again on the way back to the huts, and they did not watch the plane take off.

They repeated to Helen and Mary everything Smith had told them, including the fact that they had been ordered not to.

"But it's completely inhuman," Helen said.

Mary said, "I don't understand what they mean by indoctrination."

"I think I do," John said. "I can't be sure, but I'm going to assume the shots he talked about that are given during the first week are some kind of hypnotic drug that induces acceptance of given information. I do know that experiments have been tried along those lines for many years. Usually this type of hypno-therapy was unsuccessful, but we know now that the government had all kinds of drugs, including serums to prevent the diseases Dietrich mentioned, prepared and ready for use. It could well be they had found a successful hypnotic drug. Well, it won't be long before we can go hand-in-hand through dreamland with the rest of the zombies of the New Order. I can hardly wait."

Four hours after the plane had departed a ship arrived off the island and anchored just outside the lagoon. It was a big ship, about fifteen thousand tons, John estimated, and almost immediately after it had dropped anchor, parties of men, dressed alike in summer khakis, were climbing into landing craft that had been swung out from the davits. The landing craft quickly headed for the beach. When the first parties disembarked, the four who were watching noticed that some of the men wore the collar insignia of the Leaders, others had chevrons on their sleeves. They assumed that they were the Citizens, and this was later confirmed for them by one of the Leaders. He spoke to them politely and correctly, but rather coldly.

The landing craft maintained a shuttle service from the ships to the beach. As each squad left the landing craft, the men moved off behind their Leaders. Arnie was right, they moved briskly enough, but there was something mechanical, almost automaton-like about their bearing. They obeyed instantly and automatically the instructions of the Leaders. By the time night came, they estimated that over five hundred men had landed.

The next day they could see for themselves that what Bill had guessed was indeed true. From the platforms on the East and West hills the ugly mouth of a 105-millimeter recoilless rifle gaped over the low parapet commanding the entrance to the lagoon. The guns were mounted on jeeps. During the day they heard the sounds of construction-in-progress behind the huts, but when they attempted to walk along the path toward the runway—from which the sounds were coming—they were stopped by a Leader wearing the same insignia that Smith had worn, and were politely but firmly told they were not to go any further. He also requested them not to move more than fifty yards from the huts until they had been interviewed by the World Leader.

Late in the afternoon the landing craft began ferrying in women. They were all dressed in khaki shirts and skirts. Helen and Mary, who were naturally interested in them, estimated their total number at about three hundred. They moved up the path toward the runway, passing quite close to the huts but completely ignoring the four people who watched them. They moved in frightening silence.

On the morning of the third day two hundred more women landed. These were dressed in white shirts and skirts. They did not take the path the other women had taken, but went into the vegetation about five hundred yards to the east. This was the end of the landings. The ship that had brought these men and women sailed about an hour after the last landing.

During the next eleven days the group of four found themselves increasingly restricted in their movements. All the Citizens were now armed with automatic rifles, and four of them were stationed outside the huts to ensure that the four didn't move far from them. John tried approaching them, but his preliminary greetings were unanswered, and in no case did any of the Citizens speak to them.

Once a Leader brusquely told them that they would have to wait as they were until Commander One arrived.

John asked him just what supplies there were under the East hill.

The Leader said, "You notice all the Citizens are carrying automatic rifles?"

"Well, yes. I also noticed they didn't bring them ashore with them."

"All right," the Leader said, "multiply the amount of power you've seen about ten million times, and that's what's under the hill." He did not explain further, but instead told them they were not to approach the sentries who had been posted, as he put it, to protect them.

On the afternoon of December 23 the submarine arrived. A landing craft put out from the beach and picked up a party of men from the submarine. It quickly returned through the lagoon, landing the men on a jetty that had been built in the past few days. A man wearing three chevrons on his sleeve jumped onto the jetty and made the launch secure. There were six men in the launch, four of them carrying automatic rifles. They disembarked first. John said quickly, "Helen, get the binoculars."

Within seconds Helen had brought the binoculars and John focused on the jetty. One of the remaining two men climbed onto the jetty and then assisted the last one. Arnie said, "This must be the big boy. Do you think we should salute or something?"

John lowered the binoculars. "Jesus H. Christ," he said softly.

Because the man who had assisted the World Leader onto the jetty was someone they had known on the submarine as Lieutenant Perkins.

And the World Leader himself was someone they had known as Commander James Geraghty.

INTERLUDE: Nanyang, Honan Province, December 25, 1965

Li was sitting alone in his communications room. On the desk in front of him were three telephones. One was a normal telephone, though with a scrambler device that operated through the switchboard installed in the villa. The second was a direct line connecting him with Marshal Chuang. And the third was a direct line to the Chairman in Peking.

Li glanced at his watch. He had set it to American Eastern Standard Time, and although in Washington it was 23.55 December 24, here in Nanyang it was already a few minutes before noon December 25.

The phone connecting him with Chuang buzzed discreetly. Li could not stand the high shrilling of telephone bells, so all the phones were fitted with a low-toned buzzer. Li stretched out his delicate, long-fingered hand and said quietly, "Comrade Li speaking."

Chuang's voice said, "They're in position, all of them."

Li smiled. It was better than he had hoped. "My congratulations, Marshal. I will inform the Chairman immediately."

"Just wait one moment." Li winced as Chuang's harsh voice grated over the wires. He simply could not understand why Chuang had to shout into the telephone as if he were giving orders to a squad of his stupid soldiers. Chuang continued, "What's the word from Peking? Have the Russians launched?"

Li said, "I don't know. As soon as I have definite information I will of course pass it on to you."

"And even if they haven't, we go ahead as planned?"

"That, of course," Li said, "would be the Chairman's decision, but I think you can take it for granted we shall. Perhaps you don't agree?"

"You know perfectly well what I feel. I made it clear to you at our last meeting. Keep me informed."

Li heard the telephone slam down at the other end of the line. A natural and perfect boor, he thought, but he had done his job. No doubt he would be necessary in the next couple of years. After that . . .

He replaced the phone that connected him with Chuang and picked up the one that would give him direct access to the Chairman. He knew that the Chairman would be waiting anxiously for this call, and indeed within seconds he heard the Chairman say, "Li, is that you?"

"It is, Comrade Chairman, and I am proud to inform you all is ready." He listened for a few moments, then said, "My thanks, Comrade Chairman, my most sincere thanks." He listened again, and said, "Excellent. So you were right, as always. You will inform me? Thank you, Comrade Chairman. My congratulations on your prescience."

He replaced the telephone quietly and settled back to wait. The Chairman had informed him the Russians were in the final stage of countdown. He thought he would not have very long to wait.

He was correct. Ten minutes later the phone connecting him with Peking buzzed. Li picked it up and identified himself. It was not the Chairman. Obviously, Li thought, for the next twenty minutes the Chairman would have no time to spare from the active direction of the operation. He murmured a brief acknowledgment of the news, and replaced the receiver.

There remained only one thing to do before he went down the hundred or so steps to the elaborate and spacious quarters that had been prepared for him and his personal servants. He did not think for one moment that Nanyang would be the target for any form of attack. Peking perhaps; Shanghai perhaps; but not Nanyang. However, a prudent man who valued his own life highly, as Li did, naturally took precautions.

He picked up the other telephone and informed Chuang that the Russian launching had taken place.

SAFE BASE ONE: DECEMBER 21, 1966

The cold, harsh lights shone down on the Safe Base. They shone impartially on the dark water of the dock, on the Headquarters huts where the garrison slept and ate, on the four machine-gun positions spaced across the wire, and on the line six hundred yards away that Brecht's people were forbidden to cross.

Geraghty's orders to the garrison commander had been definite. He had instructed him, in the event of any violation, to shoot first as a warning, and if that had no effect, shoot to kill. Only once, just after the submarine had sailed, had any attempt at crossing the line been made. A group of three men carrying white flags had stepped across the line toward the wire. Geraghty's orders were that white flags were to be ignored. Two machine guns had opened fire, carefully placing a short burst each side of the advancing group. The bullets had sparked and whined off the concrete. The men were told that the next burst would be to kill. They had retreated hopelessly.

Now behind the wire the soldiers were bored and were looking forward only to the day when the "Nova Terra" would return and take them away to one of the lush islands that had been described to them.

But beyond the wire, in the area where most of the remaining people had established their living quarters, there was great activity. An election was in progress.

There was no question of the Democratic candidate. Brecht had overwhelming support. Two of his strongest supporters were Barnard and Goldfinch. The Republicans had not yet decided on a candidate. But everyone felt it was only a matter of days before they nominated their man. The Democrats were apparently in the majority, but the issue was complicated by the existence of several splinter groups, two of which were headed by the sailors who had defected on the boat and maintained their defiance of Geraghty by refusing to let their beards grow.

They had plenty of food to last them for a long time, and the excitement of an election to sustain them. In this excitement they found some release, some hope that when a responsible President had been elected they would ultimately be able to create a new State.

There were a few who doubted this, but they were in the minority, and their voices were not heard. The campaigning continued, while the children who had been left behind (Geraghty had selected nobody under the age of fifteen) and their parents (Geraghty had also left the married people behind) made small Christmas decorations.

The sentries at the wire waited for any attempt to attack them before the "Nova Terra" returned.

There was no attempt.

INTERLUDE: Nanyang, Honan Province, February 6, 1966

Li was sitting in the comfortable, sound-proof, book-lined room where he had passed his waking hours since the glorious event of December 25.

He had spent the time partly in meditation on the future, partly in reading, and partly distilling exquisite thoughts into exquisite poetry.

Only one thing had disturbed him. In all that time he had received only one message from Peking, and that just after the S-Day operation had been completed. True, it had been a message from the Chairman himself, and a most congratulatory message too. Since then he had heard nothing, and when he had tried to contact Peking—there was an extension from his Peking line into this room—there had been no reply. He had dismissed this as some aggravating technical fault, and as the weeks passed he had decided that, like himself, the important men, the men of power, had probably very prudently left Peking for the country shortly after the successful completion of the operation.

He moved over and scanned the titles of some of the books. He had of course read them all, but the great quality of Chinese literature was that it could be read again and again, each time revealing some fresh gem of wisdom and culture. Today he thought it would please him to admire again the wisdom of Lao Tze. He had stretched out a slender hand to remove the selected volume when behind him he heard a violent crash. He turned quickly and angrily, for he had given strict orders that he was to be disturbed only when he himself pressed the button that would summon a servant to bring food, or tea, or whatever else he required.

But this was not a servant. For a moment he lost his composure, then as quickly recovered it. Standing in the doorway was Marshal Chuang.

Chuang came into the room. He seemed to have shrunk somehow, Li thought. His forehead was beaded with sweat, and on his face there were ugly red blotches. Li sat down and smiled politely. He said softly, "This is indeed a pleasure, Marshal. What can I do for you?"

Chuang said, his voice rougher than ever, "You've done enough already, you sonofabitch."

"Please," Li murmured, "there's hardly any need for such language." He spoke more briskly. "I must ask that you control yourself."

"I wish to hell I'd been able to control you. I'm a soldier and I carried out my orders—orders from you and that ninny in Peking. Well, I can't do anything about him—he's dead."

"Dead? I don't understand. Marshal, you don't look at all well. Perhaps some refreshment . . ." His hand moved slowly to the button, pressed it three times. It was the emergency signal, the signal that would bring his full staff to his aid, not in their capacity as servants but as trusted bodyguard.

"But you're going to understand," Chuang said. "And you can press that goddam bell as often as you like. No one will come."

"No one?"

"No one," Chuang repeated. "They're all dead." He unbuttoned the flap of his holster and took out a heavy automatic pistol. "Now understand this. All over the country people are dead and dying. My own soldiers are dying. I am dying myself, but I'm going to make sure that you die first."

For the first time Li felt actual physical fear. He was, he thought, in the presence of a madman, and a madman armed with a dangerous weapon. Perhaps he could play for time, stall Chuang until he collapsed—and certainly he appeared on the point of collapse.

"Come now, Marshal. Please sit down and rest; I myself will fetch you some refreshment. If my servants are dead, then I must act for them to entertain an honored guest."

Chuang cocked his pistol. "Oh no, you bastard. Walk through that door and you'll find a dozen of my soldiers waiting for you. They're very anxious to see you, the great Li, the philosopher, the great thinker, and, apart from that fool in

Peking, the man they have to blame for everything that has happened."

A thought suddenly struck him. He uncocked the pistol and shouted an order in Cantonese. Eight infantry men with rifles and bayonets filed silently into the room. They were followed by an old, grizzled sergeant who had been in charge of Li's personal bodyguard for the past twenty-five years.

Li saw that all the troops were Cantonese. He sighed and relaxed in his chair. Well, he thought, if they were to be the firing squad, at least he hoped they would aim truly.

Chuang said, "I warned you it might go wrong, and it did. The Americans and the Russians *both* went for us. We are finished. I doubt very much if one per cent of the population will survive. And you are to blame."

"But," Li said, "it was your plan."

"Under *your* orders." He switched to Cantonese and gave an order to the sergeant. Then he spoke to Li again. "You don't understand Cantonese?"

"No," Li said. He looked round the room. "If I am to be executed, please take me outside. It would be a tragedy if any of these exquisite books were damaged by bullets."

"Who mentioned bullets? Outside millions are dying a slow death. The order I just gave was to kill you with bayonets. Slowly."

For a moment Li did not understand. Then as four of the soldiers took him from his chair and threw him on the table, while the sergeant and two others unclipped the razor sharp bayonets from their rifles, he understood.

Two hours later he was dead.

THE ISLAND: DECEMBER 24, 1966

J.G., formerly Commander James Geraghty, now World Leader and Commander One, was in good humor when he summoned Anderson and Levin shortly before noon the day after his arrival on the island. He was very satisfied with the state of the island. The guns were in position, the radar was working, and perhaps most important of all, the team of twenty doctors he had brought with him had examined all the Selected Future Leader Breeders and reported them to be in excellent shape after their voyage. Leader One Perkins had reported the state of morale to be high among the Leaders, Citizens, and Women. The construction work on the island was complete. It was no longer an undefended island, but a tight, well-equipped base.

He had set up his H.Q. in a hut about a hundred yards from the runway. Outside the hut the new flag of the United States of the World flew at the head of the newly erected flag pole. The flag had at its top left quarter a replica of the old flag of the U.S.A., while on the rest was a white globe set against a deep blue background. On a separate flagpost about five yards away was Geraghty's own personal command pennant. The pennant was crimson, and on it were the four silver stars denoting his rank.

When Anderson and Levin were brought into his office by Perkins, he noted with momentary displeasure that they were not wearing the regulation uniform. He quickly reminded himself that of course they had probably not yet been instructed what to wear. He also noticed they did not stand at attention or pay him any particular mark of respect, but again he did not hold this greatly against them. After they had been indoctrinated they would know better how to conduct themselves in the presence of a superior.

He said quite mildly, "I've decided to overlook the irregularities you committed while you were here. And though I have to reprove you officially, I may tell you I've decided not even to record the fact in your documents."

John said, "I wasn't aware we were guilty of any irregularities."

Geraghty waved his hand. "That's why I've decided to overlook them. I fully understand that you must have felt cut off from the world during your time here. So I'm going to overlook them."

Arnie said, "But what the hell irregularities are you talking about?"

Geraghty's voice lost something of its affability. "I didn't want to go into details, but since you mention it, just one of them was permitting Evans and Nichols to live together."

"But," John said, "how could we stop them?"

"I'm taking that into account," Geraghty said. He smiled. "Well, now, it's good to welcome you both aboard. Please sit down. And since I've known you both a long time—after all, you were in my submarine quite some while—I'm not going to stand on ceremony. From now on you may address me as J.G."

There was a tap at the door and Perkins entered. He saluted. Geraghty said, "Perky, what is it?"

"I thought I ought to remind you, Commander One, that the noon service is about to begin."

Again Geraghty smiled. "Forget the Commander One, Perky. I've talked to these men, and since I've known them a long time I've told them they may address me as J.G."

"Well, that's fine. But I wanted to remind you it's only a minute before noon service, J.G. Shall I switch you into the circuit?"

"Certainly," Geraghty said. As Perkins moved behind the desk and pressed a wall switch, Geraghty said pleasantly, "We have a compulsory noon service each day. Very good for morale. But"—he looked directly at Arnie—"you don't have to worry, Levin. It's strictly nondenominational. We have a very liberal regime. On one of the islands we have a Jewish chaplain."

A hidden speaker made a few preparatory noises and then the strains of "Onward Christian Soldiers," sung by hundreds of voices, crashed through the room. Geraghty sat back until the hymn had finished, then motioned Perkins to switch off the speaker. "My favorite hymn," he said. "I have it played at the start of each service. It really describes what we are. But perhaps you don't know what I mean?"

Both Arnie and John shook their heads.

Geraghty leaned forward expansively. "Twenty years from now we figure there'll be only a few communities left in the world besides ours. But if they have managed to survive for twenty years, it will mean the areas they're living in will be survival areas, where there's no trouble with long-term radioactive fallout. We will find those communities by air reconnaissance—we have plenty of fuel available for the job—and we will then send organized parties to occupy the areas. It will be the first step in staking our claim on the whole world. The inhabitants of those communities—they're certain to be very primitive, by the way—will have to be eliminated, but that's an unfortunate historical necessity. The main thing is, you will be able to play a part in it. I shall lead the expeditions personally."

"But—" John Anderson began.

Geraghty cut him off. "I know just what you're going to say, Anderson. You're going to say it's colonialism. But it isn't, really. You see, all those areas where we establish settlements are automatically part of the United States of the World. There's no question of colonialism."

"But there is of exterminating innocent people," Arnie said. "Hasn't there been enough extermination?"

"Levin," Geraghty said, "you don't seem to realize our responsibilities. We *have* to survive. As our population grows, we will need fresh areas in which to develop. Logic should tell you that."

Arnie said, "Tell it to the people who are exterminated."

"You'll understand it better after you've been indoctrinated." His voice became brisk now. "That brings me to your future. You realize you have both been selected as Leaders Four? Provisionally, of course."

"Yes," John said, "Smith told us."

"All right then. Within a week we will arrange indoctrination for you."

John said quickly, "And our girls?"

"What girls?"

"He means Helen and Mary," Arnie said clearly.

Geraghty said, "*I* mean Dimarco and Girard. Dimarco we can probably use here, she's a trained nurse, and she'll be useful to look after the S.F.L.B.'s. . . . Girard? I don't quite know where we'll assign her, but we'll find her a suitable place."

John looked quickly at Arnie. Before Arnie could speak, John said, "No, you'd better realize this right now. I don't intend to be apart from Helen, and the same goes for Arnie and Mary."

Arnie said quickly, "Say that again."

"I am trying to be patient," Geraghty said. "But I won't be much longer. You must realize there are no marriages any more. With you and Dimarco it might just have worked out, Anderson. But for you, Levin, and Girard, it would have been completely impossible anyway."

Again John spoke before Arnie could. "Why?"

"For the same reason it will be necessary to exterminate the people in any communities we discover."

Arnie said slowly, "You unbelievable sonofabitch."

Geraghty ignored him, and said, "It's very likely in the isolated communities I have mentioned there'll be men and women of different color and blood from us. So they have to be exterminated. We've had this racial problem once before in the world, but this time we can make sure we don't have it again."

John said, "And suppose we don't choose to be indoctrinated?"

Geraghty shrugged. "I've tried to be reasonable with you, but this I'll tell you: You either accept what I say or you don't stay on this island."

Arnie pushed back his chair and stood up. So did John, who had looked hastily at Arnie and seen it was too late to stop him. Nor did he feel any particular wish to stop him.

"And I'll tell you this," Arnie said. "Fuck your island, and fuck your new order, and fuck you personally, you unbelievable schmuck." As he spoke he seemed to grow in physical stature. He turned and walked out of the room.

Geraghty, unmoved, looked at John Anderson. "And you?"

"Everything he said goes for me. Double if you like." He too left the room.

When they had gone, Geraghty said to Perkins, "Give orders for the four of them to be confined in one room under armed guard." He waited while Perkins phoned the necessary orders, then went on.

"Indoctrination might not necessarily work on those two. Don't forget it didn't work on about five per cent of the people we selected at S.B. One. Well, I *won't* have them on my island."

"And," Perkins said, "that fool Smith told them about the Chinese. I know he told them not to tell the women, but I'm sure those two would have ignored the order."

"They're a menace."

"But they needn't be," Perkins said. "I have an idea I'd like to put to you, J.G."

Geraghty looked at Perkins with interest. "Let me have it, Perky."

Perkins began to talk rapidly. As he talked, Geraghty's expression softened, the doubt left his eyes, and when Perkins finished he was smiling.

"How long will it take to prepare the boat?"

"Not more than an hour."

"All right, go ahead with the arrangements."

An hour later, Perkins went to the room where the four were confined. Without wasting words, he presented them with two possible courses. Either they would obey the World Leader's orders, or they would leave the island. They could have the use of a launch, which Anderson could handle; there were other islands to the west similar to this one. By sailing due west, he explained, they would hit one before night. They had five minutes to decide.

John looked at Arnie, then at Helen, then at Mary. "Do we need to vote on it?"

The other three simultaneously said no. John went on, "But I'm not going to say it. I think it's important the youngest of us should say it. You agree, Arnie?"

"I agree. But perhaps the Leader One wouldn't care to hear it from the product of miscegenation."

"I don't care who I hear it from. I just want the decision."

Helen said, "Tell him, Mary."

Mary stepped forward. She seemed very slight and frail, but her voice was firm. "We will leave your island, the four of us together. We will find a place where we can live like human beings. You and your Commander can go to hell."

"All right. You will have a full tank of gas, enough to take you two hundred miles. Supplies, all you're going to need and can carry, have already been loaded in the boat. You will leave exactly five minutes from now."

"Wait a minute," John said. "What about our personal belongings?"

"Everything you will need is on the boat. You have my word for that."

They waited in silence for two minutes, then Perkins said, "Time to go." He led the way out of the huts and down the beach toward the jetty. Two Citizens carrying automatic rifles walked on each flank of the party.

When they arrived at the jetty they saw that much of the small launch was filled with stores, which had been covered with some kind of plastic sheeting and securely lashed down. John noted quickly that the launch was riding low in the water. He assumed it was the weight of the stores but there was also a suspicion that this was a trap. One way he could find out. "You're sure the gas tank is full?"

"You have my word," Perkins said.

"I'm not sure I accept your word. I want to check personally."

"Go ahead and check."

John climbed into the boat, unscrewed the filler cap of the gas tank and saw that Perkins had been telling the truth. The tank was full. "It's okay," he said. "Come on board."

Helen, Mary, and Arnie got into the launch. John started the motor. One of the Citizens cast off the rope that secured the launch to the jetty. Perkins watched as John backed the boat away from the jetty and began to turn it toward the mouth of the lagoon.

As the boat moved slowly across the lagoon, they saw hundreds of men and women wearing khakis pour out onto the beach. There did not appear to be any women among them wearing white. Within seconds the men and women had been drawn up in military formation on the beach, and stood as though on parade with the Leaders positioned in front of them.

Arnie said, "Just like a goddam firing squad. Except that they're not carrying guns."

John headed the boat out through the mouth of the lagoon. They passed easily through the mouth and into the open sea beyond. Mary was sitting close to Arnie, and Helen to John. As John swung the boat until the compass indicated a due westerly heading, all of them looked back at the island.

Just in time to see the red flashes from the guns on the East and West hills. Just in time to face the blackness.

DEC. 25, 1966

THE END